TRAIL
OF THE
FALLEN

Also by Bart Paul

NONFICTION

Double-Edged Sword: The Many Lives of Hemingway's Friend, the American Matador Sidney Franklin

FICTION

Tommy Smith High Country Noir Series
Under Tower Peak
Cheatgrass
See That My Grave Is Kept Clean

TRAIL
OF THE
FALLEN

A NOVEL

BART PAUL

ARCADE
CrimeWise

An Arcade CrimeWise Book

First Edition

This is a work of fiction. Names, places, characters, and incidents are either the products of the author's imagination or are used fictitiously.

Arcade Publishing books may be purchased in bulk at special discounts for sales promotion, corporate gifts, fund-raising, or educational purposes. Special editions can also be created to specifications. For details, contact the Special Sales Department, Arcade Publishing, 307 West 36th Street, 11th Floor, New York, NY 10018 or arcade@skyhorsepublishing.com.

Arcade Publishing® and CrimeWise® are registered trademarks of Skyhorse Publishing, Inc.®, a Delaware corporation.

Visit our website at www.arcadepub.com.

10 9 8 7 6 5 4 3 2 1

Library of Congress Cataloging-in-Publication Data is available on file.
Library of Congress Control Number: 2022934940

Cover design by Erin Seaward-Hiatt
Cover illustration by Denise Klitsie

ISBN: 978-1-950994-52-6
Ebook ISBN: 978-1-950994-63-2

Printed in the United States of America

When you're wounded and left on Afghanistan's plains,
And the women come out to cut up your remains,
Just roll to your rifle and blow out your brains
And go to your God like a soldier . . .
—Rudyard Kipling

TRAIL
OF THE
FALLEN

Just at dark Tommy carried Hendershott up the slope to the cave. The lieutenant was dripping from two wounds Tommy could see and more that he couldn't, and he grunted with every step Tommy took. With ten yards to go, Tommy stumbled on the dried carcass of a pack burro half-buried under a load of firewood. Hendershott swore and dug his fingers into Tommy's neck as Tommy fought to keep his feet. He rolled the lieutenant into the cave and propped him against the rocks then tended the wounds as best he could. The mouth of the cave had a small lip like a sill that gave them some cover, but not much.

Tommy could see the black shapes moving toward them across the plain like ghost warriors, the closest taking up positions in the boulders at the foot of the slope. He crawled back outside the cave, keeping hidden by the rocks. The wound in his thigh began to sting and twitch. He got to the dead burro and cut the burlap sling loose from the homemade sawbuck with his skinning knife. It looked like it had been a nice enough little burro and reminded him of home. Tommy was halfway back to the cave with the wood before they noticed him and sent some fire his way. When he didn't return fire he could hear their voices, laughing and mocking. One stood up and said something in Pashtun that made his boys laugh. Then another made a gesture recognizable in any language and turned his back, shaking his weapon in the air. The Kalashnikov rattled in the rocks when Tommy shot him. Tommy built a small fire at the mouth of the cave, just enough to take off the chill for Hendershott. It went on like that for three days.

Just before dawn on the fourth day they came again, but slowly this time, almost leisurely, keeping their distance, their shouts faint, but confident that they were out of range. Tommy picked three that were clustered close together toward the rear, family men most likely, and sighted from one to the other to the other, from the second to the first to the third, until he had a rhythm. As Hendershott wheezed and gurgled behind him, Tommy fired three times fast and even the faintest shouting stopped. From far down the slope, Tommy heard one last voice, mocking and faraway like an echo. The voice was in English, and it was calling Tommy's name. He heard the gunship overhead and heard Hendershott moving behind him. Then hell came knocking.

I
THE BLACK FLAGS
OF KHORASAN

Chapter One

I woke up with the sweats again. It had stormed during the night, and fading moonlight lit up the new snow. It had been almost two years since I'd come home, but the night sweats and bad dreams had come for me the first time just days before when I was alone in the canyon closing up our new log house at the pack station for the winter. I'd known men who'd had the nightmares both in-country and back home and remembered the old guys I'd met two winters before in Walter Reed who'd had them since the battle for Hue along the Perfume River, and I remembered the Gulf War vets messed up from depleted uranium. I'd heard the crying in the night. I'd seen the fights with orderlies in the corridors. I'd known all of that, but it wasn't going to happen to me. I thought I was different. But now my sheets were soaked and the shivering wouldn't stop. Neither would the dream. The dream of the cave. I knew it was only a dream and that it had never happened. At least not that way.

The days were getting short. I wrapped myself in a

Pendleton blanket and turned on the generator then flipped on some lights and stripped the bed. I told myself it was four thirty on a nice black fall morning and the day ahead would be fine. While I was waiting for the coffee maker I'd set up the night before, I shuffled through the log rooms, making a mental checklist of what I had left to do. Walking past the bedroom door in the dim light, I caught my reflection in the mirror over Sarah's dresser. Wrapped in the blanket, I looked like a starving Chiricahua waiting for his beef ration from a crooked Indian agent in a bad 1950s western. I wanted to take a shower to wash away the fear sweat, but I'd drained the pipes the day before. I set the sheets, some clothes, my tool boxes, and bags of anything a mouse would eat on the deck to load into my truck. By then the eastern sky was gray at the canyon mouth.

The truck was packed and the diesel idling when I walked across the fresh snow toward the outhouse. I thought I saw some movement at the edge of the tamarack across the creek. Something black that stood out against the shadowy snow on the pine boughs. Something that could've been a man. A big wind swirled the loose dry snow into my eyes, and I got into the truck and drove out of the yard. The wind died as fast as it came and left the sky clear with the first of the blue dawn. When I looked back through the dirty rear window, whatever I thought I'd seen against the trees was gone. Maybe it was only a shadow, motionless in the wind.

A quarter mile down-canyon through the yellowed aspen I stopped the truck at the wooden bridge. I took a shovel from the truck bed and began pushing the fresh powder off the boards into the water in parallel tracks so if I had to come back and it hadn't stormed again, the snow mashed down from the tires wouldn't leave two tracks of ice under my wheels. It was a narrow bridge, and I knew folks could slide off it if they lost traction. I'd seen it happen.

I shoveled fast, wanting to get back into the truck, but the flat edge of the shovel caught on nailheads and splintery wood and made it slow going. I was almost to the log abutment on the far bank when I looked out across the meadow. I thought I saw the black shape of the man again, hobbling at the edge of the trees. I took a couple of deep breaths and walked toward the truck without looking back. The wind swirled and rushed again in the tamarack, and I told myself that I was hallucinating. That what I heard above the groaning of the wind in the trees was not the echo of a voice calling my name.

It wasn't till I got in the truck that I paid attention to why I'd been heading to the outhouse by the corral in the first place. I'd hidden my dad's old Remington .270 in those rafters that summer so it was close and handy but out of sight. The last place a thief would look. It meant too much to me to leave it there. But I'd given myself the fantods so bad that was exactly what I was doing now. I wasn't turning back. Not that morning.

I got out to lock the steel gate on the pack station road behind me and took a quick glance at the snow for footprints but didn't see a one. That just made the fantods worse. Like what was dogging my tracks didn't leave any trace of their own that a human could see.

I pulled into Paiute Meadows about a half hour later. It had snowed in the valley, but the snow hadn't stuck. I parked on the side street next to the Sierra Peaks and got out. Then I looked west down the main street past the gas station at the end of town, towards the mouth of Aspen Canyon. A black line of storm clouds had formed above the western peaks, covering the Sawtooth ridges in the time it had taken me to drive the two blocks from the gas station. I turned away and hurried inside the Sierra Peaks for breakfast.

I sat at the counter. A couple of people I semi knew nodded and I nodded back. I ordered a chicken-fried steak with home fries and over-easy eggs and black coffee while I glanced at the big TVs on the walls. The TVs were new. Both the two old cafés in town were trying to look like sports bars. The results were mixed. One screen was tuned to an Irish turf race with the sound off, and another was tuned to an NFL pregame show. The third screen at the end of the room was covering some breaking news. Crime news, it seemed like. The sound was off on that, too. Helicopter footage made it look like a mass shooting or hostage taking. I picked up my plate and coffee and moved down a few stools at the half-empty counter for a better look. It was live coverage of a prison break over in central California. I flagged down the waitress and asked her to turn up the sound. Once she did, it still was hard to figure what was what. Nobody talking to the camera knew anything. Accounts varied. Witnesses contradicted witnesses. The first statement from the Sacramento County Sheriff's Office rep was that eighteen convicts had busted out of prison in a laundry truck. They'd shot the truck driver and stole his clothes. A local news guy announced from inside a studio that the first clue there'd even been a breakout was when California Highway Patrol had found the laundry driver's body in a ditch a mile from the lockup. The TV switched to a news reporter standing in front of what looked like the prison. He read a statement from the corrections department. All it said was that they were figuring they had a short count and would have more information as things got clear. Meanwhile, folks shouldn't jump to conclusions. An announcer from cable news headquarters started talking over helicopter shots of a gray stone prison, then shots of a dam and a reservoir. I stared at the screen and poked at my gravy with a piece of toast. When they switched to new footage, I got a bad feeling.

Now all three screens were switched to aerial shots of the prison. I ate slow, keeping my eyes on the screen while I kept feeling the stares of two guys in a booth behind me—like I was somehow involved or at least knew more than they did. I was pretty sure I knew exactly where all this was going down, so maybe I was involved just a little bit. Now a man in a suit ID'd as from the California Department of Corrections started an outdoor Q-and-A with a reporter. The wind was blowing the prison guy's hair, and both he and the reporter looked cold standing out on the wet asphalt. He said the same thing as before. The prison was on lockdown and the count was still ongoing. The reporter grilled the guy hard about reports of heavy gunfire, like he didn't buy a thing the prison guy said.

I saw a number on the screen that folks could call with tips. Then they went silent and a voice-over cut in, and the footage switched to a suburban neighborhood. There was lots of smoke and confusion. It was the aftermath of a shootout between escapees and local law. The officers were outnumbered. A black-and-white was on fire and a second was wrapped around a light pole, and bodies were in the street. One of the bodies wore prison clothes and might have been a dead escapee. Whoever these folks were, they were seriously hard-core.

A guy in uniform stood in front of a cluster of mics and ID'd himself as the Sacramento County sheriff. He said there might be as many as eighteen or twenty runners, so the prison statement about a bad head count was crap.

The picture cut back to the prison. There was smoke rising from behind the stone wall and what looked to be a main gate was swinging wide. The sheriff said that roadblocks were being set up and the situation was in flux.

The waitress followed me down the counter with a coffeepot in her hand and her eyes on the flat screen.

"Anybody hurt?" she said.

"Looks like two or three dead so far." Just saying that brought back the old dread. "But I doubt it'll end there."

"Where is this?"

"Folsom."

"Isn't that where your wife's ex is locked up, Tommy?" She finally looked at me. "The guy you shot to pieces a year or two ago?"

"Yup."

I left a twenty on the counter. The two guys watching me from a booth nodded to me as I walked by. I nodded back. I got the feeling every damn customer was watching me go.

The Frémont County sheriff's office and historic stone jail where my wife, Sarah Cathcart, worked as a deputy was on the corner a block away. A TV was on in the squad room there, too. I saw Sarah sitting on the edge of a table, watching. She reached her hand out to me without looking and kept her eyes on the TV screen. I took her hand in mine.

Sarah's boss, Mitch Mendenhall, shuffled over our way, one bootlace dragging. He nodded in my direction then focused on the news. A bigger-than-life-sized cardboard cut-out of him in uniform leaned against the wall telling folks to RE-ELECT MENDENHALL FOR SHERIFF.

"Holy crap," he said, "I don't envy that Sacto sheriff one little bit."

"Rough night, Mitch?"

"Fundraiser down at June Lakes," he said. "Host had a margarita machine then a blindfolded whiskey tasting plus an auction." Mitch popped a couple aspirin and swallowed them dry. Then he disappeared in his office and came back holding a decanter. He held it out to me.

"Guess who won the blindfold taste test?" Mitch said.

I took the decanter from him. The label said Pappy Van Winkle.

"This is a fine bottle of bourbon, Mitch."

"Yuck. Bourbon's nasty," he said.

"You want, I'll take it off your hands. The whole deal sounds rigged."

"You can't believe how much some of them bottles went for at auction," he said. "Tell you what . . ."

"Mitch?" Sarah said. "Any word on the names of these renegades?"

"I'll leave it to you in my will." He winked at me like it would be our little secret.

"You break the seal on that bottle," Sarah said, "the US Attorney could decide this election for you—for taking a bribe."

He laughed.

"Mitch," she said, "the convicts?"

"I figured you two'd be askin', so I already checked with a public affairs gal down there. Some real bad actors." He looked right at Sarah. "But the ex-husband is all tucked in at the prison infirmary."

"Sick or shivved?"

"Blood poisoning, Tom," Mitch said. He turned to a shaved-headed moose of a deputy writing a report at a desk by the door.

"Probably from one a Tommy's two-seventies from when he shot him in the foot, huh Sorenson?"

"Before my time." The guy named Sorenson grunted and kept hitting the keys.

"You sure it was Kip Isringhausen?"

Sarah tensed just hearing me say the ex-husband's name.

"Yup," he said. "The gal said old Kip's on a lotta meds, so they're keeping him real quiet."

"Thanks for checking, Mitch," Sarah said.

"Real quiet," Mitch said, "for now." He laughed and stood up like it hurt.

After a few minutes the coverage repeated and repeated. The name of the dead truck driver was being withheld until family could be notified, but one of the law enforcement officers sprawled on the street had been identified, and his brother was being interviewed. That was pretty grim. The brother spoke for ten or fifteen seconds then broke down and couldn't talk anymore. Sarah led me over to her desk and we sat together.

"Did you get the cabin all buttoned up?" she said, trying to sound normal.

I nodded yeah.

"I'm going to miss that canyon the next few months." She gave me a sweet look. "Way more privacy than at Dad's."

I squeezed her hand but didn't say anything. Mitch was walking back our way holding his phone.

"I'm serious, Mitch," she said. "You better get your campaign sign out of here, too, before someone busts you for electioneering on county property."

He just waved her off.

Sarah turned back to me.

"Let's not get ahead of ourselves on this." She nodded toward the TV screen. "There's nothing so far that has anything to do with us."

"I know. I'm heading back to your dad's. I'll swing by the school later and pick up Audie."

"Okay." She held my hand with both of hers now. "If she hasn't burned down the fifth grade."

"Always a possibility."

Mitch stopped at her desk looking at his phone. "First two IDs on the runners," Mitch said. "Gilbert Orosco, halfway through a ten-to-twenty for armed robbery, and Chester Livermore, first-degree murder, kidnapping, and raping a kid. Both from over in California."

"We're kinda in California, too, chief."

"We're in the good side of California," he said. He looked

up from his phone. "This big-city shoot-'em-up is a long way from sleepy old Paiute Meadows."

"As long as these guys don't start heading east toward our side of the mountain," Sarah said.

"Let's hope it stays that way," said Sorenson.

"Scared, big guy?" Mitch said.

The phone in his hand buzzed, and he walked back toward his office. He didn't see Sorenson flip him off.

"Well, baby," Sarah said, "Kip on the loose somehow was always going to be our worst nightmare. If he *is* on the loose."

"Yeah."

"But this has nothing to do with us."

I hadn't told her about my nightmare yet.

We spent half the year, Sarah and I and our baby Lorena, and a ten-year-old orphan foster kid, Audie Ravenswood, on Sarah's dad's ranch in Shoshone Valley forty miles north of our pack outfit. Audie's mother had been a teenage prostitute whose murder in Reno had left the kid alone in the world. Alone except for my awesome new wife, who guarded that kid like a cranky she-bear. Together with my mom and her boyfriend, Burt Kelly, a Marine packing instructor at the Mountain Warfare base up by Sonora Pass, we helped Dave Cathcart with his cattle out on a winter grazing permit and kept the place squared away and profitable. Together, we all spread the ranch work around and got it done. Dave called our random bunch a goddamn redneck hippie commune, but his health had been spotty and we could tell he liked having his daughter and granddaughter and old friends close.

Mom and Burt lived on his place in the double-wide that used to belong to Sarah and her first husband, Kip, the Folsom convict. The same convict who was on all our minds, and who we tried not to talk about. When I first came back to California from Fort Benning, I sat in that double-wide drinking Kip's Maker's Mark and trying to ignore his snide questions about what I'd seen and what I'd done and how it might've messed up my head. As we sat there, Kip was already scaring the crap out of Sarah with that talk, but I figured he'd got some of those questions from stuff she'd told him before. The way we all run our mouths about our exes sometime, even if we know we shouldn't.

I came into Shoshone Valley that morning from the south on the Reno Highway. The valley sat between the brown rocky edge of the Sierra on the left and the huge empty Monte Cristos on the right, the aspen in the high canyons yellow now from the early frosts. Out on the meadows, cattle close in to the barns and corrals grazed on the last of the green, and pockets of fog marked the course of the West Frémont River as it flowed north. In spots it looked like the whole valley was underwater with just treetops poking up through the whiteness. Early falling cottonwood leaves burned in piles along the ranch lanes, the smoke mixing with the fog on the river.

That night at dinner we kept Dave's TV on for live coverage of the prison break, but the news was already moving on to other stories with fewer live updates. The escape sounded more and more like it had turned into an old-fashioned manhunt. Like a black-and-white heist movie from my dad's day. Mom wanted to turn it off, but Sarah stopped her.

"Tommy and I should keep on top of this," she said. "Just in case."

"I know," Mom said. "I just hate that we have to fill our thought with this horrible stuff."

Burt got up to take his plate into the kitchen. He gave Mom's shoulder a squeeze, but his eyes were on me.

"Hey, Tommy," he said, "you sure that Isringhausen psych-job isn't traveling with these cons?"

"Not from what we heard so far."

"But would he bust out if he had the chance?" He looked from me to Sarah. "Would he come after you two?"

Just then, Audie walked into the living room from the bedroom Sarah and I shared with the baby. She'd probably been Instagramming her fifth-grade-Instagram-girl-mafia about boys. Junior high boys. Sarah said she was already tightening her cinch and screwing down her hat for a long decade ahead of us with that child, and we still had a ways to go with the whole adoption business. Audie climbed on the couch next to Dave. The grown-ups all watched her, seeing if she would ask us what we were talking about and wondering what we would say.

I looked back to Burt.

"I expect Kip would come at us if he had the chance."

Burt'd been in Desert Storm. I guessed he'd be out at their double-wide cleaning his AR-15 right after dessert. Sarah got up and took her department radio into our bedroom. She was gone about five minutes.

"So far the rough count is twelve convicts still on the loose," she said, "not eighteen."

16

"But still," Mom said, "twelve is a whole lot."

"It was thirteen, Mom, but one of them took a bullet."

"Lucky thirteen," she said.

"They dumped the laundry truck sometime this afternoon over by Rancho Cordova," Sarah said, "then they seem to have split up. It looks like they had a stolen Econoline van and a Toyota 4Runner plus, according to a witness, a pickup waiting with supplies and weapons. All of the vehicles hot, all with stolen plates. The witness wasn't sure about the make of the pickup, only that it was blue and long, like maybe a crew cab. And the woman saw a lot of firepower." Sarah sat on the arm of my chair, just calm and professional, looking at her iPad.

"There was naturally huge confusion," she said. "A truck from a mattress recycling charity pulled out of Folsom just before the breakout and local cops thought they had another escape vehicle. They pulled it over, but the driver checked out and his load was nothing but old mattresses so they let him go."

"Not enough Lysol in the free world to make me sleep on a used jailhouse mattress."

Sarah made a face and smiled at me then went back to processing the facts. "FBI has a BOLO out on the Econoline and the 4Runner. These guys obviously had outside help, including using pretty common vehicles for the getaway. But there was what seemed to be a fair amount of organization from the inside, too. A lot of discipline. The woman witness said it was almost like a military operation. Cool, efficient, and methodical." She turned to me. "What do you think, baby? You're the soldier."

"Looks like they're heading down towards Sacramento."

"It's easier to lose yourself in an urban area," she said.

"If that's really where they're headed."

Dave got off the couch and walked to a window. "Snowin'," he said.

"What's the weather like down at Folsom?" Burt said.

"It's snowing from Placerville on up," Mom said. She smiled at Burt. "Maybe we'll have a white Christmas this year. Why don't you start us a fire, Burtie?"

That old boy was way too big to be called Burtie, but he didn't seem to mind if it was Mom saying it.

"The Sacramento County sheriffs said one of the twelve was a lifer, an ex-soldier called Billy Jack Kane," Sarah said. "Now a skinhead badass who killed two Mexican guys barehanded in a biker bar down in Taft. He's new to Folsom, but they think Kane might be the main man—or one of them."

I thought I saw Burt pause a step on his way out to the mudroom. Or maybe I just imagined it. I looked up at Sarah.

"Where're you getting all this, babe?"

"The US Marshals Service," she said.

"Folsom's a state pen," Dave said. "What the hell are the Feds doing messing in?"

"Since nine-eleven," Sarah said, "the marshals have taken over most all of our fugitive operations nationwide. They'll be running a joint task force on this."

Dave sort of snorted. Audie mimicked him, and he laughed.

"Hey, Dad, you didn't mind the FBI's help when Kip almost killed you a year and a half ago," Sarah said.

Dave walked back to the couch and sat next to Audie.

"You got me there," he said. "That agent Aaron Fuchs and Tommy here saved my bacon, so old Fuchs is okay with me."

"Aaron Fuchs is *not* old," Audie said.

"Figure of speech, Sis," Sarah said.

She read a text on her phone.

"The joint task force is establishing a perimeter from Rancho Cordova to El Dorado Hills," she said.

Dave looked at me. "Where the hell is that?"

"One of those strip-mall big-box towns in the foothills east of Sacramento."

"The perimeter is established by verified sightings," Sarah said. "The task force will be widening it soon enough."

Burt stood at the mudroom door with an armload of split kindling. For a big guy, Burt walked awful soft.

"The US Attorney and marshals have already started interviewing family members and prisoners on the inside," Sarah said. "We can learn a lot about every one of these clowns and whether this was an organized act of this guy Kane's skinhead gang—"

Burt dropped his armload of wood on the floor about six feet from the stove. The room got quiet.

"The WhiteFighters," he said.

Sarah just stared at Burt. "How did you—"

"I knew his brother," Burt said. "Ricky Lee Kane. He was a Marine."

"My god, Burt," Sarah said. "The brother could be the key to all this. We need to talk to him fast."

"You can't," Burt said. "He's dead."

Chapter Two

I got up and started walking towards the kitchen. I felt wobbly, like I needed fresh air. Sarah was the only one who paid me any mind, but she didn't say anything, just watched and looked worried. Mom asked Burt if Ricky Lee Kane, the brother of the escaped convict, died in combat. He shook his head.

"The ATF shot him in Idaho maybe six months ago."

"But what for?" she said.

"Making bombs," he said. "And selling weapons."

Mom didn't ask him any more questions. In years past she had some pretty rough-sawed cousins near Boise Valley, but she hadn't spoke of them in years.

I went into the kitchen and poured myself a Jack on the rocks in a plastic cup. Sometimes that worked as well as fresh air. I was setting the bottle back on top of the fridge when the cup just collapsed in my hand. I guess I was holding it harder than I figured. I cussed loud and could feel the folks in the living room staring. Things were quiet as I mopped the bourbon up with a paper towel. I got a coffee cup and tried again. Once I'd built another drink, I leaned against the doorjamb trying to look all casual and semi-human. All this seemed to take forever.

"Selling weapons from who?"

Burt didn't answer me. I asked again louder.

"He washed out of the Corps sniper school," Burt said. "Some hassle on a survival exercise right here at Sonora Pass." He bent over and picked up the stovewood. He set it real careful in front of the stove like he was embarrassed for throwing it down.

"Kane went after his Red Hat instructor with a knife," Burt said. "He was lucky he didn't get shot on the spot. We'd all be better off if he was."

"How come?"

He looked around the room a minute before he answered me. Like this was a real sore subject.

"He stole weapons. High-end, state-of-the-art ordnance."

"Like what?"

"You heard of the Mk 13?" he said.

"Oh, yeah. Your guys' new sniper rifle."

"Yeah," Burt said. "The Mark thirteen Mod seven. After time in the brig for assault, Ricky Lee gets court-martialed and discharged. Right away he gets a crew together and hijacked a bunch of those sniper rifles. At least a dozen, maybe two or three times that. Snuck 'em right off the base in a lady visitor's truck."

"Inside help?"

"Oh, yeah."

"I never heard that."

"Hell, Tommy," he said. "That's nothing the Corps wants to advertise. They got enough trouble with finding those sex traffickers down at Pendleton."

"Any of these rifles get recovered? You know, used in some crime or sold in an ATF sting?"

"They vanished without a trace," Burt said. "Every last one of 'em. They'd be kinda hard to conceal, so Marine CID figures Ricky Lee hid 'em close to the base, planning on picking 'em up before too long. He was in Idaho meeting a buyer when he got killed."

"Damn," Dave said. "What a waste of the taxpayer dollar."

"When he got capped up there," Burt said, "the secret died with him. Feds found a couple of his accomplices shot dead execution style."

"How much we talkin'? Value-wise."

"Black market value?" Burt said. "From a hundred grand to over half a mil, depending on how many they scored. Some folks say there's even more of 'em missing. Then you add nightscopes and suppressors for every unit. An exact count has never been released."

I walked over to the chair I'd been sitting in. Sarah patted the seat for me to sit back down with her. She took my cup then took a sip. Just as if my fantods and the wasted whiskey in the kitchen was no big deal.

"Has too much time passed?" She handed back my cup. "Maybe it's a cold trail."

I took a gulp. "No trail worth that much cash is ever cold for long."

"Do you think there's any tie-in with the escaped-convict brother?"

I just shrugged.

"So, Burt," Dave said, "how come an old packer like you knows so much inside dope about this hardware?"

"I got a hunting buddy in Marine CID," Burt said. "There was plenty of talk when the rifles disappeared. Then folks get transferred in and transferred out. It kinda faded after a bit."

"Be interesting to see if there's been increased chatter in the underground arms market in the past twenty-four hours," Sarah said.

"Or goddamn ISIS," Dave said.

My hands kinda stiffened. Sarah flinched when she felt it.

"We're talking about super-accurate, super-long-range sniper rifles. Way over the thousand-yard range of the old M40s. Value depends on who's holding them. Non-state actors could use 'em for political assassinations. The Middle East? DC? Who knows? And if one gets in the hands of the Russians or Chinese, within a year our kids are gonna be getting shot with knockoffs of our own hardware."

"Damn," Dave said. "A guy could sure rob a bank with a half dozen of them puppies."

"Chump change. You could almost buy your own bank, Dave."

"So who else?" Burt said.

"One of the confirmed escapees is a Russian national." Sarah scrolled her phone. "Vanya Vasiliev." She looked at the rest of us. "Contract killer. Murder in the first."

"Maybe this dead Kane character knew your ex, Sarah." Dave said. "Didn't Kip wash out of the Marines, too?"

Sarah ignored her dad. "There's an ATF woman named Sanchez who'll be on the task force, Burt," she said. "Friend of Aaron Fuchs. You should talk to her."

Sarah and I lay in bed together not sleeping, not talking.

"I'm not doin' so good." I could barely hear myself say it.

"I know, honey," she said. She spoke in a half whisper so as not to wake the baby in the crib across the room.

"How could you know?"

"Other than you feeling hot to the touch, yelling in your sleep, shivering, sweating, stuff like that, you're just as normal as pie, babe."

"Think maybe it's . . . I don't know . . . PTSD?"

"I'd be surprised if it was anything else. You've gone through a fair amount of hell the last couple of years." She put her hand on my chest. "And a lot of that hell was after your discharge. Right here in god's country."

I told her about the hallucinations out at the tree line that morning. About night terrors. And how I got so shook I left the Remington in the outhouse rafters.

"Well, that is *totally* not like you," she said.

"I'm going back up there first thing tomorrow to get it."

She got up on one elbow. "I've got a day shift. I can pick it up when I'm done. Save you a trip."

"I need to go back there."

"You don't need to face your fears on my account. I know how strong you are. You can't let this tear your world apart."

"I can't *not* do this."

"You want to tell me about the nightmares?" she said.

24

I told her about the dream of being trapped in a cave so small I couldn't stand up, and of nursing Lieutenant Hendershott back from the brink. Of having no food and no rounds to spare, and only the firewood I took off a dead burro to keep us from freezing. Of my boot tracks in the snow leading right back to our hiding place.

"Did any of that really happen to you?" she said.

"Yeah, pretty much."

"I remember . . ." she stopped herself a minute before she plowed ahead. "I remember after I texted you at Fort Benning when Dad was missing. When you got here, Kip was asking you what it was like. You know. Combat and stuff."

"He was just probing for weakness."

"That didn't bother you?"

"Not at the time."

She gave me a look like she didn't quite believe me.

"What were you thinking about, then?"

"You." I stared at the ceiling. "You and him."

"Okay."

I could tell I'd made her uncomfortable.

"How long were you in the cave for real?" she said.

"Seventy-six hours, give or take."

"How did you pass the time?"

"Hendershott talked history. Nonstop. He'd studied how the hard-core believers we were fighting figured they'd see an army coming from the east, an army from a thousand years ago, carrying black flags and bringing . . . I don't know . . . the second coming of god knows what. Some damn savior. The believers had to join that savior army even if they had to crawl through the snow to do it. Stuff like that."

"Sounds creepy," she said. "So what did *you* talk about?"

"Nothin'."

"Typical."

"I might've talked about the Ghost Dance here in our part of the world." I traced her cheek with the back of my hand without looking at her. "But maybe I dreamed that. I could see enough real true believers and black flags right down the hill from us."

"How did you finally get out of there?"

"Being in the cave made it hard to send out our coordinates. When I finally could, an AH-6 came in and lit up that hillside. Fried those bad boys. Almost fried us, too, before they lifted us out of there."

"What about Hendershott? Did the lieutenant make it?"

I didn't say anything.

"Honey?"

"I don't know. I try to remember, but I just can't. I just draw a blank."

"Oh, honey. Is that the only thing you don't remember?"

"No."

She put her arms around my neck, and we just lay there for a while.

I was dozing off by the time she spoke again. "What about the voice calling your name?"

"That was only in the dream. And, maybe the last couple days here, too."

"Who did it sound like?"

I was too embarrassed to answer her right away. She just snuggled up and let me be quiet.

"It sounded like your . . ."

"Like Kip?" she said.

"Yeah. Kinda like Kip."

"It's okay, baby," she said. "It's okay. This is one nightmare we can share. I hear him in my imagination all the time. Like he's out there in the dark. Stalking me."

"When I shot him, he was stalking you for real. I thought I was gonna lose you."

"I know, honey." She put a hand on my chest. "I know. Me too. Remember, this is not some moral failing. This is just some crap you brought back from your deployment, all mashed up with what you and I went through here. Together."

"I know that." I had to laugh. "When I'm awake, anyway."

"You've dodged this bullet a long time," she said. "It'll pass."

"I know you're worried. The drinking and all."

"There are other ways to tough this out."

"Sometimes it's the only way I know."

"As long as you know I'm here if you need me."

"I know, babe. Sometimes it's the only thing I *do* know."

There wasn't anything left to say. I ran my fingers down her bare back. "Sometimes you're hot to the touch, too."

"That's different," she said.

I headed out at 7:30 the next morning to drop Audie off at the school at Rickey Junction three miles up the road. She was sulky about a note from her fifth grade teacher about bad language.

"You're pissed off at me," she said.

"Never."

"Even when I rip some douche a new one?"

"'Specially then."

27

"So what do I do about this?"

I took the paper from her and took out a pen. "How 'bout I'll sign it, and you'll think twice before you open your mouth."

"That's sorta what you do, right?"

"Not nearly enough." I signed the paper. Before she took it I reached into her backpack. "Now what do I do about this?" I pulled out the antler-handled skinning knife I'd had since high school.

"Honest, Tommy, I only . . ." She started to cry. "I wasn't stealin' it. I just wanted to carry it—like you do. I was gonna give it back, I promise."

"I know, Snip. But I don't want you to get in more trouble in school."

"Or home. I know. Sarah would freak."

She watched me set the sheathed knife on the truck's dash. She took the paper back I'd signed, reading it to herself. Then she laughed. "Will this make you happy?"

I knew she was setting me up for a line from an old Henry Fonda cowboy movie she watched almost every day after school on Dave's DVD. She had the parts with the bad broncs and homemade booze and skinny-dipping waitresses pretty much memorized.

"Yes, Audie. That would make me just super happy."

"'Well whatever makes you happy just tickles me plumb to death.'" She laughed and kissed my cheek goodbye.

I could hear her rowdy cussing fade away as she held up the sheet of paper and ran across the parking lot. Clusters of bigger kids parted to let her pass.

"Outta my way, bitches!"

Chapter Three

Overnight, Paiute Meadows got another dusting of snow that was already blowing off. The ridges and crags above the valley floor stayed white from the second early-season storm of the fall. I stopped at the Sierra Peaks to refill my thermos cup and check their three TVs for updates on the prison break. The network said that one of the convicts' hot cars, the Econoline van, had been sighted that morning at a place west of the prison called Citrus Heights. An hour later there had been two sightings of the 4Runner, one south of Citrus Heights near Fair Oaks, then later, farther south at Rancho Cordova. So they were heading south, maybe to avoid the building storm, not east over the mountains. Not yet. No one seemed to have a clue. Then in a breaking news announcement, El Dorado County sheriffs' investigators said they found the mattress recycling truck in a ditch below Latrobe Road off Highway 50. They recovered a note from the cons in the truck having sport with their pursuers. The note was taped to the steering wheel and the steering wheel was covered with blood. A box spring on top of a pile of used mattresses had a slit down the center of the cotton cover like maybe someone had been hidden inside. The sheriffs found the body of the driver a hundred feet up the ditch. The deputies figured there had been at least one convict in that truck after all and were seeing if they could recover any DNA from the scene. The mattress truck was the first vehicle out, before the laundry truck escape and shoot-out. I could sense a couple of folks watching me as I walked out with my coffee.

I turned off the pavement onto the timber harvest road. The snow had made windblown ridges along the washboard grade. It would be tough going if it kept up another hour or two. Fifteen minutes later I stopped to unlock the gate on the downgrade to the bridge and watched our new log house through the light snow. I always thought if we didn't have our promise to help Dave on his ranch, it would be good to spend part of every winter here, just isolated as could be. I was trying to hold on to that thought when I stopped at the bridge. There were no tire tracks out ahead of me, so I put the old Ram in first and powered slow up onto the planks. I only lost traction once—just long enough to contemplate the foolishness of what I was doing. I passed the cabin and circled the truck so it was facing the way I came. Then I got out and left the diesel running.

I studied the snow along the corral fence, watching for any footprints. The pack station was six or seven hundred feet higher than the valley floor, so if there had been any tracks from the day before, they would've been covered by the overnight snow. Finally, every few feet or so I saw shallow depressions half-filled with snow that might've been footprints. Between each of those I saw semi-round imprints—like a post or pipe that had been jammed into the fresh drifts. Or like a child's footprint alternating with an adult's track. The weird impressions led along the corral fence and stopped at the outhouse. I had no clue what sort of loping animal or hopping magpie or gimpy psycho might've made those tracks, but I knew my dad's rifle would be gone. I yanked the outhouse door so hard I almost pulled it off the hinges. I glanced up to see what I already knew and slammed it shut.

I walked with my head low, following the crazy depressions in the snow until they faded out at the bare ground under the tamarack that grew beyond the corral. I kept walking out across the snowy pasture to the bank of the creek. I stopped and studied the spot fifty feet back from the opposite bank where I thought I'd seen the black figure or shadow the morning before. The creek flow was steady and quiet and shallow this time of year, the ice thin and easily broken. I stepped off the bank into the shin-deep water and sloshed across the creek, not stopping till I reached the first bunch of tamarack.

At first there was nothing to see. I looked through the branches and studied the fresh snow on the ground, but there was no haint, no one-legged boogeyman on a pogo stick bouncing across the snow, no bad dream come to life. I looked back across the creek and the meadow to the corral and the outhouse. My dad gave me that rifle the fall when I was eighteen, and he and I both knew that he'd taken his last hunt. That Remington meant everything to me. Whoever took it had to know exactly where it was hidden, so it had to be a flesh-and-blood human being watching the cabin. Unless I was so far gone I'd taken it myself and couldn't even remember. For a second I wished the rifle was there so I could jam the muzzle under my chin and just end all this nonsense. I was that mad. Freezing wet boots didn't help my disposition. Behind me, where that shape of something in black had messed with my brains, was the snow on the tamarack boughs just as pretty as a Christmas card. I made myself think about my wife and my baby and our sweet foulmouthed ten-year-old leppie girl and the new log house, and I felt ungrateful. Then I pulled myself together and took a second look. At the edge of the trees, just as faint as could be, I saw a few more of those ever-so-slight depressions, covered like the others with the morning's new snow. They led away from me into the trees, where they faded off just like the others. According to the FBI, Kip Isringhausen had lost part of his foot from a bone infection where I'd shot him the night he was captured a couple of years before. So maybe I wasn't hallucinating. Maybe I was only half-crazy. Kip couldn't have made it over the Sierra unless he could fly, so I didn't know what or who the hell made those tracks, but the tracks were real. Someone or something had stood where I was standing and called to me from the trees. Just like someone must've been hiding in the back of the mattress truck to ambush that driver. It was scary, but it was real. That somehow made things better. I shivered like a wet dog and walked back through the creek toward my truck.

Sarah was on the phone at her desk when I stuck my head in the sheriff's office. Sorenson sat at a workstation staring at a screen. I could see Mitch sitting behind his desk in his office talking to somebody sitting off to the side I couldn't see.

"Well you know my concern, Aaron," Sarah said. "Anything to do with Folsom Prison sets off alarm bells for Tommy and me, even if it's over a hundred and fifty miles west of here. Okay, thanks."

She looked up at me.

"Aaron said the marshals ID'd more of the escapees. Besides the four we already knew about, Kane, Orosco, Livermore, and Vasiliev, there's a nurse named Tito Esparza. He's in for major prescription drug dealing and theft from hospitals, plus assault with intent and attempted murder. Nickname—Angel of Death. Dennis Wang, a psycho meth cook from the desert out by Hesperia. He's also involved in racketeering and big-time prescription opioids. Plus, Wang is a pilot. Sometimes he'd fly his own product up from Mexico or the Caribbean. Wang's smart and might be another instigator of the break."

"Any more on the Russian killer?"

"Vanya Vasiliev—drugs, murder, RICO violations. A hair-trigger Russian mob enforcer."

"So, muscle."

"Right," she said. "And the guy who died in the shoot-out with the local cops, Levon Hardgraves, originally from West Virginia? He dismembered his wife and buried her in his mulch pile over in San Ardo."

"A real scumbag smorgasbord," Mitch said from his office.

Sarah ignored him. "So that's seven we've got names for."

"And the mystery mattress-man makes eight."

"At least Aaron doesn't think I'm paranoid," Sarah said. She looked sorry the minute she said it.

"Yeah. I guess paranoia's totally my department."

She looked down at my soggy boots. "Did you get your dad's two-seventy?"

I didn't answer.

"What—is it gone?" she said. "That's crazy, honey."

"No trace."

"How can that be? If it was there . . ."

"Aaron say anything about the location of those guys?"

She was trying to process the whole rifle thing without making me feel worse, so she didn't answer right away.

"Yeah," she said. "Not a sighting, but close. A carpool mom called in a burning Econoline van on a residential street just west of Shingle Springs," she said. "It burned right down to the frame. Aaron's forensic guys are heading there, but they won't have much to work with."

"He have a team working on the mattress truck?"

Sarah looked a little surprised. "We don't know yet."

"Which way was the Econoline heading?"

"East parallel Highway Fifty," she said.

"Either they're just scattered to the winds, every man for himself—"

We looked up when Mitch walked back out of his office following a black guy about forty in a US Marshals windbreaker, ostrich cowboy boots, and a new Vegas Raiders ball cap.

"—or they've got a route all planned out," the marshal said.

Mitch looked sour. "Frémont County Deputies Sarah

Cathcart and Dale Sorenson—US Deputy Marshal Rod Ridgely."

They all shook. The marshal looked me over. I didn't introduce myself.

"The marshal will be the joint task force rep if we get any action up here," Mitch said.

"Cool," Sorenson said.

"Deputy Ridgely thinks these cons are crisscrossing Highway Fifty," Mitch said, "driving back and forth to throw off pursuit."

"Like this is a game?" Sarah said.

"I think they're heading up the west side of the Sierras," Ridgely said. "Where there's more back roads than people. Overnight we had security camera footage of one of the original stolen cars—the Toyota—in the parking lot of a place called"— he paused to look at his pad—"the American River Winery. Got pretty positive IDs of two of the guys in the vehicle."

"If they've torched the van, they probably dumped the Toyota by now, too."

"It looks like it, sir." The deputy reached out his hand. "You must be Smith."

I nodded that I was, and we shook.

"This morning, another carjacking." He stopped to let that sink in. "A Chrysler minivan taken at gunpoint from Cameron Park, just south of the winery. Witnesses said they beat up the driver bad, but there's no trace of the guy now. Too much rush-hour traffic. The 4Runner was set on fire a couple miles away. So there's some misdirection, but they're keeping close to Highway Fifty." The guy looked up from his pad to me.

"Aaron Fuchs calls you a 'resource.'"

"Aaron's wishful thinking. Just here to keep my wife company."

"That's bull. Agent Fuchs thinks you're a hunter. A guy that can track fog across wet pavement, mister."

"Not hardly."

"So, give me an opinion, tracker-man."

"These guys spent over twenty-four hours driving in circles just to throw you off. West to south to east."

"It *is* like a game," Sarah said. She spoke so soft they didn't hear her. But I could hear the fear.

"So where could they be headin'?" Mitch said.

"Oh, sorry, Sheriff," Ridgely said. "I forgot you were still here. Any of your guesses are as good as mine. South Shore Tahoe, Reno to the north. Placerville to the east. LA, Bakersfield, Vegas, freakin' Disneyland to the south. They're already in their second county jurisdiction." He laughed. "Hell, Sheriff, you *could* be next."

"We're hours away from the main action," Mitch said. "You sure you're not trying to beef up your role here, son?"

"This is the biggest prison breakout in the west in decades," Sarah said, a little louder this time. "The Marshals Service has to touch every base."

Ridgely turned on Mitch. "You think I want to be stuck here in this dump with you a hundred fifty miles from the action? If you do, you're whacked, Sheriff." Ridgely smiled. He pushed past Mitch and headed for the door, rapping his knuckles on the cardboard Mitch on his way out.

"Oh, Marshal?" Sarah said.

Ridgely turned.

"These mountains are correctly known as the Sierra, not the Sierras."

Ridgely started getting scowly, looking for a fight.

"You wouldn't want folks to think you didn't know the territory." Sarah smiled just as sweet as could be.

Ridgely looked at me then busted out laughing. "She's funny."

His phone chirped, and he stopped to look at it. He turned back around.

"El Dorado sheriffs just found the half-burned wallet from the driver of the Chrysler," he said, "but there's no trace of the guy himself." He nodded like he was talking to himself. "These scum-buckets *are* messing with us." He looked back at Mitch and me. "Just playin' games."

"So what's our next move, Deputy?" Mitch said, a bit more respectful.

"Expect that the task force will be expanding the perimeter ASAP," Ridgely said.

"Expanded which way?" Mitch said after him.

"*Every* which way, Sheriff." Ridgely pretty much repeated what he'd said a minute before and passed out his department business cards, "Eyes and ears, people. Eyes and ears. We gotta get ahead of these gangsters before we all look like chumps." He looked at Sarah again and laughed on his way out.

The glass door closed behind him.

"He's as rude as Audie," Sarah said.

"Nobody's as rude as Audie."

"Placerville?" Mitch said. "Holy crap." He looked at the two of us. "I got the feeling I'm losin' my home-field advantage in a dang election year."

I kissed Sarah goodbye and told her I'd be doctoring cattle when I got back to the ranch and that I'd call her later if she wanted a ride home. She looked more worried about me than she did about the prisoners inching our way. She nodded and watched me go.

The prospect of a hard winter had me preoccupied with all the things I still needed to do and wondering if I might keep the pack station open later next fall, weather permitting. Anything to get my mind off the prison break and federal cops and my dad's missing Remington. I had two empty propane bottles in the bed of my truck so I drove over to the NAPA at the end of town to fill them before I headed home. I unloaded them at the big outside tank then went into the store to roust out someone to fill them. Helen, the counter lady, was talking to a couple of women who'd given her a piece of paper with a list of things to buy.

"I've got the diesel lines and hydraulic fluid in stock, but I'll have to call the Gardnerville store for some of this other stuff," she said. She searched her computer screen. "I can have them here by three." She looked up at me. "Be with you in a sec, Tommy."

The women acted like maybe a mother and daughter, a rough-looking pair. The younger one was cranky and did most of the talking. She handed Helen her credit card and scowled at me like I might try to slow her down, and like I best not try. After a minute Helen left the counter and disappeared into the shelves. The younger woman looked over at me then nudged the older one. I caught them both looking my way, the younger one kind of laughing. The older one gave me a grim, squinty glance like she'd be happy to stake me out on an anthill. For a quick second I thought I recognized her, though I knew I'd never seen her before.

"Hey, Helen, you're busy, so I'm gonna go fill a couple of propane tanks. I'll tell you how many gallons."

"Thanks, Tommy," Helen said from the back of the store. "I forget you used to work here sometimes after school."

I could almost feel those two witches' eyes on my back as I headed for the door. I couldn't get out of there fast enough.

It was starting to snow again when I walked out to my truck after paying for the propane. The two hostile females were stowing a box of replacement stuff for what had sounded like a backhoe or excavator in the trunk of a beat-up Camry. They hadn't been dressed for tractor repair, but that was none of my business.

I drove back toward Shoshone Valley alone with my violent thoughts. Then just before Hell Gate summit twelve miles north of town, Sarah called me on my cell.

"We just got a report of a carjacking somewhere south of Fifty before it bisects Highway Forty-Nine," she said. "It could be one of a dozen roads, but the next big town is Placerville. The victim was only eighteen. He was beaten badly and left in the snow to die, but he was still alive and described his two attackers pretty well."

"Any of 'em our convicts?"

"It sounds like," she said. "The descriptions match Billy Jack Kane and Chester Livermore. Those two were cellmates for a short while this spring. The car they took from the boy was a red Jeep Cherokee with a Chico State bumper sticker, and they were driving east toward El Dorado." There was a pause, and I thought we'd been cut off for a second.

"So once they hit Forty-Nine, they could go north to Placerville or south to god-knows-where. They're still doing a lot of zigging and zagging."

"Babe?"

"Yeah?"

"Face it, hon," she said. "They keep coming east. Like they're coming this way."

The road was wet but clear, the snow not sticking yet. North of Hell Gate, the Reno Highway made a long downhill curve, past an abandoned Forest Service Guard station then a dirt road turnoff to Hanging Valley. In summer, cattle grazed that canyon on the old mining sites and dozens of small meadows along the beaver ponds that today were already getting covered with new snow. I could see the abandoned barn from the 1880s sitting just below the highway, the tin roof about to blow away in the next big storm. Just off the pavement at Sonora Junction, a Marine pickup was parked next to a boxy black and green articulated personnel carrier with rubber tracks. Two Marines in coveralls worked on the vehicles' underside where the two separate units hooked together. It looked like a lousy job to have in the roadside slush.

By late morning when I got to Dave's ranch, the snow had

tapered off. He was picking up a load of mineral blocks in Gardnerville, and Mom and Burt were shopping at Costco, so I had the place to myself, which I always sort of liked. I got myself a beer, let Sarah's Aussie out of the house, and saddled my good red gelding. I rode slow through the pasture east of the headquarters, checking the calves for foot rot, pink eye, or respiratory problems, but my brain was a million miles away. A solitary pair of Canada geese had flapped out from the ditch in front of me where they'd been half-hidden in the yellowing grass. They started beating their wings to fly out of my path and pretty soon were flapping overhead away from me toward a line of willows, wingtip to wingtip, gaining altitude all the time and barking like a pair of strangled hounds.

We'd be weaning these calves before long, but I wasn't thinking about that. I was thinking about vans and trucks full of killers skirting the Sierra foothills dodging roadblocks and helicopters, and I was thinking about what Sarah said. Wondering why a dozen hardcases would be heading our way—if that was what they were doing.

I spied a red calf with droopy ears and his head down. He looked as poorly and distracted as I felt. I checked my doctoring bag, took down my rope, built a loop, and went to work. Throwing a rope from the back of that fine red horse always perked me right up. Nowadays it was about the only thing that did.

It was past lunchtime when I rode back and unsaddled in the barn. Mom's car was parked in front of the ranch house, where she was unloading groceries. Before I went up to grab a bite,

I checked the gelding's feet. It had been less than three weeks since I'd shod him, but I checked them anyway, you know, just in case, then put him in the horse corral behind the barn instead of turning him out in the pasture right away.

I was walking across the snowy yard toward the house when I thought I saw something move out of the corner of my eye, something beyond the barn out by the abandoned harness shed. I decided it was nothing. Maybe just a bit of reflection caught by my Ray-Bans. Then I saw it again. I whipped my head around and saw nothing but shadow and snow. A quarter mile distant I saw a ratty blue Ram extended-cab pickup parked under some cottonwoods along the fence separating the lane from our mares and colts. I couldn't make out who was behind the wheel or if there was anybody inside at all. I looked at the horses, running my eyes over a pair of registered two-year-old fillies, thinking how slick and healthy and well put-up they looked, and looking forward to starting them in the spring. When I looked back up the lane the blue truck was gone.

I was getting hungrier now, but instead of grabbing some lunch right away, I walked back behind the barn and caught the gelding I'd just turned out. I tied him in the alley and pulled both front shoes then cut polyurethane snow pads to fit and nailed them back on between the iron and the hoof. Just in case. That would keep snow from balling up if I found myself riding in deep drifts in the high country and needed better traction. Just in case anybody asked.

42

Chapter Four

I flopped down on a kitchen chair. Mom poured me a cup of coffee and made me a ham-and-cheese sandwich. Dave's big TV was on in the living room.

"This Folsom escape just gets more and more weird," she said. "Now they're saying thirteen convicts are missing."

"Including the guy killed in the shoot-out?"

"Including him," she said.

"The thirteenth guy escaped with the other guys, or after?"

"Not after," she said. "Before. A half hour before the big laundry truck."

"The guy in the mattress truck?"

Mom set Lorena in my arms.

"I think so," she said.

We were both quiet for a minute. I nuzzled my kid. She was fussing after just waking up from a nap.

"It does sound like some bad prison breakout movie,"

Mom said. "A convict released from the infirmary who never got out of his bunk. Another con carving a gun out of a bar of soap." She looked up. "What's that all about?"

"Maybe for a fake gun like Dillinger in that old Warren Oates movie."

Mom pondered that a minute. "So just this morning, when they think the prisoner in the bunk is dead, they find the corpse of a guard in his bunk instead of him. They figured the guard was only killed this morning after the other bunch skedaddled."

"So the guy from the infirmary is missing?" I felt like my stomach just dropped on the floor.

"They're not sure."

"Mom." I took her hand. "The guy from the infirmary was Kip."

"But they said the missing man was named Ingalls."

"That's Kip's real name, Mom. Remember?"

"Oh," she said. She spoke so soft I could barely hear her. "Oh, my Lord. I knew that."

I dug out my phone and Ridgely's card and called him. I didn't want to terrify Sarah with bogus information. Ridgely said there was major confusion at the prison. A guard had been shanked and stashed in a prisoner's bunk. There had been other attacks on guards after the initial break. And there was confusion about just whose bunk it was. It wasn't the only confusion in yesterday's first few hours. Ridgely told me he'd try to get an update from Folsom for me ASAP. The official word for now was that Kevin Ingalls wasn't among the escapees.

"Having such a big bust-out has the rest of the cons

totally shook," Ridgely said. "There've been two really violent incidents in the yard, so there's a general lockdown. With a prison population that big, chaos rules."

"One last thing you might want to check."

"Shoot," he said.

"See if the FBI forensic folks found any DNA yet from that mattress recycle truck. That might tell you which escapee was the first guy out."

He asked me who I thought they'd find. I said it was just a hunch, but maybe Ingalls.

"If he was the first guy to clear the wall," he said, "that might confirm this whole business as his deal."

Ridgely told me about other escapes he'd worked on, but none was as big or successful as this. So far. I thanked him and asked him to not get Sarah riled for nothing. Not until we knew for sure.

"Hell, Sarge," he said. "you're not doin' a very good job tampin' down your own freak-out. You're the one I'm worried about, bro, not your wife."

Mom looked up as a sheriff's SUV came down the lane in the distance. I thought it was Sarah and wanted to talk to her alone, so I topped off my coffee and went outside without my coat. Even with the early snow, the cottonwoods still carried most of their green, and the fast-drying leaves made a rustling, rattling sound in the wind. The SUV stopped, and I saw it was Mitch. I hadn't much cared for the sheriff since he used to roust me when I was a kid, so I never knew what to expect from him. He was always fair to Sarah, though, and I was grateful for that, even if she said it was because since I went into the army he was a tad more respectful of me.

He got out and started studying the sky and the cottonwoods and anything else to keep from looking me in the eye.

"You busy?"

I said I had a minute.

"Wanna take a little drive?"

"Where to?"

"I been thinking," he said. "If these gunslingers have made it into El Dorado County and there's a chance they're heading this way, maybe we should, you know, check for possible areas of ingress and egress and all that bullshit."

We? When Mitch Mendenhall said he's been "thinking," it was usually worrisome.

"Hold on."

I was in and out of the ranch house in ninety seconds, buckling on my Beretta nine and pulling my coat on over it and squaring my hat. Mitch nodded like he was glad I'd be armed though I didn't think that he'd be itching for a firefight if he could help it. A showdown with a margarita machine was about all the danger he could handle.

"That your Beretta, Tommy?" he said.

"Yup."

"Surprised you ain't carrying your old two-seventy."

"Wasn't planning on this little detour."

"Want me to wait here while you run in and get it?" he said.

"No. I'll be fine."

He squared his own duty belt like we were Wyatt and

Doc and crawled behind the wheel. When we pulled up to the Reno Highway a mile west, he just idled at the stop sign.

"You think Highway Fifty?" he said. "El Dorado county sent out an alert there was a sighting of that red Jeep in Placerville."

"A positive or a maybe?"

"Maybe a 'maybe,' I guess."

"We are a *long-ass* way from Placerville, Mitch."

He pretty much ignored me. "This morning I get a call from the FBI office in South Shore. Your pal Agent Fuchs. Actually, the call was for Sarah, but she talked to him like I wasn't much there. From what I made out, it was something about missing Marine sniper rifles."

I watched the mountains. Mitch watched me. We still idled at the stop sign.

"So you too, huh?" he said. "I get froze out of maybe the biggest case in my career? Jeezo, Tommy."

I filled him in on just the basics of the missing rifles, just like Burt had told Sarah and me.

"I'm glad that's on the Feds' radar."

"Well, cripes," he said. "That's a big deal, then, right Tommy? Now everybody's up to speed but me? That's bull-crap. This is my dang county." He was puffing. "I shoulda been *told*."

"No argument here."

"Well, why wasn't I, god dang?"

I didn't have a good answer. I asked him where we were headed.

"East Fork, up in Alpine County," he said. "Been talkin' to Sheriff Flint Richmond up there. We're gonna coordinate

our departments, develop integrated communications sys-
tems, compatible frequencies, strategize operations, maybe
even set up defensive perimeters and command-and-control
centers in the event of possible criminal incursion."

"Just the two of you?"

"Hell, yeah, Tom. Don't laugh. He's as pissed as I am
about the Feds leaving us out of the loop like we were a bunch
of rubes."

Truth was, Mitch had got so much mileage out of this
prison break I wouldn't've been surprised if he'd planned the
thing himself.

We drove without talking. When we passed the Marine
auxiliary housing complex up above the highway, he tensed
up more.

"So what's the plan, Mitch? You're antsy as hell."

"Forget the Marines a sec," he said. "You know this Kip
character. You remember I testified at his sentencing hearing
after you shot him to rescue Sarah and her dad."

"Oh, I remember."

"So if he was part of this escape, you think he wants
revenge? Am I in trouble? I mean from Isringhausen?"

"No more than the rest of us."

He was quiet. We'd never been friends or anything close
to it. "I been getting phone calls," he said.

"Yeah?"

"Yeah. Some female. Like 'my time was coming,' stuff
like that. You think it's connected to this Folsom deal?"

"Wouldn't be surprised."

"It's weirding me out, I tell ya."

"I imagine it would."

I didn't mention my hallucinations or my dreams. It's not like they had anything in common with Mitch. Why would they?

A couple of miles farther on, Mitch pulled off the asphalt and pointed to a green highway sign.

"Monitor Pass?"

Mitch looked happy. "Richmond and I both got to wondering," he said. "If those bad actors made it over the mountains, is this a way they could come out?"

"Anything's possible."

"I been lookin' online," he said. "Says this is the newest and maybe most isolated pass over the mountains."

"Newest to be paved, maybe. Not new to the Paiute or mountain men like Jedediah Smith."

"Well, it comes out right near the Cathcart ranch." He looked at me. "Right in your front yard."

"If you could've found that online, so could a bunch of escaped convicts. Is that what you're thinking?"

"Sure am." He gave me a wobbly grin across the Mossberg 12 gauge locked between the seats.

We were opposite a two-lane road that spilled toward us out of a narrow canyon less than half a mile from the highway. Mitch looked nervous.

"So," he said, "we go up this road?"

I sometimes forgot that Mitch was from Orange County in Southern California and had zero curiosity about this part of the country.

"So, this Sheriff Richmond's expecting you?"

"Not yet," Mitch said. "I didn't want him to think I never been up here."

"Oh, for chrissakes, Mitch."

He took a deep breath. "Well," he said. "We gotta do something."

"Sometime doing nothing is a better plan. You know, patience."

"I don't *do* 'patience.'"

I pointed to the narrow cut. "Then drive."

Mitch looked up. The road disappeared around a curve in less than a mile. He turned left off the Reno Highway and crept into the canyon.

"Don't look like much," he said.

The road climbed the side of a rocky gully, then the gully opened out, overlooking a treeless valley. At the far edge of the valley, dead cottonwoods marked the sites of abandoned ranches and cow camps. The road climbed and turned back on itself across bare ridges then climbed some more. We gained altitude fast, though Mitch was driving slow. He went on about roadblocks, the US Marshals, and the county elections coming up. He was a guy that needed to be talking so he felt like he was doing something.

We could see burned-over ground and remains of the black trunks of scorched trees. New snow settled on Indian paintbrush growing through the rocks and dead mahogany and the sage that grew near the road. Snow was fresh on the pavement and covered the yellow line. Mitch slowed to a creep.

"Want me to drive?"

"I'm okay," he said. Then he slowed down some more.

The treeless country sloped down on the right, and we could see the far-off East Carson River drainage that gave the town of East Fork its name. When we got to the Alpine County boundary sign, Mitch stopped.

"This the pass?" he said.

"Couple miles farther."

"How come the state line don't follow the top of the dang mountains?" he said. "A straight line from Tahoe to the Colorado River is just retarded."

"Great question." It was about the smartest question I'd ever heard him ask.

We got to another steep piece of road, but Mitch just poked along, riding the brakes and looking green at the gills.

"Stop here. I'll drive a bit."

This time he didn't give me an argument. We traded places, but in less than a mile I stopped. We looked back over boulders and sage and sandy peaks a thousand feet below us till in the distance we could see a patch of flat pasture framed by the steep walls of the canyon mouth like a gunsight. That pasture was the north end of Dave Cathcart's ranch.

I checked the GPS on my phone and told Mitch how close we were to East Fork. From the Reno Highway to Monitor Pass was a three-thousand-foot climb, so I wanted to get over it quick before the snow got too heavy.

After coming off the summit, we pulled into East Fork less than a half hour later. It was the county seat and had almost three hundred folks living there year-round—according to the sign. But you wouldn't know it from the main street. The place looked pretty well deserted. Like it had shut down for a winter that hadn't even started yet.

The woman behind the counter of an old-time general store checked out Mitch's uniform. She said we'd just missed the county sheriff by five minutes. She'd been burglarized the night before, and Sheriff Richmond was off following a lead at a place called Hope Valley. I poked around the store, seeing what they stocked. Mitch watched the woman follow me around the store. She was wearing slippers and a robe like she just got up.

"What got taken, if you don't mind my asking?"

"A couple of nice Yeti mugs," she said, "flashlights, batteries, some ammo, some candy bars, beer and vodka, a cooler, Red Bull, cigarettes, that kind of stuff."

"What kind of candy bars?"

She gave me a strange look. "I dunno. Snickers. Three Musketeers. Twix. All those, I guess."

"What kind of ammo?"

"Are you a deputy?"

"No, ma'am."

"Mostly nine-millimeter," the woman said. "A box of three-oh-eights." She poked around a locked plexiglass case that had been ripped off the wall. "I think we had one box of forty-four Mags. That's missing."

"Okay, thanks."

"You do kinda sound like a deputy."

"Sorry."

Mitch drifted around the general store a bit longer, like maybe the candy bars were going to be given away if he waited long enough.

"We should go."

"Yeah," he said. "Where is everybody?"

Mitch slipped and almost fell on a patch of fresh ice in a shady corner of the board porch. I let him get into the passenger side again. He was quiet till we started down the switchbacks.

"You really think maybe these jailbirds will try coming over to our side?" he said.

"It's possible. Or maybe the woman coulda been burgled by teenage snowmobilers."

Mitch stared down at the narrow cut a couple thousand feet below us. Then he laughed.

"Imagine if those cons came down this crappy-assed road and some local law was waitin' at that narrow canyon and stopped 'em in their tracks. Kinda, you know, trapped 'em. That hero lawman would be a shoo-in to win an election, I bet."

"That hero'd have to trap 'em by tonight. Tomorrow morning at the latest."

"How come?"

"This pass usually is the first one closed once the snow starts."

"Don't tell Sarah yet," he said, "but when me and sheriff Richmond set up our own 'eyes and ears' bi-county task force"—he nodded to himself—"we might just surprise all of you."

I got out and let mister "bi-county task force" drive once we hit the Reno Highway. Heading back south the last few miles toward Dave's, we passed under a row of old cottonwoods along the pavement, their dying leaves rattling in the wind like every other cottonwood in the valley that fall. Nailed to one of the trees was one of Mitch's life-sized election signs waving at us. A black cloth was wrapped around the cardboard head like a turban so all we could see was the painted eyes. From a distance it made me think of the black shape in the pack station meadow. The cardboard was nailed on the north side of the tree so we hadn't seen it on our way out. The cottonwood looked leafed out—the branches heavy with dark leaves. I heard a squeaking, rustling, clattering sound as we slowed. Mitch drove off the pavement into the fresh snow and hit the brakes. The sound stopped in an instant and every leaf jumped sideways and flew up into the next tree just like I was hallucinating again. Then the noise started just as fast and just as loud. The limbs of the first tree were bare, with not a leaf on them.

"What the—?" Mitch said.

"Starlings. Hundreds of 'em."

"That's creepy," he said.

He jumped out of the SUV, and I followed. Mitch had to stretch to reach the cloth wrapped around the cardboard head. He unwrapped it and stepped back.

"This ain't funny. Makes me look like some danged ISIS guy."

There was a bullet hole in the cardboard forehead. Mitch stared at it like somebody just walked over his grave. I picked up the black cloth, and we got back into the SUV.

"Well *that* was weirder than crap."

He had no damn idea.

"As long as these guys don't start crossing over to our side of the mountain," Sarah said to Mom for the dozenth time, "we probably don't need to worry."

Night came early and she looked worried all the same. Then came the snow, heavier now. Monitor Pass would be closed by morning. We sat in Dave's living room staring at the news. Even Audie stopped being a smartass and just watched us watching the screen. I walked into the kitchen to pour myself a goodly jolt of Jack Daniel's. Sarah kept her eye on me until I sat back down.

No one on the news mentioned the name Kip Isringhausen, but his living ghost was all around us. When Dave and Sarah had first met him, he seemed like he had money to burn. He said it was from selling a horse trailer dealership over in the San Joaquin, so he was looking for new business opportunities on this side of the mountain. He left out the part about the cocaine dealership and the pot farms up in the Monte Cristos. The double-wide Mom and Burt lived in had been Sarah and Kip's newlywed house, and he'd paid for it in cash. After six months or so, he scared Sarah so much with his coked-up paranoia and violence she moved back into her dad's house—the ranch house we lived in now. Her dad disappeared right after. That's when Sarah texted me at Fort Benning and asked me to take some leave and come home. Nothing more than that. And when I did, that's when Kip went on the warpath. I knew then I'd never let Sarah out of my sight for more than a few hours as long as he lived. I was wondering if the double-wide was still in his name.

I walked to the front porch of the old house and fired up the propane barbeque. Burt trimmed the fat off a couple of tri-tips while Mom made sweet-potato fries in the kitchen. She said Burt had to watch his blood glucose, but I'd taught Audie how to microwave wild rice and whip up a mess of garlic butter so the rest of us could carb out along with our protein. Dinner was always pretty loosey-goosey at Cathcart's, but everybody helped and, if Burt was our yardstick, we weren't exactly starving. I was wire-brushing the crust off the grill and trying to stay focused when Audie asked me to reach the mother-loving garlic in a high cupboard, but that wasn't quite how she said it.

"*Audie*," Mom said.

"Shit, Grams," Audie said, "Tommy knows what I meant."

Mom came out to the porch a bit huffy and muttering something about a convent school—and we weren't even Catholic.

"Come on, Ma. The kid does pretty . . . *darned* good for somebody raised in a whorehouse."

"You told me it was a gentlemen's club and not . . ." She shook her head. "Oh, never mind." She was still talking to herself when she cleared the door.

That night at dinner we filled in the rest of the family on where things stood. Sarah asked her dad about moving in with a Paiute Meadows rancher friend and her son for a few days, but he wasn't buying it.

"I'll be goddamned if I get chased off my own place by a damn rumor," Dave said. "Those sonsabitches could be anywhere." He was quiet a sec. We could tell he was angry. "I never did like that Kip anyhow."

We all knew *that* wasn't exactly true.

He was getting wound up, so Sarah let it drop. She took out her radio and disappeared into our bedroom to check with her office. That was beginning to be a habit.

"Hey, Burt. The snow's barely sticking on the ground, and your guys already busted a Sno-Cat. Saw one off to the side of the Sonora road on my way home."

"You best believe that's a big stink, Tommy," Burt said. "Some fool on the base took it for a joyride. Vandalized the hydraulic steering linkage."

"You don't know who did it?"

"Not yet," Burt said.

Dave laughed. "You find that guy what took it, he'll be in a world of hurt."

"And it's really not a Sno-Cat," Burt said. "It's some Scandinavian deal. They call it a S-U-S-V. Small Unit Support Vehicle. Susvee for short. Goes damn near anywhere."

"You guys up the creek without it?"

"Naw," Burt said, "we got six more on the base."

"Of course you do," Dave said. "You're the government."

"They all got some age on 'em," Burt said. "Talk is they'll all get replaced when something new comes along."

"Hey, Burt," Audie said. "Will you take me for a ride in one of them?"

"I got better access to government mules," he said, "but I'll see what I can do, Ace."

Sarah came back into the living room.

"What's the news?" her dad said.

"Well, it's kind of curious," she said. "You know the convict who died in the shoot-out with Sacramento County officers just a mile from the prison? The guy who put his wife in the mulch pile? Preliminary ballistics indicate he was shot in the back with a forty-four Mag. Those deputies don't carry forty-four Mags."

"A deputy coulda been carrying a private piece," Burt said.

"Or the wife-killer coulda been killed by his own crew. The burglars who trashed the East Fork general store stole a box of forty-four Mags last night. Maybe they needed to restock after the breakout."

"Why would they do that?" Mom said. "Kill their own, I mean?"

"First, they create a big scare. Freak out half of California with the big breakout, then trim the team."

"Makes sense," Burt said. "I bet Tommy's right. If they're going after stolen Mk thirteens. It's a bigger share for the guys that're left alive."

"Unless this is really just a smokescreen for revenge," Sarah said, "against us. Then none of this matters."

"I'd say both revenge *and* stolen guns. Kip's a damn multitasker."

"This is not funny, hon," Sarah said.

Audie had been sitting with Mom, big-eyed and amped by all the grown-up crime talk. Then she jumped up and ran into the kitchen. We heard her rattling around out on the porch then heard the door to the mudroom slam. She marched back into the living room carrying a rifle and stood next to Dave's chair.

"Come on, Grandpa," she said. "Let's get the sonsabitches."

"You shouldn't leave that around where a child can handle it," Mom said.

Sarah eased the rifle out of Audie's hands.

"Tommy . . ." she said. There was no color left in her face.

"I don't have a clue, babe."

"What the hell's going on?" Dave said.

Sarah handed the rifle to me. "This is Tommy's rifle," she said. "From the pack station." She looked at Audie. "Where'd you find this, Sis?"

"On the mudroom porch. Leaning in the corner." She looked from Sarah to me like she was about to cry. "Am I in trouble?"

I shook my head no.

"What's going on, you two?" Burt said.

"It means he was here," Sarah said. "Kip was right here in the house."

Chapter Five

Neither of us got to sleep for a long time. We just held each other and listened to the sounds an old house makes in the night. Sarah's dog, Hoot, had the run of the house, and we could hear him walking out of our room and down the hall to Audie's or Dave's. Sometime just before dawn, packs of coyotes would come down close to yip and howl, maybe raiding the barn for ground squirrels in the grain bin. Sometimes they woke us up. When they woke up Hoot, he barked like hell until the coyotes quit, then he tossed out a few random barks as we were dozing back to sleep, just to let the coyotes know he was on the case. That night one of the yips was high and sharp like a human whistle.

The next morning Burt changed his schedule so he could stay at the ranch with Mom, Dave, and Lorena. That made Sarah and me more at ease. Audie wanted to stay home from school to help Burt stand guard. He said he'd be happy if she did. He said she was tougher than any dozen escaped killers.

"Oh, Burt," Mom said. "Don't say such things. She's just a kid."

"In Afghanistan, girls not much older than Audie carry a Kalashnikov with one hand and balance a baby on their hip with the other."

"*Tommy*," Mom said. "They do not."

Sarah had a long cell-phone talk with Aaron Fuchs, telling him about finding the Remington, and what that meant. One lone escapee or an ally? Or the whole shootin' match? We decided I'd go with Sarah when her shift started. Sarah told Burt she'd call him when we got to Paiute Meadows and pass on any updates. She didn't make a peep for the first twenty miles through West Frémont canyon, but from what she had pried out of Jack, she figured something was up. The river looked pretty and Christmassy with fresh snow on the banks and the boughs of the Jeffrey pine, but Christmas was a long way away.

"I'm trying not to just completely lose it," she said. "First Kip escapes, then he's in our *house*."

"*Someone* was in our house. We don't know it's Kip. He coulda had some crony swipe the rifle the morning of the escape, then plant it in the mudroom just to mess with our heads. To make it look like he was one of the escapees."

Sarah looked at me, not knowing what to think.

"He coulda engineered the whole thing from inside his cell."

Then I told her about the blue truck parked at the edge of our horse pasture the day before.

"You know this has always been my worst nightmare," she said. "I'd hear a noise outside when we're in bed and—"

"I know. But he's still human. More or less."

"Yeah," she said. "And whether it's from the inside of Folsom or the outside, he's got help."

"Even Kip would've needed help to stage a breakout like this. But just to plant the rifle, maybe he got some local guy he knew when he was married to you."

"Please," she said, "don't bring that up."

"Sorry, babe."

She was quiet for a bit. "Sometimes I think you blame me."

"Never. I put you in that shitty situation when I signed up for that third tour. I blame myself for being a commitment-phobic jerk. Never you."

"Well, at least we're clear on that." She leaned over and kissed me on the cheek and almost drove us off the pavement into the river.

The truck was flying when we came up the slope toward the Sonora Junction, each of us alone with our own thoughts. The sky over Sonora Pass was gray, but no snow was falling. As we made the curve by the CalTrans yard, I couldn't help notice that the Marine mechanics had got their job done. The S-U-S-V that had been parked by the side of the road was gone.

The sheriff's office was crowded. A pair of long plastic tables with PROPERTY FRÉMONT COUNTY PUBLIC LIBRARY stenciled along the edge sat on either side of the squad room facing Mitch's office. A blank whiteboard was propped on an easel on one side of Mitch's door. A flat screen TV with the sound off sat on the other side. More chairs were crowded around the room in no particular order. Agents from Alcohol, Tobacco, Firearms, and Explosives elbowed US Attorneys and FBI SWAT personnel for seats at the tables. Federal Bureau of Prisons staff sat next to a couple of my pals from the Forest Service. All of the squad room workstations were occupied, mostly by folks on their phones. Everybody wanted to know why the task force had convened here in Paiute Meadows on such short notice and wondered what the hell was going on.

US Marshals crowded around their boss, Rod Ridgely, at what became the cool kids' table, while he leaned against Mitch's doorway, talking on his phone. You could tell who was from what agency by the letters on their windbreakers or ball caps. Finally, Ridgely put his phone in his pocket and walked over to the whiteboard, waiting for folks to quit talking.

Sarah and I stood off to the side, not saying a word.

Ridgely listed the cons' known route on the whiteboard, from Folsom to El Dorado Hills to Cameron Park to Shingle Springs, then heading up Highway 50 towards Placerville.

Mitch sat on one of the plastic chairs in the middle of the room next to my dad's old team roping buddy, Frémont County deputy sheriff Jack Harney. Mitch looked steamed that he was kicked to the curb so publicly with the election getting closer every day.

Ridgely walked through a quick list of alternate routes from Auburn to Fiddletown but kept going back to Highway 50.

"Seems like," he said, "we didn't focus at least part of our search far enough east. Not by a long shot."

He nodded at Sarah. "Deputy Cathcart? Care to fill us in?"

Sarah straightened up, standing tall and tough in full uniform. She gave a quick summary of my stolen rifle getting planted in our mudroom.

"The Remington two-seventy showed up last night just forty miles north of where we're sitting this minute," Sarah said. "The escaped cons are literally in our backyards."

Ridgely had to quiet the room before he explained what the cat-and-mouse with the .270 meant. That the cons or their allies were close, and that Sarah and our family were possible targets. The escapees were on the move, heading east.

"That's why everybody in this room has gotta re-think," Ridgely said. "Re-focus."

He checked a message on his phone and told the room that the task force leader was just a few minutes out, so sit tight. In the meantime, he fielded a few more questions.

Finally, Ridgely looked beyond Sarah and me through the glass front door of the sheriffs' office. In no time the crowd of local, state, and federal law had turned one-eighties in their clanking, squeaking folding chairs. A Reno TV crew waiting outside pointed their cameras and microphones at a heavyset, gray, seen-it-all, done-it-all, cowboy-hat-wearing non-horseman. The guy pushed through the door and gave the crowd the once-over, making a growling noise that might have passed for human speech.

Ridgely introduced the guy as his boss, the task force leader, US Marshal Arvin Waingrow. I was relieved to see FBI Supervising Agent Aaron Fuchs at Waingrow's elbow.

Waingrow let the press follow him in, and that told me all I needed to know. He rambled on a bit, mostly boilerplate BS about the joint task force and the marshals' role as lead agency and all they had done so far—all organizational crap, no red meat about catching bad guys. He brought out four uniformed sheriffs' officers, one from each of the counties that were involved so far, or were about to be. The four introduced themselves and their counties: Sacramento, El Dorado, Amador, and Alpine. Three were deputies. Sheriff Flint Richmond from Alpine County was there in person. He was the guy Mitch was hoping would help get him back in the game. Richmond asked Waingrow point-blank for an FBI evidence-gathering team to give the East Fork store a once-over on the outside chance any of the convicts had actually come that far into his jurisdiction. Waingrow stayed pretty deferential to Richmond, as the sheriff's reputation as a scrapper was well known.

"What's next beyond those four jurisdictions?" a reporter traveling with the task force said.

"We are," Sarah said, so everybody in the room could hear. "Right here. Frémont County. As of last night. At least one convict—or a coconspirator. Who knows how many more." She retold the story of my stolen .270 appearing in the mudroom again for the late arrivals and explained the significance of an ally of the escaped convicts rooting around on a county officer's back porch. Then Aaron surprised a lot of folks by introducing Mitch Mendenhall of Frémont County, California, now the fifth county sheriff in the game. The most surprised person in the room was Mitch himself. He made it halfway to his feet then sat back down with a little wave, trying to look casual, like being a ground-zero guy in a big-time manhunt happened to him every day.

A second news van from a South Shore TV station pulled up onto the red zone by the glass front door. Waingrow told a deputy sitting on the table to keep them out for now. They griped until Aaron ignored Waingrow and let them in. They were from his backyard, and he obviously wasn't going to piss them off. Fuchs was kind of a quiet guy, but when he talked, folks listened.

Ridgely straddled a chair backwards and stretched his legs while his boss took questions. Waingrow got about four words out when Sarah stood up and pointed to the silent TV.

"Audio," she said. "Turn it on."

The whole room froze. Mitch stumbled out of his chair and grabbed a remote from the table.

A woman in a breaking news close-up was sobbing, saying something about her child and a bus.

She kept crying, "My baby . . . my baby."

Through the static on the screen, a local news guy said something about a place on Highway 50. The room stayed quiet. Aaron was on his phone as he stepped into Mitch's office with Waingrow right behind. After a minute Aaron stuck his head back into the squad room.

"The convicts have hijacked a middle-school bus ten miles west of Placerville."

"Oh, god," Sarah said.

Aaron and Waingrow huddled a bit longer inside Mitch's office, both with their phones in their hands. The other law enforcement folks stayed as quiet as they could, trying to hear.

Aaron came out first.

"No word yet of any casualties."

The room exploded in chatter, then Aaron held up his hand, and things got semi-quiet again.

"Any positive IDs on which escapees were involved?" Sarah said.

Aaron said no, just a tough-looking bugger, armed and no-nonsense.

"We're matching up descriptions with images of our known runners," he said, "plus some photos a few of the kids took with their phones."

"Brave kids."

"There's still about eight children unaccounted for," Aaron said. "Assumed to be still on the bus."

"So, hostages?"

"Waingrow says it's too soon to call the kids hostages," Aaron said.

"Well, what the hell would you call 'em?"

Sarah started to say something when the woman being interviewed howled and the office went dead silent. Then Waingrow started talking, more to news crews than the task force.

He said the hijacked bus was from a school district just west of Placerville, adding that Marshall Ridgely would keep the agencies apprised of any new developments. Then Waingrow huddled with Ridgely a minute or two before hustling out the back entrance to Mitch's office, head down, taking no questions, apparently heading for Placerville. The coverage repeated after he left.

"So," Sarah said, "we're on our own."

"We're on our own."

Local newscasters said the bus had disappeared down one of the narrow roads of the western Sierra foothills and could be heading east towards the Sierra Crest. On what roads or highways, they didn't know. A guy from the Bureau of Prisons said one more Folsom inmate apparently had either escaped from the prison infirmary or had been miscounted when he got returned to his cell.

I saw Sarah mouth the name Kip and shake her head.

Sarah and I left pretty soon after that.

"So why wouldn't that jerk call the kids hostages?"

"That would indicate we're losing ground," Sarah said, "not gaining it."

"Do we have any protocols in place in case crazy-assed convicts show up on our doorstep?"

She put her arm around my waist and shook her head no. It had stopped snowing, and what had fallen in town had turned to ice and slush and mud.

We stepped off the curb to make room when a news crew came outside to do a remote in front of the county sheriff's logo on the exterior wall. A young reporter gave a savvy rundown of the bus hijacking and said all law enforcement was now concentrating in Placerville. Ridgely walked out behind them talking to a woman in snow boots. Those two stopped when they got to us.

"I don't like your boss," Sarah said.

"What can I say," Ridgely said. "The guy's a tool."

The woman stared at Sarah then reached out her hand. "Deputy US Attorney Kathy Avakian. Eastern District, California." Sarah took her hand and shook it.

"Marshal Waingrow and I were supposed to take our show on the road to South Lake Tahoe with Supervising Special Agent Fuchs," the woman said. "Brief the team there. The break-in at that little town store and convicts in your kitchen moved the goalposts on us."

I must've laughed.

"And you are?" she said.

Sarah introduced me, but the lady didn't seem to have much use for civilians. She looked at Ridgely. "Heading for Placerville, Rod?"

"Yeah. Meeting Waingrow there. He wants my 'assessment.' You know, boots on the ground. How to allocate resources and all that cool stuff."

Avakian told him to watch his back then splashed through the slush to her car. Sarah watched her go.

"For boots on the ground, I should take the cowboy, here," Ridgely said. "You wanna go with me, Smith?"

"I think just now Sergeant Smith's place is with his family," Sarah said.

"Oh-*kay*, then," Ridgely said.

"Even money," she said, "the convict missing from the Folsom infirmary is Kip Isringhausen. He is also my ex-husband. This would have sounded pretty far-fetched a year and a half ago when he was on the gurney bleeding to death from gunshot wounds."

"Courtesy of the Sarge, here?" Ridgely said.

"Correct," Sarah said.

Ridgely laughed.

"It seemed stupid for him to promise to escape from prison when Tommy had just put four rounds in him and almost killed him," she said. "But down deep I think we both knew, if anyone could pull off busting out of Folsom, it would be Kip." She said again just how much of a threat the .270 in Dave's mudroom meant. The whole thing had her pretty shook.

"So this shit is no joke to you two," Ridgely said.

"Definitely no joke."

Sarah nodded down the street toward the Sierra Peaks. "Want to grab a bite with us before you go?"

"Best boogie on down the highway," he said. "I'll call you when I get to . . ." He made a face. "Did you good folks know that Placerville used to be called Hangtown?" He touched his fingers to his throat and made a worried face. "That's some messed-up shit, California."

We watched him walk off to a sparkly new Range Rover.

"I'm gonna run into the Sporting Goods and pick up some beef jerky, a six-pack of Sierra Nevada, and a box of .270 soft-points. You want to grab us a booth?"

"No," she said. "I'll stay with you." Then she stopped in her tracks. "Why are you buying ammo? Planning a trip?"

I just shrugged.

We were walking through the slush carrying my stuff back to Sarah's truck when Mitch charged out through the glass doors and hollered at us that all hell was breaking loose in Placerville and we needed to come see it.

We hustled back inside the sheriff's headquarters, pushing through the remaining lawmen and broadcasters in the squad room to get to Aaron. Everyone had their eyes on the screen, a jiggly aerial shot of a hovering FBI SWAT helicopter, probably by some Sacramento news chopper.

Mitch led Aaron and the rest of us into his office. Sorenson and Jack gathered up folding chairs, and we all sat elbow to elbow and watched the monitor. A woman wearing a sidearm and a ball cap stuck her head into the doorway.

"Is this a private party? Or can anybody join?"

"This is ATF Special Agent Isela Sanchez out of Sacramento," Aaron said. We nodded all around.

We could see frantic parents and worried reporters on Mitch's widescreen. Aaron read from his phone that a half hour earlier, a highway patrolman had spotted the carjacked Jeep Cherokee turning off Route 50 a few miles west of Placerville. The Jeep stopped at an In-N-Out on a rise above the highway where any cops could be seen coming from either direction. A pair of women ordered twenty Double-Doubles and extra fries and no drinks, to go. They paid cash then drove eastbound toward Placerville, bold as brass. The CHP officer radioed his position then followed the Cherokee till it turned off the highway. The Jeep pulled over and stopped next to a patch of old oaks, leaving its headlights on in the fading light. The CHP unit dimmed its own lights and waited at the edge of the oaks. When there was no movement from the Jeep by full dark, the officer eased past it slow and shined his spotlight across the Jeep's interior. It was empty. Nothing connected the Jeep to a missing school bus yet, so the patrolman just watched the Cherokee from a distance and waited for backup.

Placerville was an old-timey gold rush camp with a meandering downtown of pre–Civil War brick and frame buildings. A winding semi-new highway ran parallel to it, connecting Carson City to Sacramento along the South Fork of the American just like it had for a hundred fifty years. Steep hills covered with nice old wooden houses rose up on all sides of the town. A highjacked bus couldn't move fast in that country, but there were still a million places to flat disappear. Aaron kept reading from his phone, looking up every little bit to tell us what the cable folks were saying so we could make sense of the jiggly video taken by their local news chopper. The bus had been spotted rattling across the twisty highway just east of the old downtown, a good mile from the last sighting. It disappeared into the growing dark just as fast, and the hunt was on.

The FBI chopper pilot located the hijacked bus through the tree canopy. With the help of the news chopper flying above it, the Feds tracked the bus through woodsy neighborhoods where the roads got narrow and the turns got steep. The bus settled into a steady pace around thirty to forty, and even that was too fast for the terrain. The law enforcement ground pursuit vehicles were only headlights hundreds of yards behind, but they were gaining ground and numbers every minute. The bus picked up its pace, racing through the trees until it twisted so fast through one turn it looked like it would flip.

"So where the hell are they now?"

Aaron showed me a map he was scrolling on his phone.

"If the cons are on that bus and you Feds keep pushing 'em uphill, any chance you can trap 'em?" I looked at the other folks in the room.

"What's on the ridges where that bus is heading?" Sarah said.

"An airport," said Sanchez.

We all kept staring at Mitch's TV, trying to make sense of what we were seeing as the FBI helicopter banked back and forth in the dusk, its image shrinking as the news chopper rose up fast to stay out of its way. Red and blue flashes in the trees lit up the first FBI SWAT armored vehicles. The FBI chopper image was crisp and sharp now as it climbed. I could finally see the slow flashes of a rotating landing beacon on a ridge in the distance.

The bus broke out of the oak and pine and hit asphalt on level ground. It turned parallel to a chain-link fence, picking up speed like the driver knew where he was going. Beyond the fence we could see rows of the dark shapes of windowless buildings.

"Hangars?" Sarah said.

Special Agent Sanchez nodded.

Flying low, the FBI chopper lit up the roofs of the hangars then hovered above the treetops. The bus made a sharp turn into what looked like a rolling gate in the chain-link and plowed right through the gate without stopping. When the trees appeared to drop away as the news chopper rose, a big empty space opened up ahead of the bus. The clearing stretched a half mile out ahead. One-half airstrip, one-half deep ravine. The bus slowed, dragging chain-link and razor wire behind it.

"That's the runway off to the left," Sanchez said.

We could make out the painted stripe on the asphalt as the FBI chopper swung back into our line of sight then began to gain altitude and circle again.

"You been here before?"

"Yessir," Sanchez said. "We conducted an illegal explosives sting here a couple of years ago. Fertilizer bombs."

I asked her if the stolen Marine rifles had shown up on her radar.

"Definitely mine," she said. "Otherwise, *nada.*"

She said she'd had her people checking bad-apple Marines that Billy Jack Kane's little brother Ricky Lee had served with. Guys who might have some knowledge of what happened to the rifles from that heist.

"It's too much of a coincidence that a dozen bad guys bust out of Folsom and head right toward that Marine base," she said. "But now Waingrow is nervous. He doesn't want to scare folks with rumors of top-of-the-line weapons in the hands of murderers."

"If you knew where they were stashed, you could use 'em as bait."

"Don't think I haven't suggested that, Sergeant," Sanchez said.

"And?" I looked across the room at Aaron. When folks I didn't know called me by my old rank, I was never sure if that was a good thing or a bad thing.

"Above my pay grade, apparently," she said.

On the screen two figures stepped out of the shadows and jogged to one of the hangars. The news chopper circled but didn't focus on the hangar until a section of wall swung up like an oversized garage door and lights popped on.

A twin-engine plane rolled out slow from the hangar and headed for fuel pumps, lights off except for dim emergency ones in the cabin. The fuselage flashed in and out of our field of vision from the landing beacon. In the dark I counted four windows along the sides of the fuselage, maybe five, and caught a quick look at what might be the pilot and one other guy as the plane pivoted away from the hangar.

"What d'you think, Aaron? What kind of plane is that?"

"Hard to tell," he said. "Maybe a Piper Navajo?"

It turned again as it got close to the pumps. The two people on foot started dragging a hose toward the plane. When they got close, one of them started fiddling with something on the tank.

"The hell?"

"Credit card authorization," Sanchez said. "After five p.m. the pumps aren't manned. Credit card only."

"Well, I'll be goddamned."

For the first time we could hear the muffled sound of a cop's bullhorn but couldn't make out the words.

"It's too small," Sarah said.

"To be a Piper?"

"To fit a dozen escapees—and maybe little kids to boot."

While we were talking, the school bus came rolling out on the asphalt, barely visible on the side of the screen. Flashing lights of cop cars circled a hundred yards down the asphalt like they were trying to block off the runway. Red and blue lights glowed on the body armor of SWAT and Homeland troops pouring out of their armored transports.

We heard a reporter off-camera ask if law enforcement knew if all the kids were safe. There was cross-talk but no clear answer.

"They better watch it," Sanchez said, pretty much to herself, "or this could turn into another Waco."

I looked over at Sanchez. She was maybe in her forties. She wore boots and Wranglers and a ponytail hanging out a ball cap. Her short parka would let her get to her duty Glock pretty quick.

I looked back at the screen. The school bus rolled into a skid about fifty feet down the airstrip and jerked to a stop with the passenger door facing the plane. The plane's landing lights popped on, and the whole place lit up. In the brightness we could see that one of the two folks at the pumps wrestling the hose was a woman. She looked like she might be the younger of the pair I'd seen at the NAPA a few days before. Then just as quick the exterior lights went dim. It was like the pilot just needed a quick look to get his bearings.

Even with the jiggly news camera and jumpy lighting, I could make out convicts crowding the steps of the bus from the inside. I didn't see any kids.

The first cons down the bus steps were armed, jumping the twisted chain-link and stumbling toward the plane. The two who got there first wheeled around and opened fire at guys behind them still jammed on the bus, now pushing and punching to get out of the line of fire. A couple were gunned down as they hit the asphalt. Another stumbled over the chain-link and was hit as he fought to keep his balance. One more thrashed in twisted razor wire.

Most of the cons weren't armed, and maybe that was part of the plan. In the flashing dark they must've thought it was gunfire from the law coming up behind them, because they kept stumbling and staggering toward the lights. Bodies dropped, blocking the bus steps long enough for five or six shooters to sprint the rest of the way to the plane. I made a rough estimate that maybe a dozen escapees had been in that bus, but the real number was anybody's guess.

"My god," Sarah said. "If any kids were inside . . ."

The two at the pumps stopped fueling, whether full-up or not. The plane turned and taxied away from the bus, making a slow creep toward the center of the runway. The headlights of the cops came up fast. The news chopper got one more good image of the pilot as the plane turned. He was an old white guy wearing a white uniform shirt. He had a gun to his head. Then his body gave a jerk and the plane made a hard stop and we couldn't see him anymore till a door opened and somebody pushed his body out. He landed hard and didn't move. It was an Asian guy who'd capped the pilot and shoved him out the door. We got a good look at him when he jerked his pistol and fired up at the news crew. He looked so close that Sanchez flinched at the shots popping on the screen, and she didn't look like a person who flinched easy. The news chopper rose up to get out of range. The last thing I could see on the ground was the pilot's white uniform shirt oozing dark.

More lights flashed as two highway patrol cars, a sheriff's SUV, and the personnel carrier from FBI SWAT charged into camera range, pouring fire. We watched what looked like Homeland troops in full tactical gear fan out around the bus and start blasting away. A highway patrolman ran right in front of them waving his arms and shouting at them, like maybe he was warning them about possible kids still on the bus. Then fully automatic fire ripped the front of the bus from the plane, taking out anything that twitched. One of the Homeland personnel lay on the asphalt, not moving.

Mitch turned up the volume so we could hear what the cable news people were saying. There was still no mention of the kids.

The TV camera made a jerk to the side then the image went to static. It took almost a full minute for them to get back online. The image was almost pitch black till airplane landing lights popped on again and stayed on. The twin-engine started picking up speed.

"They forgot about the damn plane."

The news guy said pretty much the same thing I did. He speculated that the stalled bus made an easier target.

Aaron turned to me, grim as hell. "What a joke."

When no one was left alive in the bus to fire back, law enforcement finally started targeting the plane, but by then the cons inside had secured all the doors and stopped returning fire.

The flat top of the ridge gave way to a steep slope at the far end of the runway. We watched the plane clear the end of the airstrip, the land falling away under it as it gained altitude, then it banked and disappeared into the dark.

With the plane gone, Homeland agents in their heavy gear advanced on the bus and started stumbling up the steps over the bent chain-link, the bodies, and the razor wire, firing a last few rounds at the men inside who were past firing back.

Sarah and I followed Aaron, Jack, and Sanchez back into the squad room, where a few cops and reporters were still watching shoot-out coverage. Mitch paced around in his office then plopped back down at his desk. We could see him staring at his TV like he knew that the Placerville slaughter meant that the last chance he had for good publicity on the crime-fighting front had just slipped through his fingers. Fate dealt that hand two and a half hours and a hundred-plus miles too far west. Short of some big grandstand play—the kind that could get a fella killed—Mitch would end up a footnote in the county records, nothing more. Except for us letting him know we were just outside his office, we let him be. From where I sat, I could see him reach into his desk drawer and pull out the bottle of Pappy Van Winkle he'd won at the election fundraiser back what seemed like a thousand years before, and just stare at it, nothing more.

Cable news only had the coverage we'd just seen live, so they started replaying it as they added commentary. One of the local announcers said the shoot-out was a victory for law and order, and the lady from the network said that it was a disorganized slaughter from start to finish. The network cut to US Marshal Waingrow standing in a snowstorm under a pop-up tent surrounded by cop cars and flashing lights at a mobile command roadblock somewhere on Highway 50 east of Placerville.

"—for now it looks like the few surviving escapees have made their getaway by air," Waingrow was saying. "We've got a confirmation from the Hangtown Middle School." He paused like he was milking the suspense. "Every one of the kids that was on the bus . . . is *safe.*"

There was some scattered applause from a couple of Highway Patrol officers standing behind him, then the coverage switched back to Placerville.

A reporter stood with two kids about twelve. They said they thought there was a substitute bus driver, a mean-looking guy who missed three of their stops in a row. When the kids started yelling, the driver pulled a gun and called them brats and told them to shut up. Some of them started to cry.

They were on a dark road when the bus stopped. More bad guys were waiting. Some of them wanted to keep the kids as hostages, especially the girls. A guy with an accent told everybody to get off the bus. He told the kids to run and not look back if they knew what was good for them. The two kids on the screen looked pretty composed.

The footage cut back to Waingrow again, snow on his Stetson, listing the spots where the hundreds of personnel from the joint task force would be canvassing the west side of the Sierra Nevada in pursuit of the desperadoes. He mangled his geography a bit but described the plane okay and gave out the ID numbers on the tail with the usual Do Not Approach warning, advising folks to call the hotline number running at the bottom of the screen.

The one reporter on-site in the woods with Waingrow asked him if this was a random collection of convicts who saw an opportunity and took it or something more planned.

"To the best of our knowledge," he said, "this escape was coordinated." He was reading off a tablet. It didn't sound like anything he would've written. "Perhaps planned by a ruthless white-power prison gang." He scanned the tablet again a few seconds.

"The gang calls itself the . . . Whiteflight. It first surfaced at Huntsville Prison in Texas."

Special Agent Sanchez turned her face away from the screen and raised her left arm and muttered "bullshit" into the sleeve of her parka like a kid. Jack laughed.

"What a dork," she said.

Waingrow listened to one more question that got lost in the wind and the pines. "Yeah," he said. "This could be an act of domestic terrorism, but it's too early to be real sure. We're looking into that, too."

The squad room had pretty much emptied out, so I peeked into Mitch's office. I saw him parked at his desk, staring at his expensive bottle of bourbon. He finally poured a shot and took a swallow. Then he made a face and spit it into his wastebasket.

Sanchez turned to Aaron. "Nobody's said jack about stolen Marine rifles. But sooner or later," she said, "these bastards are going to make a move on that ordnance."

"He didn't even get the gang's name right."

"It *was* all planned," Sarah said. "But not the way Waingrow meant. The bus. The plane. Newly stolen vehicles ready and waiting. Then sacrificing half of the crew on the bus to be slaughtered by lawmen or gunned down by their own guys."

"I'd say every bit of it was planned."

"What kind of coldhearted bastard does something like that?" Sanchez said.

Sarah looked at me like she knew the answer. Like there was only one coldhearted bastard we'd ever met who could do something like that and like it.

Sanchez zipped up her parka and stretched.

"Where you heading?" Aaron asked.

"Wherever I can get a tostada and a shot of tequila in this town," she said. "Then in the morning I'm gonna retrace Ricky Lee Kane's steps for the millionth time."

"We do need more boots on the ground," Aaron said. "You guys be safe."

"We've got too much ground and not enough boots," Sanchez said.

We watched the two Feds leave.

"So, what next?" Jack said.

"Find that plane."

Chapter Six

Waingrow had made it clear early the next morning in a long group text that the stolen airplane had given the remaining escapees a long reach, so he didn't want the task force to rule anything out. Not prison gangs or ties to any crime flare-ups in the eastern Sierra—specifically Reno. Not any meth-dealing elements in Silver Springs and not robbery crews or even anti-government militias. He mentioned ATF Agent Sanchez's role for folks who didn't know her and explained she was investigating a tie-in with weapons allegedly stolen from the Marine base the year before by Ricky Lee Kane, the late brother of one of the escapees. The mention was blunt. If those rifles were out there, letting them fall into the wrong hands could be a damn nightmare. Waingrow obviously didn't want to be accused of missing a trick, so by mentioning everything, he focused on pretty much nothing. He wrapped up by claiming that such a big breakout from a famous lockup like Folsom had half the states of California and Nevada totally spooked, and just because some counties hadn't sustained any casualties, there was no way to guarantee that citizens could anticipate they'd be safe until the bastards were either killed or caught. He was Captain Reassurance, but for *el jefe* the text was surprisingly un-crappy. Sarah and I both figured Ridgely must've wrote it for him.

Sarah was on the road to Paiute Meadows again early. Marshal Waingrow had also called for another task force briefing in Frémont County, this one chaired by Deputy US Attorney Kathy Avakian. Waingrow would be heading up a more visible and obviously way cooler briefing in El Dorado County where the big casino there had a nice lunch buffet. Aaron was repping the FBI at that one because it was in his own backyard.

Avakian wanted to parlay with Mitch, Sarah, Jack Harney, Deputy Sorenson, and the undersheriff from Mammoth. Sarah left the house less freaked and more positive than the day before. I told her I'd catch up with her shortly after noon.

After an early breakfast, I saddled up a nice bay colt I'd started that fall. Audie was out of school for the weekend, so I got her mounted on the old mare we'd given her. She, Dave, Mom, and I rode out to gather the main bunch of Dave's cows and calves and push them to a pasture next to the corrals. The calves would be vaccinated the next day and we'd wean them soon after, once the vaccine was well in their system. In a month, the cows would be trucked to Dave's grazing permit out on the high desert for the winter where they'd calve in the spring.

Usually, Dave would hard-ass me for bailing on him in the afternoon, but now he acted relieved that I'd be sticking close to Sarah.

We spread out as we rode, crossing dry ditches cut through yellow grass and early snow. I tried to force my mind on the cattle and on keeping Audie from getting too chargey, but a plane full of armed gunsels kept the rattle going in my brain. Audie had appropriated an old hat of mine. She said I wouldn't miss it as it was so beat to crap. I said, all my hats are kinda old, Snip. She says, well, gimme all of 'em then. I didn't want to get into an argument with the kid, as I seemed to lose every time. I got a laugh just looking at her. The hat, Sarah's old chinks that hung down to her stirrups, her yipping and popping her romal against her right boot. Those boots were new on the first day of school but now were already all run over and worn to hell. We weren't horseback more than a few hours, but it did finally take my mind off the slaughter at the Placerville airport.

By midafternoon I slipped into the sheriff's office and leaned against the back wall. Even with wet boots and dragging spurs, I tried not to draw too much attention.

US Attorney Avakian stood at the whiteboard outside of Mitch's office droning on about changes in the joint command structure. When Avakian was partway through making the job of elite law enforcement hunting a gang of escaped killer convicts in America's high country seem boring, ATF officer Sanchez walked in from the street and sat next to Sarah.

We watched Avakian at the whiteboard drawing stuff—circles and arrows and pie charts and Venn diagrams. She said she was looking for patterns with the help of FBI profilers. As each escapee had been got positively ID'd, they were assigned an investigator from the US Attorney's office. They would open a separate case file from the other escapees, and the investigator would get to know the individual's patterns, friends, and enemies, and all that, and generally get inside his head. I actually thought that was a pretty smart idea. The attorneys would study overlapping groups of friends and enemies, relatives, and partners in crime who could be indicted then leaned on for information or betrayal. The description got a tad boring toward the end, but you could see these attorneys knew their stuff.

Avakian stayed low-key until it looked like she was losing the room. Then she paused for breath and held up a little piece of paper. She said it was a printout of a fuel receipt from the Placerville airport. She said what Isela Sanchez had told us the day before—that after five in the afternoon, the only way to access the pumps was by credit card.

"The name on the receipt was Tiffany Ingalls, age thirty-seven. Last known residence . . . Santa Barbara, California." She caught Sarah's eye. "The sister of presumed escapee Kevin Ingalls. Known to you folks as Kip Isringhausen."

Once her team accessed the account, the name on the receipt also matched recent purchases of hydraulic fluid, hoses, clamps, and stuff special-ordered from the NAPA in Paiute Meadows. Avakian said they were trying to match what type of equipment those hoses and valves could be used for.

"In looking for similar names, and names of purchases along this 'outlaw trail,' my staff came up with a Marjory Ingalls, age sixty-eight, of Carpenteria, California. This woman's credit card was used in a telephone charter of a twin-engine Piper Navajo from Pine Top Aviation of Truckee, California, five and a half weeks ago." She looked at Sarah again.

"Chartered from where to where?" Sarah said.

"From Placerville to Oakland."

"So they had a getaway plane they'd already used, waiting and paid for," Sanchez said. "A lot of planning. Lot of expense."

"Correct," Avakian said. "Since Mrs. Ingalls had hired this same aircraft before, and the pilot and plane returned intact, when she chartered the same aircraft a few days prior to the Folsom getaway, there was zero connection. Just a satisfied return customer. The Pine Top folks didn't think a thing about it."

"The bad guys must have been early or the plane must have been late," Sanchez said, "which would be why it wasn't fueled yet."

"And how they knew where to find the gas pumps in the dark," Sarah said.

She leaned over and spoke so only I could hear. "My former mother-in-law making nice with a charter pilot her son was about to murder. Unbelievable."

"You ever meet the mom?"

Sarah shook her head. "No, thank god. But this witch is one jump ahead of us until we figure this out."

"We are drawing up indictments of these accomplices as we speak," Avakian said.

When the US Attorney was done, we waited to see what Ridgely had to say. It was late in the day. He sat back with his boots on Sorenson's workstation and gave us rubes and locals an update on the search perimeter. They were nice boots, expensive but with no stirrup wear on the instep and no trace of mud or manure. I was thinking that probably the closest those boots got to cattle was Ridgely watching highlights of a Texas Longhorns football game on ESPN. As easygoing as he was, this guy was a walking, talking example of the Federal-State pissing contests I'd grown up hearing about from Dad and other stockmen over water and grazing and trespass my whole life.

Mitch joined me at the back of the room, fiddling with his phone. He didn't look like he'd been paying attention to what was being said. The only one of us who *did* look halfway happy was Ridgely. If he'd made a round trip to Placerville, driving half the night, he still looked fresh as a damn daisy.

". . . so Oakland International is obviously a head-fake," he said. "But we've got eyes on the ground watching all its charter traffic just in case. Actually, all airports both commercial and private within range are covered," he said. "The marshals' service or local officers have staked out most of the smaller public-use airstrips, and we're still waiting for reports from Lee Vining and Lone Pine in the south and Plumas County up to Susanville in the north. I'd bet within a day, our range will expand as far north as Shasta and south to Mojave. Any place within reach."

"I looked up those Pipers online," Mitch said. "Some of those buggers got a humongous range, so those boys could be in Nebraska by now. So you got nothin', is that what you're sayin'?"

"Not exactly," Ridgely said. "You're assuming they left

Placerville with a full tank. Plus, a new Ford King Ranch pickup was stolen last night from a town called Beckwourth"—he stopped a second and checked a note from his pocket—"not far from one of the Plumas County airstrips. Same technique as the three carjackings we've seen in the last couple days. If this theft was connected to our runners, that would put them an hour or so north of Reno, not freakin' Nebraska, and open up a whole new search area up there."

"Well, jeezo-christ," Mitch said.

There were more groans from folks in the room. Ridgely was sticking to the facts, so things were tolerable till Aaron and Waingrow and a couple more of his marshals stomped back in with new snow on their boots. Waingrow glanced over at me standing off to the side for a second then looked back at the Frémont County staff. "You about done here, Deputy Marshal Ridgely?"

Ridgely nodded yeah.

Waingrow took a few questions. Sorenson asked about skinhead gangs. Jack Harney reported on the high alert status of folks at the Frémont River Paiute reservation and that was about it. Waingrow looked at his notes. "Okay, people. Our focus needs to be on recapturing these"—he looked down at a legal pad—"seven remaining felons and their accomplices. We got six dead, so we're making progress."

"With all due respect to you folks, sir . . . weren't those dead cons all killed by their fellow prisoners?"

"And who are you, again, sonny?" He didn't say it nice.

"As you know," Aaron said, sarcastic as hell, "this is Staff Sergeant Thomas Smith, formerly US Army, currently a wilderness outfitter. He knows this area better than anyone in this room. The Bureau has relied on the sergeant's knowledge *and* temperament more than once."

So Aaron wasn't hiding his annoyance super well, either.

"Just to be clear," Waingrow said, "you got no function here."

"Wasn't asking for any."

The boss marshal didn't see Ridgely smile like a damn Buddha.

After a few more remarks, Waingrow finally adjourned the meeting and told Ridgely to gather his gear. They were driving back to Douglas County in fifteen minutes.

Ridgely stopped at Sarah's desk.

"Didn't your boss just come from there?" Sarah said.

"We'll be catching a government plane in Minden," Ridgely said. "Head back over the hill to Sacramento then drive up Fifty *again* with some Eastern District honchos to inspect the Placerville mess."

"Why not fly directly to Placerville? I hear they got an *awesome* airport."

Ridgely laughed. "Funny guy."

"Just sayin'."

"*El jefe* don't like flying in the mountains after sundown," Ridgely said.

"Still, Ridgely, I hear a guy can drive from here to Placerville in two and a half hours."

"You be sure and tell *el jefe* that, Sarge."

"Careful, then," Sarah said.

"Like I got a choice?"

"What does he need you for?"

"I'm the detail guy, mister. Brief the pooh-bahs of the

90

regional task force so they can brief the DOJ in Washington. Calm those troubled waters. And know the details so *el jefe* don't have to."

"Better you than me, buckaroo."

"High-profile mayhem makes folk insecure," he said.

"In the army we had a name for your job."

"So I've heard," Ridgely said.

After he left, Sarah got on her phone to check on her dad.

"Tell Burt I saw his boys got that Small Unit Support Vehicle repaired."

Sarah listened a minute, then signed off.

"Burt told me it wasn't fixed," she said. "It was stolen."

She'd told her dad we were going to catch dinner in Paiute Meadows, then she told Mom to tell everyone there we were fine. Aaron and Isela Sanchez stopped us at the side door to the Sierra Peaks.

"Got a minute?" she said.

"Sure." I felt both of them were checking me out. "What's up?"

"The ATF would like to pick your brain," Isela said.

"I only know what you know."

"Come on," Sarah said. "We were about to get some dinner."

We took a booth under a banner that said in big letters DON'T FORGET TO VOTE. Three of us ordered rib-eyes. Isela ordered shrimp scampi and caught me making a face.

"What?" she said.

"I always thought it was safer to order seafood if there wasn't a bunch of mountain ranges between you and the ocean."

"My guy never actually orders seafood," Sarah said.

"Before I met these two," Aaron said, "I didn't even know what a rib-eye was. I was more of a sand dabs or sushi kinda guy."

"They got this thing called refrigeration," Isela said. "You ever been on the deck of a commercial fishing boat, you better hope to hell they freeze the catch and keep it frozen till they get your dinner on the plate." She laughed. "Just funnin' you guys. My uncle ran a trawler down off Loreto."

"Dorado or yellowtail?" Aaron said.

"Guns mostly," Isela said.

"So you come to your vocation naturally," Sarah said.

"Smart *and* pretty," Isela said.

The Sierra Peaks had a smallish bar off the dining room with its own entrance to the sidewalk. When things got busy, a big bartender named Cedric brought the drinks to the tables himself. Isela had ordered Jack on the rocks, but not until I did.

"So where do you think Ricky Lee Kane hid the guns he stole?" she said.

"Why ask me?"

"Don't get all bashful," Sarah said.

"Since the breakout, folks think Sarah and me know too much."

"Don't you?" Isela said.

"I figure what you guys figure. That Ricky Lee stashed them pretty close to the base, but because of his dishonorable discharge, not so close that Marine training units would spot him coming or going."

Cedric put the drinks down then kinda hesitated, like maybe he expected me to say something.

"Hey, Cedric. This early winter cut into business much?"

"Naw, Tommy, it's all good."

He gave us all a wave then walked back to the bar.

"What was that all about?" Aaron said.

"Like I said, folks think we're some sort of experts."

"It's just my husband's fan club," Sarah said.

Isela was itching to talk, so I got back to it.

"I'd guess the rifles were stashed close to the base but not too close. I figure we can rule out those miles between the Reno Highway and the base. Rough weather rules out anyplace west of the base up to Sonora Pass. I'd say that puts you within a dozen miles on either direction from Sonora Junction. Ricky Lee probably had a spot picked out and some boys waiting to help him hide the goods."

"Does it matter which state he hid them in?" Sarah said.

"Not really," Isela said. "It's all federal as far as we're concerned."

"Typical."

"Ignore the husband," Sarah said.

"Any likely guesses?" said Aaron.

Isela took a pocket notebook out of her jacket and started scribbling. Old school, even for me.

I moved my drink and turned my place mat over and started drawing a crappy-looking map with the pencil from my tallybook. Equally old school. I drew two intersecting roads. "Here's the Sonora Junction." I drew a circle. "Now here's the Marine base. If Kip was in on the heist, I'd say search the Monte Cristo mountains just north of here." I made some wavy lines for mountains then drew an X in the middle of them. "When Sarah and I were tracking Kip, trying to find her dad, we stumbled onto a pot farm of his up one canyon. Then, Feds found a girl's corpse—a girl who'd burned Kip in a Santa Barbara drug deal—dumped in a mine shaft on the east side of the range."

"Still in her bikini," Sarah said.

Isela grimaced. "So maybe Kip would go back to a hide-out he knew," she said.

"But I'm guessing he was already in the joint when the rifles were swiped."

"I can check on that," Aaron said. He took out his iPad.

"So if Kip was in prison during the heist," Isela said, "there's no way Ricky Lee could have navigated the Monte Cristos without him?"

"Too much country back there. And too steep. They'd either get lost or drop off a hundred-foot ledge." I drew another circle. "Here's Hell Gate Pass. There's two-track roads that run south and west from the old pack station, but it's right on the highway. Not a lot of cover."

"Is this the West Fork of the Frémont?" Aaron said. He followed the place mat to the upper right corner.

"Right. From the Sonora Pass turnoff to Shoshone Valley it's twenty winding miles with steep canyon walls boxing you in. You go beyond that another ten or fifteen miles, there's lots of open country west of Monitor Pass, but it's way too far from the base with too much exposed road."

A kid waiting on us brought salads. I set mine off to the side of my homemade map. Isela leaned over the table, studying the scribbles. The only place I hadn't drawn on was in the upper left.

"So what's this empty space over here?" she said.

Sarah was watching me. She'd already figured it out.

"That's where you'll find your stolen Mk thirteen sniper rifles, I expect."

We were all silent a bit, just staring at my map. Aaron asked where it was. I got a fresh place mat. I started at the Marine base and sketched the Sonora Pass route. Then I marked a dirt road that went a long way up a wide canyon less than a mile south from the Sonora turnoff.

"What's up there?" Isela said.

"A million places to hide," Sarah said.

"What's it called?" Isela said.

"That's Hanging Valley," said Sarah. "Right under our noses."

"Describe it."

"The dirt road up the canyon is well maintained. Farther up it climbs through timber along a creek. You said the guns were stolen in late winter. If the snow wasn't bad, this would've been a quick way off the highway then out of sight into the backcountry."

"So, access to a paved road but close to some empty country, too." Isela said.

"Yeah. Where you could see pursuit coming and disappear."

"Any commercial activity?" Isela said. "Vacation homes?"

"In summer, folks run cattle the first few miles. There

used to be a cow camp, too. Maybe some sheep. Back a way there's ruins of mines and some nice meadows for grazing, plus beaver ponds and such."

"What did they mine back there?" she said. "Silver?"

"Molybdenite."

"What the hell is mo—?" Isela tried to pronounce it.

"Molybdenum disulfide," Sarah said. "M-O-S-Two. Similar to graphite." Sarah gave the woman a shrug—like she was just born knowing that stuff.

"Sorry I asked," Isela said. "They don't still mine it?"

"Not for decades," Sarah said.

"What's up there this time of year?"

"Late deer hunters, early cross-country skiers, snow campers, cowboys huntin' strays they missed before the snows, nature photographers. You name it."

"Is there a back way out of the canyon?" Aaron said.

"Not by vehicle. Even horseback it's *rough* country."

"An outdoorsy boy like Aaron here could climb out over Flatiron Ridge," Sarah said, "at the head of the canyon, right, hon?"

"Maybe in July."

"Look," Isela said. "We could be getting ahead of ourselves. These guys haven't been sighted since they flew out of Placerville. They could be a thousand miles away in any direction."

"Not if the guns were with 'em."

Isela pondered that. "True."

"They're here, or they're close to it." I told her about Kip's mother and sister at the NAPA. Repeated my story about Dad's .270 stolen from the pack station outhouse and told them about the blue pickup parked off in the distance a half mile from our ranchyard. And now the stolen Marine

Susvee. I left out my hallucinations of masked warriors in black like Johnny Cash on crack.

We finished up and Aaron got the check.

"You want Tommy to show you the canyon?" he said, pretty much out of nowhere. "That way if your crew has to move on it, you'll know what you're dealing with." He looked at me. "I know you're itching to. Scouting with Isela would make you semi-official."

"Like my guide," Isela said.

Sarah gave Isela a tense look that the ATF lady didn't notice.

"I'll contact Ridgely tonight," Isela said. "See what support he can give us—and how soon."

"When are you thinking?"

"Tomorrow morning work for you," Isela said, "for kind of a drive-by? Get the lay of the land. That'll give me another full day to line up a chopper. Then do a thorough recon."

Sarah sipped her pinot noir, not taking her eyes off me.

Isela and Aaron kicked around some details, and I told Isela where to meet me. She left first, heading back to the sheriff's office.

I looked at Aaron and laughed. "Dorado or yellowtail? Shit, Aaron. You're full of surprises."

"You're not the only Mister Outdoors here anymore, babe," Sarah said.

Sarah and I usually took turns driving when we were lucky enough to be driving together. That night she was behind the wheel with a fuzzy half moon rising behind us and flecks of snow swirling in the headlights. I studied the country on either side of the highway, knowing it was always changing if you knew what to look for. A dozen miles north of town we crested Hell Gate Pass, the shallow divide flanked with crumbling vertical rock spilling toward the pavement. Sarah's Silverado zipped downhill past the boarded-up juke joint at the hot springs, then past the gravel turnoff into Hanging Valley.

"You mad?"

I watched the early moonlight shining across open hills to the west above the Marine base then toward Sonora Pass and the Sierra crest.

"What was your first clue?" Sarah said.

Next morning, I got back to the junction about fifteen minutes before ATF Agent Sanchez. I pulled off the paved road and looked over the country. Hanging Valley spread out wide by the highway with both pine and pasture easy to see from the pavement even with the new snow. I knew from gathering cattle and leading pack trains of deer hunters in high school that trails spiderwebbed along the creeks and pastures and disappeared into the timber and over the ridges. Places to get lost and places to hide.

I was back on the road in less than a minute. The rising sun hit the clouds from a new storm that was coming in fast, first bright orange from the sunrise then purple then gray then black. In another few minutes, Hanging Valley would be socked in with little left visible from the road.

Around the bend I pulled over at the Sonora Junction. I parked close to where I remembered the all-terrain Marine Susvee had sat, then I got out to study the ground. Some Cal-Trans equipment from their maintenance yard had criss-crossed through the gravel since the Susvee had been there but I found its tracks easy enough.

I kicked the snow with my boot toe now and then to see if I'd missed anything. I found where vandalized hydraulic lines had dripped into the gravelly ground before the snow had covered it, and where the wide rubber tracks had dragged the tarred gravel as someone drove it off. Where the tracks hit the highway they left parallel black smudges in the asphalt. That made me think whoever was driving the thing maybe didn't have too many hours experience on that machinery. Once I walked out onto the road, the smudges appeared to turn south. Then they faded out under all the tires that had passed over since. I looked back toward Hanging Valley then west toward the pass and the training base. Everything was close to everything else, just a few miles from the canyon to the base. I stepped back as a tractor-trailer hauling sand hissed by in a sharp wind on its way south.

Isela pulled up in her rental Chevy and we hopped into Sarah's pickup. We passed the old barn downhill from the highway and turned onto the dirt road another half mile on. The road ran high on the left shoulder of the canyon, and I cruised along at about thirty on the trackless snow but dropped to half that before long. I liked how Isela didn't say much, her eyes scanning the wide valley below us on the right. When she noticed I'd drained my Yeti, she refilled it from her thermos.

"Hope you like it black," she said. She was quiet for a minute, then, out of nowhere, "I rode horses as a kid." She kinda smiled to herself.

We followed the road as the canyon narrowed and were in aspen and Jeffrey pine soon enough.

"In Oakdale."

"What?"

"Where I rode horses as a kid. Oakdale, in the Central Valley. A Portagee rancher ran a horse camp for kids there."

We were quiet a while longer.

"You fly over these mountains from Sacramento to Reno, you forget how much country there is up here," she said. She lowered her head for a better look out the windshield. "Forget how far you are from human habitation. How easy it is to disappear up here."

"City people think it's easy to hide yourself in empty country, but you stick out to folks who live there. They can spot a person who doesn't belong a mile off."

"You counting on that?" she said.

"Yup." I drove on a bit more. Thinking more than driving. Now it was me looking out the windshield, scanning the country.

"What would it take for you and Ridgely to bring some force up here? To flush out the cons if the guns turn out to really be their play?"

"If there's any hint these guys are within spitting distance, I can bring force to bear." She looked out at the new snow and took pictures with her phone. "The marshals are the lead agency, but we each have our own turf. I'll be giving

Ridgely a heads-up about this place to make sure it's on his radar, if it isn't already." She took more pictures then put her phone in her pocket.

"Did the marshals set up the fake buyer in Idaho?"

"*I* set up the fake Idaho buyer," Isela said. "Ricky Lee had sold explosives to skinheads up by Hayden Lake before."

We went over what would be a good landing spot for a chopper if we could get one by the next morning, and who should go with us if we got the go-ahead. Her choice was Sarah to represent the local law and Ridgely, if we could track him down, representing the task force.

"Yeah. I was the agent on-site at Hayden Lake when our takedown of Ricky Lee went sideways," she said after a pause. "It was a sting. He didn't know what hit him."

She didn't say anything for a minute.

"I did want to take him alive, though."

"This deal gets froggy, we might all be sorry you didn't."

We pulled out of the trees below rolling meadows.

"You're the only one around here who thinks like I do," she said.

"It's 'cause I think you're right. This used to be my business. I know what that hardware is worth. And what it can do."

"You and Billy Jack Kane both."

"What'd you mean?"

"I thought you knew," she said. "Before he got sent to Folsom, Billy Jack had been in the army, too. Ricky Lee was trying to follow in his big brother's footsteps, except in the Marines."

"Doing what?"

"Being a sniper," she said. "Billy Jack Kane was an Army sniper. Just like you."

Chapter Seven

Visibility dropped fast. We kept climbing, winding through trees we could barely see on a road that went from rock solid to mush with the turn of the wheel.

"I think we've gone about as far as we need to."

Isela had been leaning her head against the passenger window looking a million miles away till she jerked upright when I talked.

"Okay by me," she said.

The road dropped into a gully. I crossed over a rusted-out culvert and almost got us stuck backing up. The low-hanging morning light was just a dirty yellow cloud with a bright-white eyeball-searing smudge of fog where the sun was supposed to be.

"It'll be good to take a chopper up here to check for any sign of our runners." She laughed. "And with Rod in the loop, Waingrow can't hard-ass you."

"I just want to rule out this canyon—or put a target on it. Either way."

"You don't think we'll be ruling anything out, Smith. You think we'll find the freakin' mother lode."

"Don't you?"

"I wouldn't be here if I didn't. Finding the rifles and the cons both? Sweet."

She laughed and topped off my Yeti with the last of her coffee. We were back at the Sonora Junction about thirty minutes later. I walked her to her car as we went over details we'd need to cover the next day—providing she could get task force support for a chopper.

"A person wouldn't want to slog up that canyon in the snow on foot," she said. "Especially if they thought a half dozen killers were waiting for them."

"I never go anywhere on foot."

I got back in the Silverado and watched Special Agent Sanchez wheel around and drive off south into the storm. She was kind of a character, but I liked her. Weird sense of humor and tough as a boot.

The black sky rolled behind me, keeping pace with the Silverado like it was chasing me. A light snow started to fall again. I stuck to my own thoughts, winding north in the canyon of the West Frémont. At the bottom of Shoshone Valley, ten miles south of Dave's Ranch, the canyon opened up at a wide spot on the highway called Three Flags. It wasn't much more than a few bungalow motels and a chainsawed life-size grizzly in front of an Indian trading post where tourists could buy their kids Minnetonka moccasins or rubber-topped tom-toms and where the last grizzly was shot more than a hundred years before. Down the road a quarter mile more, I passed a grocery with gas pumps out front. I got out and bought a cardboard cup of coffee for the last twenty-five miles. I didn't see many customers.

There'd been no trace of the escapees since Placerville, so I tried to put the convicts out of my mind and think about fall chores. Out on the winter permit there were spring boxes to rebuild and water tanks to repair and floats to replace. Back at the ranch there'd be steers to ship and yearlings to doctor and fences to mend, all before any more big snows. I tried to keep the hallucinations in the distance, but there were times when I was working alone and far from headquarters when they'd creep up on a guy and tap you on the shoulder.

About five miles from the ranch I saw I had a text from Mitch. He said he'd got a heads-up by text from Alpine County Sheriff Flint Richmond. Mitch had been saying that the guy's hide was chapped as much as his was. Richmond was mad that the Feds—every damn kind of Fed—were tramping all over his jurisdiction when he was the designated law—the *only* law in his county as far as he was concerned. Richmond was a rawboned old hardnose who'd climb down to hell and back to follow a lead or protect his turf. Mitch said the guy's text claimed he'd found something suspicious in the East Fork general store break-in, but he wouldn't say what. Richmond figured the two of them oughta look into it together and leave the US marshals out of it. They just might find those escaped cons all by themselves. After all, who knows that country better than them?

The most irregular thing I'd seen up to then was how damn long Mitch's text was. I guess Richmond got him all stirred up. Mitch's text ended, "Want to come along? Come armed."

I got hold of Sarah. She was already down in Paiute Meadows, probably passing Hanging Valley when I was up in the canyon exploring. She wanted to go with me to East Fork, but after we talked it out, we were both afraid that Mitch might get himself in a tight spot acting by himself in a place where he had zero authority. She said it wouldn't hurt to keep an eye on that part of the country, especially as Richmond had that loose-cannon reputation. He supposedly packed a single-action Army Colt .45 with all chambers loaded, gunfighter style. Figured a hammer resting on an empty chamber was for sissies. And no Sig Sauers for that cranky old fart.

Sarah sounded in a good enough mood I figured I'd tell her I was thinking of hauling a horse. "You know. Just in case."

Sarah was quiet a minute—then sarcastic. "And . . . why?"

"I'll take your old trailer. Look like some retiree local or maybe a weekending tourist out for a pleasure ride."

"So you want to have a horse—just in case?" she said.

"Well, yeah. Without you, a horse'll give me somebody to talk to."

"Baby, you are *so* weird." I could hear her laugh over my crappy cell service. "I'm sure that's just a super-good idea, hon."

"I knew you'd like it."

"Make sure you only observe, okay? Kip's crew could be anywhere. And—"

"And don't do anything stupid?"

"That would be a good plan," she said.

"Okay. I love you."

"Love you too, babe."

I thought back. In the ten-plus years I knew him, I never got a text from Mitch Mendenhall before. Not once.

At the ranch I filled Burt in on what I was up to and asked to borrow his truck. Then I hitched Sarah's old Cal-Poly Miley two-horse to Burt's F-250 and put on a feedstore ball cap instead of my buckaroo 10X beaver, along with my letter-man's jacket from high school to add to the non-horseman gunsel factor. Then I saddled and loaded my go-to gelding, a horse I wouldn't mind betting my life on. Sarah would laugh at me in the jacket, the ball cap, and her old trailer, but I was hoping that looking even the tiniest bit different than usual might buy me an extra split second if I walked into trouble in that little town. Sometimes that's all the chance a guy gets. I'd told Burt where I was going, but I didn't tell him what I was doing. Not all of it, anyway, though when he saw me buckle on my 9mm and slide the .270 into the saddle scabbard, he walked around his Ford like an insurance appraiser in a body shop. This whole meet-Mitch thing seemed *all* wrong. But he wanted me in the little general store in East Fork, California, and I didn't want to let him down.

Two roads led to where I was going. The steep curvy nine-mile-or-so climb from the cleft in the mountain I'd driven up with Mitch a few days before was out. The snow had closed the pass. That left a big loop thirty-some miles north of Dave's ranch that cut through the new houses south of Gardnerville out to Highway 88. I got Sarah's voicemail and was giving her an update when she came on the line. I expected her to talk me out of what I was doing, saying how the marshals would raise hell about locals freelancing, but I was wrong.

"You humiliate someone in their own house like the marshals did to Mitch," she said, "you own whatever crazy stuff they might do to get their dignity back."

That woman never stopped amazing me.

The road left the suburbs and passed a few historic ranches then followed 88 up to the West Fork of the Carson, out of the valley and into the trees, heading for the Sierra crest.

If Alpine County wasn't just next door to Frémont County I wouldn't bother, but like Sarah said, it was near enough to tempt Mitch to try something really stupid on his own. At an old gas station and store I turned left off 88 heading back south. I skirted the top of a pretty little pocket of rangeland called Diamond Valley that held a couple of ranches plus some grazing land of the Southern Washoe. That country was crisscrossed with roads, some paved, more not, some going back to the early Comstock and Pony Express days. Some of the roads I'd never laid eyes on. After winding through pine and meadow and cattle, I was back into the town of East Fork. There was no traffic and new snow was sticking on the asphalt. A restaurant in an old building had a purple chalk sign outside saying they wouldn't be open till four thirty. I passed the stone courthouse before I knew it. By the time I found a wide spot to turn the two-horse trailer around and park the rig, I was already out of town.

I climbed a patch of snowy lawn in front of the courthouse and went inside. A uniformed deputy writing a report told me sheriff Richmond wasn't there. The guy looked me over with my jacket that barely covered the butt of my Beretta and said Richmond was up in Carson City at a prison-break task force meeting. He said he'd heard of somebody named Mitch Mendenhall but never met him. The deputy and a woman on the phone in an office off the lobby seemed to be the only people in the place. I asked the deputy if he could call his sheriff for me. He said that Richmond always turned his department radio off when he was in a meeting. I asked if he could call the sheriff's cell phone.

"I saw him bring a county budget meeting to a dead stop when a phone in somebody's pocket went off," he said. "But knock yourself out."

He went back to his keyboard.

"He only uses his phone for family business." He didn't look up from his typing.

"And the service is truly horrible," the woman said.

"So, no word he was expecting a visit from the Frémont County Sheriff?"

"Not that I heard."

The guy stopped typing and finally looked up.

"Sorry. We're not blowing you off. I haven't talked to the boss since my shift started."

I walked back outside where the snow on the grass was slippery with slush. I got to the truck and just stood there a minute. Then I walked up the middle of the main street.

The old-timey general store that Richmond had texted Mitch about looked the same as it did a couple of days before, so I was wondering what the big deal was as I studied the place harder, just to be sure. It sat just two wooden porch steps up from the pavement. I opened the double doors, and a bell I hadn't noticed when it was just Mitch and me rang as I stepped inside. I was careful not to cut myself on a single broken pane of window glass next to the doorknob that I hadn't noticed before either. It looked like a clumsy burglar had paid the place a second visit. I took out my phone and shuffled around among the mosquito repellent and sunscreen and candy bars. A guy in a dirty black tee shirt stood behind the counter, but I didn't look at him. I stopped to check out more fishing and camping stuff plus canned food and cookout condiments. A room off to the right appeared to be an add-on a few feet lower than the rest of the store. A second guy, tall and scrawny with spiky yellow hair, stood at the back of that room stuffing canned food and snack food in grocery bags and stuffing his face with a Twix bar. He stared at me then turned away and picked up two full bags. His cheap jeans sagged on him enough so I caught a glimpse of a pistol butt. I stepped back and he brushed by me, setting the bags on the floor by the door. He gave me a last hard look when he headed into the back room for a second load.

I walked around the rest of the store. Both guys watched me all fake secret-like, and I watched them watch me. I stopped at a sign on a doorframe that said private. A hanging blanket covered all but the bottom two feet of the doorframe. I turned away but not before I saw a pair of bare feet in ratty slippers sprawled on the floor. There was just a bit of blood soaking into the green rug. I turned away like I hadn't seen anything and walked toward the counter. On the way I stopped at some cheap plastic rain ponchos then looked down at my phone as I closed the last few feet to where the big guy stood.

"No work."

"Huh?" I looked up. I was looking into the face of Vanya Vasiliev, Folsom tats and all. A dirty gray cigarette hung from his lower lip, defying gravity. I recognized him in an instant from all the news coverage. He almost looked like he was expecting me.

"Cell phone." He shook his head. "Don't work up here." He tried to smile, but his mouth just drooped. The cigarette hadn't moved.

I put a couple of twenties on the counter.

"How 'bout a bottle of Jack?"

He turned to the liquor bottles on the shelves behind him, taking his time. I could see the rolls of muscle on his neck and the dark skin and stubbled black hair. He picked up a bottle but didn't turn around.

"I figured you more for the Maker's Mark kind of guy."

He tried grinning again when he turned around, a bottle of Jack Daniel's in one big fist, a fifth of Maker's Mark in the other. I saw a broken tooth and two gold ones. Even across the counter his breath stunk. His lower lip still drooped. His forehead was tiny and dirty. I was trying to find something to like about the guy but coming up short.

Maker's Mark was what Kip Isringhausen drank. Or used to drink. He and I had a long boozy talk comparing Maker's Mark to Jack Daniel's one night when he and Sarah were living in the double-wide after Dave disappeared. Right after Sarah had texted me at Fort Benning, asking me to come home.

So this Russian knew who I was. He knew all about me except where I was going to die. In this town? In this store? Or maybe he knew that, too. It didn't tell me if the text from Mitch was fake and this was part of Kip's plan or not, but it did tell me Kip was even closer than anybody suspected.

"Maker's Mark is for punks, punk."

Vasiliev stopped smiling. I yanked the bottle of Jack from his fist and headed for the door without looking back. I didn't wait for my change.

The second guy stepped in from the side, blocking my path. It took me a second to decide between breaking the whiskey bottle or touching this creep. I switched the Jack to my left hand and grabbed a fistful of greasy hair, dragging his face down as I brought my knee up. Then I jumped back so's not to get any of his blood on me.

Vasiliev must have took about thirty seconds to get his pal squared away and straightened up then fifteen seconds more to make sure the storekeeper with the ratty slippers on the floor of the back room was good and dead. The bell over the door told me exactly when the two cons slammed out of the store and started scanning the empty street for me.

I'd hustled behind parked cars on the narrow pavement, not looking back right away, putting some distance between us. I got a good look from the recessed doorway of an antique shop. They were still on the covered porch of the general store with the spiked-hair guy trying to stop the blood pouring down his face. Vasiliev grabbed him by the back of his shirt and pointed down the way I'd come, then he crossed the street and walked the other direction. If he was cold out there in just a stinking tee shirt, he didn't show it. When he waited for a car to pass I ducked in a coffee shop with painted come-ons covering the glass, watercolor paintings of steaming cups at tourist prices. It was an old building, like all the buildings in town.

Vasiliev walked by the window then stopped. He was only about twelve feet from where I stood on the other side of the glass, staring in at the tables and at a guy with a goatee standing behind an espresso machine. Vasiliev rubbed his stubble and put his nose against the glass and his hands on either side of his face, trying to block the glare. The guy looked like he'd eat your liver for a latte. He also looked as dumb as concrete. I was wondering what in hell Mitch had got himself into. After thinking about it, I had to laugh out loud. Loud enough that the goateed guy turned to look at me. Goofy old Mitch Mendenhall had stumbled on a couple of the hard-assed escaped cons and maybe more. Cons that the entire states of California and Nevada were looking for, and he'd done it all by himself.

Vasiliev backed into the snowy sunlight and moved on down the street. I gave him two or three minutes to put some distance between us then walked out the back door of the coffee shop and hopped over picket fences and crossed vacant lots and frostbit flower beds, leaving footprints in new snow. I headed back to the courthouse, walking over snow-dusted grass to the front door. My footprints in the lawn had been pretty much obliterated by bigger, heavier prints—like from work boots. Inside, the courthouse was empty. The deputy and the clerk were gone. I stood alone in the entrance, just me and my bottle of Jack. I could hear calls going right to voicemail. Lights were on. A sports call-in show was talking about the 'Niners running game. A back door was open.

A wide trail of footsteps and a little sprinkle of blood led to a snowless rectangle on wet asphalt where a long vehicle had been parked. From bare spots where tires had sat, tracks headed out of the parking lot and disappeared northbound. I ran up to the road in time to see a tan Mercedes van with a county logo on the side round a curve.

I ran back to Burt's truck, checked my horse in the trailer, and hopped behind the wheel. I followed the van out of town from a good ways back, barely keeping a visual as the road wound through thin stands of timber heading toward the way I'd come. Still, it was one of those tall Mercedes, so it was easy to follow.

Since nobody on Richmond's staff knew anything about either Mitch or the convicts, I was guessing Vasiliev and the other guy were just some sort of scouting and foraging party. There was no way of knowing for sure if Kip was with them or close by, but he had to be. Nothing else made sense. All I knew for certain was he'd gone to some trouble to get to this part of the country, so close to the Cathcart ranch. Going face-to-face with the bastard was the least I could do.

Ahead of me I could see the van slow up. Either the road was bad or the van was turning off or they'd spotted me. The afternoon wind was picking up and the big gusts threw fresh powder against the windshield hard enough that I had to drop to a full stop in a mini-whiteout. It was like riding an Apache gunship through a sandstorm when you didn't know which way was up. My mind went from those Apaches back to the cave and to Hendershott, wondering what ever happened to him or if he was even still alive. The gusts faded. The van was gone, and the road ahead was clear except for light snow in the trees. I flinched when I thought I caught a figure in black out of the corner of my eye, like one of the guys wrapped in black from head to toe dancing around outside the Afghan cave. I jerked my head around, but there was nothing to see but the swirl of snow reflecting on the lenses of my Ray-Bans.

I stopped harder than I should've with a horse in the trailer. A second blast of wind hit, and I stumbled out of the truck, gulping for air, trying to shake away the dizziness from my head and from the hallucination. I leaned on the door handle thinking I'd pass out, then ripped off the seal on the whiskey and had a gulp, then another. After a minute I got back in the truck but left the door open, taking deep breaths in the raw air. I forced myself to focus on the road until I saw the van up ahead. It was a Special Ed minibus with a "watch for children" warning on one rear door and "frequent stops" on the other. It was creeping along slower now, putting me closer than I wanted to be. I maintained my speed and rolled on by it, watching it turn off to the right behind me onto a narrow strip of asphalt that climbed a pine-covered hill. I kept going on the road without losing speed. Turning off to follow the van would totally blow my cover if I hadn't blown it already. I pulled over at a wide spot in the road about a hundred yards down. I'd brought the horse in Sarah's old trailer for more of a prop or a distraction than anything, but I needed him now to catch up with the van and not get seen. That big sorrel was coming on six and glad to get out of that little trailer.

The van was on a road that curved back and forth as it climbed. I caught up with it pretty quick, keeping downhill, hoping to stay out of the line of sight of any passengers. The side windows were smoked, so it was tough to tell if I'd been spotted or not. Where my path merged with the paved road, I held back until the van was a dozen car lengths ahead of the horse. Then I stayed on its tail at a long trot. The road curved to the left around the edge of a marshy lake, a queasy green-and-yellow acre or two in the half light of falling snow.

Beyond the lake the road broke out of the trees into open ground. I pulled up the gelding at the foot of a slope in the cover of the last of the trees and waited to see where the van was headed. I could tell by watching its bumping and rocking that the road ahead was rough with broken pavement. A long strip of bare ground ran parallel to the road. Beyond that was a wall of scrubby timber. Something orange flickered against the shadows of the pines, a bit of bright color snapping in the breeze. Then I could make out what it was. I was looking at a windsock. The van drove out to the center of an empty airstrip and stopped. Now everything made sense.

Chapter Eight

The twin-engine plane sat on the airstrip tucked in against the pines. The rear doors of the van slid open, and two people, the deputy and the courthouse clerk, were dragged out by Vasiliev and the spiky-haired guy. The deputy tried to grab the second man. A single shot was fired. The woman screamed and the deputy fell. There was no telling whether he was dead or wounded.

More convicts jumped from the side door of the plane reacting to the gunshot. There was crap and trash scattered around like they'd been holed up for a couple days—since Placerville. That timeline would be about right. The deputy and the courthouse lady had been tied together at the wrists with zip ties. The last two cons out of the plane turned and grabbed a bundle of something. The bundle looked heavy and awkward. The men reached deeper into the plane and gave a last tug and the bundle fell out and hit hard. When it twitched with a big spasm, I saw the bundle was Mitch Mendenhall. One of the cons grabbed him and sat him up. He rocked back and forth, staring off into the distance. Staring right at me, though I didn't figure he could see that far.

A dark, Latin-looking guy with wild hair and a stringy black goatee carried a bag to where the county people were tied. He took a syringe from the bag and walked from one of them to the other. First he lifted the deputy's arm, held it a second, then jabbed it with a needle. Then he grabbed the woman's arm, twisted it, then laid it out flat and stuck her with the same needle, not that under the circumstances hygiene made a damn bit of difference. God knows what was in those shots. From the US marshals' briefings, this guy would be Tito Esparza, the prisoner they called the Angel of Death.

I got off my horse and tied him in the trees with the Remington still in the scabbard. I figured at least some of these bad actors would have weapons, so I wanted to learn what I could without getting myself killed. Until the first shot's fired, it's just human nature to hope you can walk away.

They hadn't noticed me walking toward them right off, so they didn't see me rack the slide on my 9mm then lower the hammer and slip it into the right-hand pocket of my old jacket. I patted my shirt pocket where I carried my phone, though I was pretty sure I'd have no service. Finally, one by one, they stopped what they were doing and stared at me walking their way in no particular hurry. Vasiliev and his partner had already seen me up close, but the rest didn't have a clue who this stranger was. I was close enough to spit at them when a scrawny person dressed in black jumped out of the plane onto the ground, almost falling when they landed. The person hobbled up to me, unwrapping what could've been a black wild rag or scarf that covered their head and face. When they were up close, the person gave the scarf a last tug so I could see who it was.

"*Psych!*"

No hallucinations this time. It was the younger of the two women I'd seen at the NAPA in Paiute Meadows. The woman who'd tanked up this plane and put it on her credit card during the Placerville shoot-out. As calm as she'd been that night, she didn't scare easy. I thought for a quick second that maybe now that the Feds had her ID from the credit card, it would make her expendable to Kip. The woman looked half-crazed, skinny and dirty and dangerous. She had an old oak crutch in her right fist. When she got close she tucked it under her armpit and hopped a couple steps with her right foot off the ground, the rubber tip of the crutch leaving round circles like the weird footprints I saw in the pack station snow. That was the morning of the breakout. It meant Kip had been planning to mess with my head even when he was still locked down in the joint. Thinking of every last detail, till a thrift-store crutch put crazy pictures in my head, like some nightmare version of Kip or the Taliban or both was haunting my dreams.

Then all the convicts froze in place and looked sideways at the rear door to the plane. Another person stepped into the doorway. It was Kip. He stared down at me like he didn't recognize me for a second.

I stared back up at him.

"You look like crap, bud."

He still wore prison pants but with a Golden State Warriors hoodie. He wore purple Crocs that looked pretty lame out there in the icy weather. His right ankle was bandaged then wrapped in a nylon and Velcro brace, probably from when I shot him a couple years before. The bandage was oozing and brownish. All told, he looked rocky and weak, a long way from the buffed-out psych-job whose Maker's Mark I'd been drinking a couple of years before. If he had a bone infection, that would explain the trips to the Folsom infirmary and give him one more reason for wanting me dead.

"Well now," he said. He looked up and down the empty airstrip. "I wasn't expecting to see you quite so soon, old Tom." He laughed or coughed. It was hard to tell.

I stared at him. Kip had changed more than just physically since his iron-pumping days. I remembered just how crazy he could get from steroids and coke. But now it seemed like coordinating the escape had got him wound to the breaking point.

"I figured your retard sheriff would fall for the fake text," he said, "but wasn't sure you would. I just wasn't sure how hard you wanted to believe it."

I stayed still, both hands jammed in my jacket pockets. Kip always liked staging his mayhem, so I figured I was safe for a bit. I crouched down next to Mitch to straighten him out and make him more comfortable. I saw bruising but no wounds. I figured Esparza had drugged him, too.

"What'd Mitch ever do to you?"

"He testified against me. Jeez, short memory?"

"I did a lot worse to you."

"And don't think I forgot it." He looked down at his foot then rubbed his left elbow semi-unconsciously until

120

he caught me staring. "Most definitely. Your time's coming. Coming for sure." But he wasn't sounding so sure just then.

The skinny woman in the fake ISIS costume walked over and sat at Kip's feet on the bottom step of the plane, giving me the stink eye. It pissed me off that this rank old hide could creep me out, even for a minute. But it was just her. No haints, nothing more.

Kip looked off into the trees where I'd tied my horse. "Just seeing if you brought backup." He shifted his weight, and I could see he was hurting.

"If you're looking for Sarah, she might not make it on time."

"I'll see her soon enough," he said.

"You know she's the only reason you're still alive?"

That got his attention. Behind him I could see an Asian guy I figured was Wang, the drug flier. I remembered him capping the charter pilot at the Placerville airport. He came up behind me, trying to look tough. I didn't turn my back on him.

"What? Like she . . ." Kip said. Right then, he was all about Sarah.

I laughed at him. "You're so pathetic. No, she wanted you dead. She figured you were out of your rabid-ass mind when I was still back at Fort Benning. But I figured it would look bad to some small-minded folks if Sarah married a guy who'd just killed her husband, even if the husband needed killing. Folks would stare at us when we went out to dinner and talk about us behind our backs at the Tractor Supply."

That got him. He started seething, breathing through his nose. Then he started sneezing, and I laughed at him. The tough-guy act is hard to pull off when a fella has the sniffles.

"I could have these boys ace you right now," he said. "So watch what you say. My sister, Tiffany, here," he nodded to the scrawny woman, "she'd go at you with a razor if I let her."

"I bet she would."

"You're the one with the cute little girl," the woman said. "The one at the school just down the road from your house." She dug a phone out of her pocket and fiddled with it. In a second she held it up. I could see what looked like Audie running past some other kids. Then I heard Audie's laugh, and heard her yell, "*Outta my way, bitches!*"

The woman walked up close to me. I could see Audie running and then the image flipped and I could see the sister inside a truck, then me, sitting in my own truck not ten feet away from the woman.

Kip looked up. "Knock it off, Tiff."

She ignored him. "I'm gonna take a bite outta *that* little biscuit."

"You don't shut up," Kip said, "I'll shoot you in the foot for real." He gave her a demented look. "Then we'll *really* be twins."

The woman turned away and shut up.

I looked as casual as I could, trying not to let the sister spying on Audie worry me, buying time, trying to see inside the plane so I could get a count. The spiky-haired guy was probably Chester Livermore, the child rapist, so it was hard not to worry about Audie. The others I could see were Kip, probably Wang, Vasiliev, and Esparza, and another, smaller Latin-looking guy I could see moving around the interior of the plane. When I turned back, I saw Kip staring at me. While I was looking I could see bullet holes in the skin of the fuselage from their escape from Placerville and a dent in one of the props from what I guessed was a rocky landing. It made me wonder if the plane had flown as far as it could. I kept my hand around the 9mm in my pocket, but I knew my only way back to my horse and the highway was to not let any shooting start. If Billy Jack Kane was anywhere on the airstrip, I hadn't spotted him, but then I'd never really seen him up close. Four or five guys shot dead in the school-bus double-cross meant that, except for him, I might be seeing all the cons that were left alive.

"You think you can take us all out?" Kip had caught me counting. "Then you're the crazy one, big guy."

"Ask me seven men from now."

That confused him.

"You tried to make me think I was crazy. I don't quite know how, but you had me going for a minute. You and this bitch." I was tense and wanted to get out of there. To get Audie.

Kip stared at me, off his game all of a sudden. "You invited this shit-storm a year and a half ago when you came barging into my world from Fort Benning."

All of a sudden he looked happy, like he'd just discovered something.

"Hold on. You're so full of shit with that 'seven men' crap. I thought you were talking about my boy Billy Jack. Since I downsized, that'd be *my* seventh guy. But you're trying to jerk me around with a goddamn *movie*. I saw *Seven Men from Now* in the joint," he said, like I'd faked him out. "That's just a goddamn movie. A badass Lee-goddamn-Marvin western."

"Wrong. It was Randolph Scott, chump. He's the hero."

In the movie, he was wound tight because his wife got killed, but he was a total badass. And at the end, Randy Scott blows Lee Marvin clean away. I looked around at his crew and the shot-up plane.

"And you ain't even close to being Lee Marvin, bud."

I had to admit, this temporary stopover in the woods was kinda genius. Probably not many folks even knew about this raggedy airstrip, and even fewer would connect it to the bloody hoo-rah a hundred miles and a couple days before.

Our talking roused Mitch. He looked up, and I could see he recognized me.

"Why don't you let the sheriff go? No way he's a threat to you."

"Since when did *that* ever matter?" Kip said.

I held my breath a second. I thought I heard a motor or something in the distance.

"I want to see how long it takes you to see the big picture." Kip wiped his nostrils with a thumb and forefinger then licked them both. "I'll give you a clue, but you gotta guess."

He stopped talking and jerked his head back. We both listened to a faraway noise in the sky. He looked jittery, but it may've just been the coke.

I had to laugh. It did sound like the buzz of a plane's engine.

Now all of Kip's crew scanned above the treetops, looking for a plane through falling snow.

"I guess Sarah's on time after all."

"Vanya!" Kip said.

"Way ahead of you," Vasiliev said.

"God*damn*it," Kip said.

The Russian threw a blue tarp over the drugged-up county lady and the wounded deputy. He weighed it down with icy chunks of asphalt and frozen chunks of dirt from the airstrip so the bodies wouldn't look like bodies from the air. I slipped my phone out of my pocket and took a quick pic of the van's license plate during their scrambling.

Wang grabbed Kip's arm, then yelled to someone inside the plane. The scrawny Mexican guy ducked his head to clear the side door and helped Wang steady Kip down the steps to the ground. From the task force briefings, the runty guy was probably Gilbert Orosco, the armed robber. Kip saw me watching how much trouble he was having with that right leg. He didn't see the wounded deputy push his head outside the blue tarp till he tripped over him.

Orosco steadied Kip. Kip pulled a Sig 9 and put two rounds in the deputy's head then yelled at Orosco to hurry and get him loaded in the van.

The noise got louder, and I spotted a chopper, not a plane. It looked like maybe a Marine Sikorsky, but it had too much altitude to tell or to know if it was a routine training flight or if the Marines were doing recon for the task force. I'd bet even money that whoever's bird it was, Sarah was sitting next to the pilot. If she hadn't known I was headed for East Fork, Kip's crew might've had an extra couple days to regroup. Either way, if it was a Marine copter, it brought me back to those missing Mk 13s. Actually, everything always brought me back to those rifles.

Kip's sister ran over to the van and jumped behind the wheel. She hollered at the cons to load up fast. They gathered up what little stuff they had and did what they were told, pushing past Mitch like he wasn't there.

It was crazed and disorganized for a minute, but I made another mental count. Kip, Vasiliev, Esparza, Wang, Orosco, and Livermore. That made six, plus the skanky sister, so maybe Billy Jack Kane wasn't part of this go-round.

Vasiliev got Kip hoisted in the side door and buckled down, then jumped in beside him. Wang climbed into the front passenger seat next to the sister. She floored it, and the van spun its wheels and fishtailed in the snow until it straightened out. When it did, Wang leaned out the window and fired two rounds in my direction. I scrunched down but nothing came close. In another minute the van cleared the end of the airstrip. I lost sight of it when the road turned down into the trees. A little shaft of late sunlight glaring off the side window of the van lit up the blood on the deputy's head for an instant then was gone so quick I might have hallucinated that, too. I'd had 'em all and lost 'em all in just minutes. But now I knew where they were—right in my backyard.

I checked the deputy. He was gone. I pulled the tarp back over him.

"Those were the for-real Folsom cons?" It was the courthouse clerk, loopy and disoriented.

"Yes, ma'am."

"Well for heaven's sake," she said.

She looked at the deputy then nodded and about passed out.

I cut her loose from the zip ties then climbed inside the plane and found seat cushions and blankets for her and for Mitch. Half of the seats were smeared with ketchup and mustard and In-N-Out wrappers like a family of raccoons had been living in the plane's cabin. Mitch called to me when I was coming off the steps.

"Did they get away?" He sounded like he was about to cry.

"We'll get 'em. You hadn't got me up here, they'd be gone without a trace—or camped here too damn close to Dave's ranch."

"You think?"

"The psycho bitch knows where Audie goes to school. I gotta get that kid outta there."

"I screwed up," he said.

"No, you did good, Mitch." I bent down and held my phone so he could see the picture I took of the van's license plate.

"Won't they steal another?"

"They won't have time." I straightened back up. "Not for a while, anyway. Right now they're hauling ass straight into the suburbs."

Standing normal made me dizzy, and I had to put a hand on the plane's wing to steady myself.

"How many?" he said. "How many of 'em are left?"

"Six, plus the sister. Maybe seven." I leaned over him to wrap him tighter in the blanket.

"Six killers," he said. He nodded his head, almost smiling. "That's pretty damn—"

I heard the whip of sucking air and the slap of impact at the same instant and felt a mist on my cheek from the fresh high-velocity hole in Mitch's forehead. I jerked my own head sideways. When I first caught Mitch out of the far corner of my eye, I thought I saw Hendershott instead and remembered the lieutenant dying from friendly fire when the AH-6 lit up the hillside and stray .50 cal rounds ripped into the snow and rock of the cave. I remembered the way Hendershott's face just vanished. I remembered it all for the first time.

For a second Mitch looked surprised as he slumped to the side. Then he looked just like regular old Mitch, and I wasn't surprised at all. Of the escaped convicts, I figured only Billy Jack Kane could've made that shot. And I'd already bet somebody's life that FBI forensics would tell that the round was a .300 Winchester Mag from a stolen Marine Mk 13 rifle. So it wasn't my imagination. The devil knows how, but at least one of the stolen rifles was *already* in play. And now, Billy Jack Kane made seven.

II
POGONIP

Pogonip: A dense winter fog containing frozen ice particles that is formed in deep mountain valleys of the western United States. From a bastardization of the Shoshone *payinappih*, meaning "cloud."—*Merriam-Webster's New Collegiate Dictionary*

Chapter Nine

I was alone in the quiet, sitting on a dry patch of dirt under the wing of the plane. I'd eased the county lady away from the dead deputy and was trying without luck to get service on my phone. I thought about Sarah and Lorena and Audie and the video taken of her at school, but I couldn't leave the lady by herself. I watched snow falling on the windshield and on the blue tarp I'd draped across Mitch's corpse and on the polyester blanket from the plane I'd wrapped around the woman. She was quivering, coming out of the drugging by the bearded con. Waiting for her to stir, I scoured the site for any sheriffs' radios or Search and Rescue satellite phones or private cell phones dropped in the getaway, but Kip's crew had policed the area pretty well. I tried my phone a last time. Plenty of battery but no bars.

I stepped over Mitch's body, careful not to jostle it, and climbed back up into the plane. It was an eight seater, and it stunk inside from more than just french fries and ketchup ground into the interior carpet, dried-up vomit and a clogged-up toilet. I made my way forward and fiddled with the cockpit radio, hoping the escapees were in too much of a hurry to disable it or had just been too strung out to think clear. Once I figured how it worked, I got hold of a guy who ran a glider charter at Carson Valley airport. He said he'd notify Sarah at her office for me. Then I asked the guy to call Jack Harney direct, in case he was closer. I told the guy to tell Jack I was sitting in the Folsom escapees' stolen Piper Navajo and that at least six of the killers were heading north just minutes ahead of me. I told him I needed Deputy Harney to park outside the Shoshone Valley School until relieved by Sarah or me, and I needed it done fast. The charter guy said he'd get right on it and wished me luck. He'd be drinking for free at the J-T Basque Bar in Gardnerville for a month with that story.

It was hard telling Sarah about Mitch when she radioed a few minutes later. I told her where I was and what happened to her boss.

"Oh, Mitch, my god," was all she could say at first. It took her a minute to steady herself. She'd worked for him since her first day as a deputy when she was right out of grad school.

"I was always afraid of something like this." She was quiet another minute. I heard her blow her nose. "He was always more small-town politician than big-time law enforcement," she said. Her voice was calm now.

He'd made her crazy, but she figured a way to point him in the right direction most of the time. They'd been through some pretty hairy stuff together in the last few years.

"He just wanted to be a stand-up guy," she said. "Like you."

132

We talked a few minutes more on the crackly radio. I told her about Audie and Jack, and told her not to worry. Jack was probably already at the school. She said the office would have the sign-out sheet ready and Audie waiting at the gate. We knew we'd be swarming with law and reporters soon enough, and this would be our last chance to talk for a while, just the two of us. I gave her the Alpine County van's license plate info from my phone and we talked about where the cons might be heading. Then she told me she loved me. Neither of us mentioned the little fact that I was lucky to have taken the dumb chance I took and come through the last couple of hours without ending up like Mitch.

I stepped out of the plane and checked on the clerk. She was still only semi-conscious, so I took the time to walk across the airstrip and fetch my horse. The woman looked up while I was hobbling the gelding close by and feeding him some grain I'd packed in a ziplock.

"My Lord," she said. "I thought I dreamed all this."

"No such luck, I'm afraid, ma'am."

I got her sitting upright and drinking from my water bottle. I asked her if she was hungry and got her some beef jerky from my saddle pockets. She told me her name was Edna and talked about her boss, Sheriff Flint Richmond.

"Did he think this teaming up with Mitch Mendenhall was a good idea?"

"I think so," she said. "But Sheriff Flint would have been in the thick of it if he knew the convicts were hiding here right up the road from us. He was spoiling for a fight."

I looked over at the tarp covering Mitch's body.

"Yeah."

A wind picked up and riffled the tarp. Then a gust blew it up from Mitch's head, exposing the hole where the back of his skull was supposed to be. I snugged the tarp down tighter. We wouldn't be alone much longer.

Sarah and Sorenson were the first officers on scene, flown in by a CHP chopper. Right behind them a National Guard Blackhawk landed to airlift Edna across the state line to Gardnerville, the closest emergency ward. She was chipper and chatty as they strapped her in. She introduced herself to Sarah and said she could drive herself home if someone would just take her to her car. One of the National Guard EMTs told her protocol dictated she be checked out. Then he trotted over to Sarah, who was examining the dead deputy.

"This storm is closing in," he said. "We'll get the lady airborne and contact Alpine County about this fatality."

"I already did," she said.

The guy thanked her and started for his chopper. He stopped to check out Mitch's body still bundled in the blanket from the plane.

"You think you could maybe arrange ground transport for your sheriff with your county coroner?" he said.

"This sheriff *was* the county coroner."

Tough as she was, Sarah was taking Mitch's death harder than she let on over the radio. The Guard chopper lifted off, spinning the snow around it that settled on the broken asphalt as it rose. We could see an SUV coming up the runway from the direction the convicts had taken when they disappeared into the trees.

"That will be Aaron," Sarah said. "I radioed him first, but

Waingrow and Ridgely and Richmond and the rest should be right on his tail—if they don't get lost." She looked around at the airstrip with the shot-up plane and the trash and tarps and Mitch's body all covered with fresh snow. "Well, this looks like a Christmas card from hell."

She walked away from the plane and flagged Aaron down. Then she, Aaron, and I huddled against the Piper as far from Mitch's body as we could get and still have shelter.

"Where's the rest of your crew?"

"I ditched them," Aaron said. "I wanted to get you two alone before the marshals got here."

I filled them in about my last couple of hours. I couldn't enlighten them much about how Mitch and Richmond figured to round up a half dozen hard cases on their own, or even if the plan was real and not another fake-out. That actually made more sense.

Aaron stood quiet, sipping cold coffee, letting my horse lip his free hand, not looking at any of us.

"You better saddle up, Tommy," he said.

Sarah looked from Aaron to me. "Why?"

"Waingrow needs a scapegoat," Aaron said. He was studying the ground, the shot-up plane, the gap in the trees he'd just driven through. The same gap Kip had just escaped into. "A scapegoat for what he's going to call a sweet little ambush that went sideways through no fault of his. Of Mitch getting killed and the convicts getting flushed out of here before we could surround them and recapture them." He turned to me. "I figure he's picked you."

"I don't see how . . ." Sarah stopped. But she did know how. *Exactly* how. It was just the way things worked.

"Makes perfect sense. I'm the freelancer in this deal. To the press I'll be the gung-ho local, the gunslinger ignoring law enforcement protocol and playing vigilante. Getting real law enforcement pros like Mitch killed."

Sarah snorted at that. She looked sad and distracted. She knew how easy that story could stick once newspapers and cable news got a whiff.

"I'll head out now. Tell Waingrow I'll be back at the ranch writing out a statement for him."

"Even though you don't work for him?" Aaron said.

"Especially that. He can hang this on me if he wants."

"He can try," Sarah said.

I looked up and down the airstrip. I could already see a US Marshal's SUV coming at us through the trees.

"Waingrow's gonna be pissed for real when he sees this place. One road in. One road out. The plane maybe out of fuel, or close to it." I looked at Aaron and almost laughed. "You coulda boxed these desperadoes in with a half dozen Cub Scouts and not fired a shot."

Aaron looked like he'd already thought of that very thing.

I bridled my gelding and tightened my cinch and stepped aboard. Sarah squeezed my free hand, and I bent down to kiss her goodbye. She pulled back with a semi-annoyed look, like she'd just noticed my jacket from high school.

"I can't believe you wore that."

"Part of my distraction."

She tried to laugh, but it came out more like a sob. She grabbed the front of the jacket and pulled me down and kissed me, tears in her eyes. I loosened my reins and headed out. She watched me ride off, circling toward the end of the airstrip away from the plane and the oncoming SUV. She would be tied up with the FBI and the marshals for a good long while. I figured Kip and his sister would be concentrating more on their getaway than harming Audie, but I still didn't want to dawdle.

I could see Waingrow through the front window of his SUV talking on his radio. He never gave me a single look—like he didn't figure some horseback guy in a ball cap had anything to do with his brand of take-no-prisoners crime fighting—not that he'd actually taken any prisoners yet or fought any crime that I could see.

He looked up, and his head whipped around when he finally noticed it was me. I touched the bill of my ball cap with one finger in a casual salute then uncorked that big gelding, flat flying down the broken road. Behind Waingrow's SUV was an immaculate Alpine County Jeep with an immaculate winch on the bumper and a shiny county logo on the door. The guy driving was totally squared away starting with his square jaw, sitting straight, white shirt and black tie, LBJ Stetson, 12 gauge pump, and mirrored aviators. I'd never really met Flint Richmond, but I figured I was about to unless I rattled my hocks.

I followed the route I'd taken coming in, dropping fast down the slope through early afternoon shadows in the sparse pine. I counted three more law enforcement vehicles heading up the hill before I hit the highway.

I jumped the horse into the trailer and hauled ass out through the trees toward the West Fork of the Carson and followed that down into the new Gardnerville suburbs, glancing back and forth up the driveways and into the backyards as I drove, just in case seven hardnose killers had stopped in for lunch or to steal another car.

I pulled Burt's rig parallel to the school parking lot and jumped out with the diesel running. I found Jack standing at the security chain-link outside the attendance office looking all business.

"This lady here has your sign-out sheet ready to go."

He gave me a thumbs-up then drove off, heading up to East Fork.

I scribbled Audie's name, and the office lady threw open the gate as Audie came running down the hall.

"Goodness, Tommy," the woman said, "the fifth graders are just decorating for Halloween, so you if you have a minute . . ."

By then we were pulling out onto the Reno Highway.

"I seen better-run jails," Audie said.

She looked at me then laughed and grabbed at the cap I was wearing.

"You look like a damn prune picker in that ball cap," she said. "That's what Grandpa Dave would say. Where we goin'?"

"Home."

She handed me a half-finished witch made from black construction paper. When she got serious, I always had to laugh.

"Better-run jails?"

Ten minutes later, I circled Burt's truck in the ranchyard and unloaded and unsaddled my horse then turned him out in the wrangle pen with the rest of our saddle horses. I unhitched Sarah's trailer, and Audie and I trotted up to the house. Sarah got back to the ranch about a half hour later. I got us both a beer.

"Hey, Sarah," Audie said. "Tommy just sprung me from school like I was some total badass."

"You are a total badass, Sis." Sarah looked whipped when she said it.

I turned on the TV to cable news and told Audie to watch and let us know if any big stories happened, then I motioned Sarah outside. We sat on the steps and I showed her the video on my phone. The one Kip's sister sent me. I wasn't sure how Sarah'd react. Me telling her about it worried her. Seeing it just got her mad.

"Did Audie see it?"

I shook my head no, and neither of us said anything. Sarah leaned against me and took my hand.

"Sneaking a video of Audie shot on school property the morning of the escape," she said, "of a *ten-year-old girl*." She squeezed my hand till my fingers hurt.

I could see Burt stepping out on the deck of the double-wide about a hundred feet off. He saw his truck, and he saw us. He waved and went back inside.

"You didn't have to stay with Mitch's body?"

"No," Sarah said. "Sorenson and I are both officially deputy coroners if we're the only ones on duty. He said he'll wait until the Alpine county ME signs off and Aaron's evidence response team is in place, then . . ." She looked up. Aaron's SUV was rolling down the lane toward us.

"He said he was going to stop by," she said. "He's

bummed. He thinks we might have missed our chance to bring those convicts in all in one bunch."

Aaron got out of the SUV and sat with us on the steps. "Beer?"

He nodded yeah, and I got him one out of the kitchen. "Any updates?"

"There's been two sightings of a tall, tan Mercedes van already," he said. "One heading north at the junction of Eighty-Eight and Three-Ninety-Five in Minden, one up by Hope Valley." He was reading from his iPad.

"Heading west?"

"Yeah," he said. "We better catch them fast. Local sheriffs manning a bootleg roadblock on Kingsbury Grade opened fire on a tan van a few minutes ago. It turned out to be a bookmobile."

"Damn, Aaron. That's only about a fifteen-minute drive from your headquarters in South Shore. What do you mean 'bootleg?'"

"Not cleared with the task force," he said.

"Trouble with Waingrow?"

"Not for me," Aaron said. "For getting the job done right. Waingrow's one of those impatient guys who always wants to look like he's got things under control. Like he's got the facts nobody else has."

"Just like Mitch," Sarah said.

"Exactly like Mitch."

"When things take too long," Aaron said, "or there's some public safety issue, Waingrow gets reckless. Starts turf wars with other agencies. And now this thing with Ridgely has him freaked."

"What thing?" Sarah said.

"Rod was supposed to be following a hot lead at an airstrip north of Reno," Aaron said. "A carjacking outside a town called Beckwourth in Plumas County, California. Now Waingrow's guys can't get hold of him, and he's sending another marshal up there to check it out. He's afraid Rod tangled with some escapees without backup. You know his type."

"A cowboy?"

"I was going to say showboat," he said.

There wasn't anything to say to that.

"I don't want this Ridgely thing getting Waingrow so skittish he forgets why Sanchez wanted to recon that canyon in the first place," Aaron said.

"Then I wish Ridgely would check in," Sarah said.

"Plumas County is to hell and gone." I checked the time on my phone. "Kip's crew could've made it almost that far by now, but they'da been hauling ass, and there would've probably been more sightings."

"And more shootings," Aaron said.

Audie ran out to the porch and hollered for us to come quick. I was worried until she yelled that there was more big doins on the TV. Then she jumped off the porch and ran across the ranchyard to the double-wide to get Burt and Mom.

We all circled around the TV screen looking at a low-speed chase. The Mercedes van from the Alpine County airstrip was creeping along a freeway that had been cleared of traffic. Rolling behind it was a mess of flashing lights. Nevada

Highway Patrol, FBI, Washoe county sheriffs, Reno police, ATF, and more. Mom, Audie and Burt came in the house from the double-wide. Burt held Lorena in her car seat. Mom looked bent-over and tired, so someone must've told her about Mitch.

Aaron stood up but kept his eyes on the screen as he checked his texts. Sarah pulled out her radio and went into our bedroom.

"This is the van you saw, right?" Aaron said. "The van that half all of California and Nevada is looking for?"

"Yup." I showed him the license plate picture on my phone.

Audie bounced up on her knees on the arm of Aaron's chair, so she could poke him with her finger.

"Any sightings of convicts inside?"

"No," Aaron said. "The windows are tinted. We're going with the assumption they're all still in there. Especially as there've been zero sightings of the cons elsewhere."

Sarah walked back into the living room pocketing her radio.

"So what's the story here, babe?"

"After Placerville, then the Kingsbury Grade screwup," she said, "Waingrow doesn't want a gunfight on the streets of Reno."

Mom offered me a cup of coffee. I shook my head no and watched the van inch by what looked like the off-ramp to the Reno airport.

"At least we finally got eyeballs on them."

"Yeah," Aaron said. "For now."

"What do the marshals say?"

"They're rolling up the freeway at ten miles an hour and they've got a deputy marshal north of here that seems to have just vanished," Aaron said. "So they're not saying much."

The caravan dragged along. Network and cable news chattered over footage of empty highway and flashing lights. I stood up and got some more beers. It had been a long day so far.

"Can I ask you what you were doing up at that airstrip?" Aaron said. "I was never too clear on that." He stared at his beer but didn't drink.

"I got a text from Mitch asking me to meet him and the Alpine County sheriff in East Fork. Like he wanted backup in case he actually found those cons. But I don't think the text came from Mitch at all. And if it didn't, I think the text he got from Flint Richmond was bogus too, or Richmond woulda been there before me, blasting away, instead of hanging with you at your briefing in South Shore. I figure this was all Kip trying to spook me."

Aaron laughed. "You didn't tell Waingrow?"

"I don't work for Waingrow, remember?"

"You don't work for anybody, friend."

"Tommy told me his plans," Sarah said. "I figured that was due diligence enough."

"I think Waingrow is a horse's ass, and I didn't trust him not to fly in with guns blazing. That would've just increased the odds of . . . that Mitch would buy the farm."

Aaron was nice enough not to point out the obvious thing—that *my* plan didn't work so well either.

"On the off chance the text *was* from Mitch, I was hoping to talk him and Richmond out of whatever they had schemed."

"Mitch was a dead man walking when you got on your horse, Tommy," Aaron said. "No matter who sent that text."

Sarah's phone chimed. She pulled it out of her pocket, listened, then tapped something and put it back.

"That was Kathy Avakian, the US Attorney. She just heard from Ridgely."

"And?"

"He said he's tracking the van, too," Sarah said. "But from the other direction. Says he's locked and loaded, still parked at the Reno Highway junction with Highway Seventy." She stared her phone. "He said he thought it best he stays put so he can backstop the Reno action from that airstrip in Plumas County."

"I swear," Mom said. "Every single one of you is just plain gun crazy."

Sarah reached over and squeezed Mom's hand.

"Avakian did ask me if that's still in Nevada or back in California."

Aaron stretched out and finished his beer. "Everybody's protecting their turf," he said.

"No wonder nobody's got caught yet. It's California, for what it's worth."

"Shush, you two," Mom said. "The van's stopping."

A news chopper hovered on one side of the van. A Nevada Highway Patrol chopper hovered on the other side. We saw a whole army of law in full battle rattle circling the van, creeping up, weapons aimed, ready to go blasting muzzle-to-muzzle with a half dozen hard-assed Folsom escapees. It was pretty much the total opposite of the Placerville mess.

"Well," Sarah said, "I guess this is it."

A helmeted guy walked behind an armored personnel carrier that crept up to within twenty feet of the van. He looked to be hollering through a bullhorn, though we couldn't hear a thing. He waited for a reply then raised the bullhorn like he was calling out again. More armored cops fanned out like they were expecting a burst of hellfire. Nothing happened. Then the driver-side door swung open.

The guy with the bullhorn shrieked at the van loud enough for the news camera's audio to pick it up. We couldn't make out much of what he said, but it was basically weapons down, hands up, and don't blink. The first person stepped out onto the concrete highway.

It was the driver, Kip's sister. She stood with her hands up, but even from the jiggly footage we could see she was holding something in her right hand that looked like a pistol. The trooper took a knee, ready to blow her away. The cop with the bullhorn shrieked at her—probably to drop the weapon. For a long second, things were silent and not moving, like everybody was holding their breath until the troops opened up on her and turned her into hamburger. She stood nervous and fidgety, the news camera swinging from her wild-eyed face to the windows of the van. We could only guess how many of the escapees were inside, and if they were ready to get down to it right then and there.

The woman's arm raised up with the black pistol in her hand and she did a little two-step dance then the laid the pistol against her head. We could see the shot's impact but not hear it as her head jerked and she dropped. A few of the FBI SWAT troops opened up on her, hitting her and spinning her around as she fell. There was another second's pause then fire just poured in on the van from all sides, ripping the sheet metal and tires and steel, shooting over her twisted body. It seemed like a long time until the firing stopped. Even the newscasters had run out of things to say.

Mom looked away from the screen.

"Sweet Jesus," Burt said. "They shot that thing all to *hell*."

"There's no more shooting from the van," Mom said.

"There never was."

Sarah caught my eye. Like she'd noticed that, too.

We watched the local SWAT and US marshals and FBI and Washoe County deputies move up to the van slow and easy. An agent pushed back the sliding passenger door then turned and talked to a guy behind him. A few more of them leaned inside then straightened up, talking among themselves. More officers checked the interior. We recognized Marshal Waingrow. He peeked inside then turned and shuffled out of camera range.

EMTs ran toward the van, carrying their equipment and keeping their heads low. The local announcer said that with all her pistol waving and all the blood, the woman's head wound appeared to be only superficial, the one round cutting a furrow in her scalp and nothing more. SWAT team metal-jacketed rounds had punctured her a few more times but her body twitched like she was trying to get up as she yelled at the folks who shot her.

"That poor, poor woman," Mom said.

"Don't waste your pity on that stringy bitch."

"*Tommy*," Mom said.

The news crews stayed focused on the woman. She sprawled next to the van. The SWAT team circled the body, crowding the EMTs. Some were shouting and waving their arms, and others just stood around watching.

"What's going on?" Mom said.

"It's empty. Kip used his sister as a decoy. Just one big fake-out."

"This is nuts," Sarah said. "Half a dozen convicts don't just disappear."

"They were never there."

Mom pointed to the type moving at the bottom of the screen. "The news says maybe they just scattered."

"If they did," Aaron said, "it's a whole new ballgame."

"It's Placerville, but this time played for laughs."

"You think they unloaded into another vehicle right after they left the airstrip, Tommy?" Aaron said.

"I'd bet my life on it."

"So, how do you find them?" Mom said.

"Find the guns." I was getting tired of saying it.

Chapter Ten

". . . with armed convicts still on the loose and, from what we have seen, still operating as a single, lethal, well-coordinated unit, several hard facts are coming into focus. First, law enforcements' response is still several steps behind these killers, a truth brought home by the entire joint federal task force being led on a merry chase by a lone woman decoy."

A guy sat at a glass table in a cable news studio, ragging about the poor showing of small-time law enforcement chasing their tails in the face of big-time criminals. When the guy mentioned that one of the high-country deputies on the hunt had been married to one of the escapees, Dave glared at his TV. When the guy started in on the lady's current husband's bloody past, and that I was the only witness to our local sheriff's murder, Dave pushed himself up from his recliner.

"I've about had it with this cufflink-wearing sonofabitch," he said. He hit the mute and scanned his Netflix menu.

Audie had been standing behind Dave's recliner the whole time. "That guy's a dickwad, right, Tommy?" she said.

"Hush, Snip. It's okay."

"Well, isn't *that* special," Sarah said.

"Least he didn't call us rubes or degenerates."

"He came damn close, babe," Sarah said.

"Oh, you kids," Mom said, "that is so unfair." She reached over and squeezed Sarah's hand.

Aaron was as pissed as I'd ever seen him—except for the time I shot up an Italian restaurant in Reno in the middle of the lunch rush.

Sarah got up and went into our bedroom to change the baby then call the undersheriff down in Mammoth Lakes with an update. He was a youngish guy with more graduate degrees than Sarah, and Jack Harney was convinced that if they called a special election to fill Mitch's job, that guy would figure he should be standing at the head of the line.

I caught her wiping her eyes as she walked across the room. I got up to stare out the window where the black sun had set. Burt came in from the double-wide and handed me an unopened bottle of Knob Creek. Dave reclaimed his recliner, and Audie climbed next to him to watch an old download of *Justified*, both of them grunting cheerful as could be whenever Timothy Oliphant emptied a 9mm magazine into some coal-country lowlife.

When Sarah came back, she, Aaron, and I sat and talked at the dinner table and I broke out the Knob Creek. As we talked, they watched me unwrap my tool kit and my cleaning kit and spread them out in front of me.

"Expecting trouble?" Aaron said.

"No more than usual."

I cleaned and oiled the Remington. Sarah watched me mount my Leupold scope.

"It's like that bozo in the blue suit was aiming his editorial right at the people in this room," she said. "Right at me."

"Everybody's covering their butts, babe. Playing Monday-morning quarterback in public is their job."

"I'm heading back to South Shore," Aaron said. "Better known as 'back to square one.'" This TV crap is just going to push the task force into doing something really stupid. Every agency wants this resolved fast before the finger-pointing gets worse, but they all want a piece of the glory."

"Maybe we can sneak a Hanging Valley chopper recon in under the radar."

"Be no crazier than schemes the marshals are probably plotting as we speak." Aaron gave me a hard look. "But now Waingrow would never greenlight anything you were even remotely involved in."

"Always a chance this TV crap'll push Kip's crew into doing something stupid, too."

"You can hope," Aaron said.

"An aerial recon with Sanchez would have been key," Sarah said.

"Yeah," Aaron said. "Too bad you're both kind of radioactive now."

I looked at my phone. "I was hopin' Sanchez was gonna stop by here, anyway."

"She sent out a group text," Aaron said. "She's got a room reserved at Stateline Lodge."

He looked at my rifle and tools spread across the dining

room table. He didn't say anything. He just stared at his glass of Knob Creek. "You can't kill them all, you know."

I didn't say anything.

We kicked around our options for another half hour, like if Aaron himself could take a recon flight with Sanchez, maybe along with one of the marshals, preferably Ridgely. He had Sarah and me draw another rough map of possible hideouts and stash spots in and around Hanging Valley for him before he left, but he didn't seem very optimistic.

Aaron had what a lieutenant pal of mine from my first tour would call one of those binary deals. Since the escapees weren't north of where the law first spotted the van, they had to be south of that spot. End of discussion. But then, that left us south of that spot, too, with no clue how close those bastards were.

Sarah, Burt, and I worked out a rotation so one of us would be at the ranch at all times and nobody was walking out alone in the ranchyard or barn. Sarah was real firm with Audie, telling her to always buddy up with a grown-up when she went outside, day or night. Sarah had brought a bunch of sheriff department radios—one for each of us, including Mom and Audie—and fistfuls of double-A batteries so we'd always be in touch. She showed them both how the radios worked, which made Audie feel like a total adult.

Sarah told her dad to take it easy, that she and I had things covered, but this was his place and his family, so there was no stopping him when he stepped outside with his old Browning Over/Under. There was a lot of hardware parading out under the cottonwoods that night, catching bits of shifting moonlight on blue steel and fresh snow.

Burt took the first watch, and I went in to crash. Sarah spent a few minutes outside talking to Burt and her dad. When she woke me to take my turn, I'd been sleeping like a dead man, which wasn't like me.

"Tommy," she said. She spoke so soft I could barely hear her.

"Be right there." The bedroom was dark, and I could hear Lorena's breathing from her crib across the room. I was fumbling for my jeans when I felt Sarah step up behind me. I heard a quick rustle of something and felt her tee shirt slide down the back of my legs to my bare feet as it fell to the floor.

"I don't suppose I need to go just this minute."

"No," she said. "You don't."

She'd given us half an hour. We were dozing when we heard voices in the hall. It was Burt.

"Tommy," he said from outside the door, "Sarah, you better get out here. There's been a carjacking—right down the road at Three Flags."

Sarah and I both jumped out of bed. I pulled on my jeans as she fiddled with her phone.

"Jack just sent this video and text," she said. "It's from the security camera at the gas station—outside the all-night minimart."

The image was grainy. It showed a woman getting grabbed from behind by two guys as she pumped gas. Her driver-side door was open.

"A woman was coming out of the minimart after buying coffee and was gassing up her car," Sarah said. She read the rest of the text. "Teenage clerk said the woman's car was blocked by a beat-up pickup. Crew cab. Two men got out. When the woman confronted them, one of the guys pistol-whipped her and dragged her into the truck. It pulled out heading south."

Sarah's police radio squawked. It was Aaron. He said he just got the message, but with a snowstorm on Kingsbury Grade, he was over an hour out.

"CHP was first on the scene," he said. "They ID'd the car the woman was driving. A rental. In ATF agent Sanchez's name. Her purse and some cold-weather gear was still on the seat."

"She was coming to try to salvage that recon flight," Sarah said. "My department's got a unit heading to Three Flags from the undersheriff's office in Mammoth Lakes, and Jack Harney is already at the crime scene."

"I've got a bureau evidence response team from my office on its way," Aaron said, "but that will take a while, too. Since Isela was ATF, they're sending another agent from her office in Sacramento, weather permitting. A deputy from Waingrow's US Marshal's office is on his way to the scene, too."

"Ridgely?"

"I don't know," Aaron said. "But Waingrow won't be far behind no matter who it is. That cable news rant about the fake-out with the van with the whole world watching embarrassed the hell out of him. He was counting on this task force making his career, not ending it."

"Sanchez have family?"

"Divorced," Aaron said. "Two boys in middle school down in Rancho Cordova."

He said he'd stop in to see us on his way to Three Flags. Then he signed off.

"So they didn't steal her car." I was snapping up my shirt.

"No," Sarah said. "Whoever it was, they left the car and stole her. She was what they wanted."

"Maybe."

We watched the video over and over, and it was superclear the woman was Isela Sanchez. One of the two carjackers looked like Vanya Vasiliev. The other Sarah ID'd as Billy Jack Kane, the mystery sniper from the East Fork airstrip. This was the first time we'd really seen him since the news of the breakout. He looked to be shouting at her, grabbing her coat and cocking a fist. She tried to kick him in the nuts, and he slammed her against her car.

Jack came on the radio. He read Sarah another eyewitness account from the gas station night clerk. The kid said Isela had fought like hell—and she had called my name.

"Did she say anything else?" Sarah said.

"Something like 'towers,'" Jack said. "The kid and one other eyewitness said the same thing. Something like 'clock towers' or 'check towers' or 'watch towers.' Something like that."

There's no Forest Service wildfire-spotting towers left around this part of the Sierra, so none of us made any sense of it.

Sarah looked at me across the bed. "Tommy?"

"I got no clue. But I bet we're gettin' close."

I got up and walked barefoot into the kitchen to start a

pot of coffee. It was about a quarter to two. Sarah checked on the baby then followed me into the kitchen.

"Do you think she's dead?" she said.

"If they wanted her dead, she'd be dead and they'd let us know it."

"You think she's a hostage then?"

"Maybe for now. Don't forget, Billy Jack Kane for sure blames Isela for getting his brother killed in that Idaho shoot-out. She may be alive now, but he's not going to keep her alive forever."

"I know," Sarah said.

Sanchez getting kidnapped and taken south would put her even closer to where she and I both figured the Marine rifles were stashed. We could let the joint task force try to figure it out and guarantee she'd be a casualty, or we could figure it out for them. Just another damn binary choice leading straight to the graveyard.

Aaron pulled into the ranchyard about two thirty in the morning. The snow had stopped for a bit so he'd made good time after all. He said he'd already made the pitch to Waingrow about a recon flight south of the Marine base, and he was waiting for the go-ahead.

"I didn't make as good a pitch as you would have," he said.

"Did the fearless leader mind getting rousted out?"

"I told him he can regroup the task force if we spy the fugitives in the canyon," Aaron said, "then plan an assault and salvage his . . .."

"Reputation?"

"I was going to say career. He screws this up, he won't be able to get a job as a toll collector on the Bay Bridge."

"How long would that take him?" Sarah said.

"If he doesn't waver, he can probably get all the pieces in place by later today, tomorrow morning at the outside," Aaron said. "So . . . twenty-four to thirty-six hours."

"And that's weather permitting," Sarah said. "You can't fly choppers in a blizzard."

"If we sight the cons' hiding place," Aaron said, "the task force has to be ready for a full-on assault."

"The downside being Isela wouldn't survive that."

"Frankly, Tommy, Waingrow has lost control of this and knows everybody is analyzing his every move. He's only pretending he's got a plan beyond vague notions of 'overwhelming force.'"

"Blizzard or no blizzard, somebody's gotta extract Sanchez."

"What are you getting at?" Aaron said.

"I was kinda hoping something quicker than twenty-four-plus hours. You know, more like a dawn raid on the enemy's pony herd, not D-Day."

He sat quiet for a minute. "I'd need to have a high probability that Marine ordnance is in that canyon," he said, "so that I can convince Waingrow to undertake what is sounding more like a commando raid than a recon flight, if that's what you're pitching."

"Tell Waingrow those guns got stashed somewhere close to the Marine base right after they were stolen, and they're just sitting there waiting for Ricky Lee Kane's big brother to retrieve them. Or waiting for Waingrow—if he has the nerve."

I told Aaron that was why Kip's crew worked their way east, over the Sierra to East Fork. And why East Fork wasn't an accident. They must've planned on staging the slow-speed chase from there to throw the law off, to pull the OJ fake-out with the sister and focus the search north, away from the Marine base, not closer. And they won't split up until they move those guns and divvy up the proceeds.

"What options do I have?" he said. "Or am I already out of time?"

"You probably don't have twenty-four hours. I could find those killers in way less time. You just can't know about it. Waingrow stumbles in guns blazing, there'll be a lot more dead guys than just Sanchez. Those cons *will* be in the wind and you'll never catch them all."

"Waingrow will do what he thinks is best," Sarah said. "Best for him, anyway."

"And what will you do, Tommy?" Aaron said.

"What *I* think is best."

Aaron stood up. Then he shook my hand and said goodbye. I tossed off the last of my whiskey.

"Anyway, that's how I see it."

"I wish I was going with you," he said.

It was a small thing, but Aaron Fuchs had never shook my hand before. He let Sarah hug him then gave me a nod and drove off out of the yard. The snow hadn't let up the whole time we'd been talking.

Sarah stopped at the foot of the porch steps. I was still standing with my hands in my coat pockets, sort of wool-gathering. I watched Aaron's taillights disappear as he turned left on the Reno Highway toward Three Flags twenty miles south. When I turned back, she was watching me.

"Coming to bed?"

"No."

Sarah gave me a look that went from bad to worse.

"If I'm going snooping back in that canyon, I better catch a horse."

Chapter Eleven

"You're not going to wait till Aaron gets word from the task force?" she said.

"They'll never move fast enough. And they'll keep me on the sidelines anyhow."

She turned quick and angry, trotting up the porch steps. I followed her, but kept my distance.

"When were you going to—?"

"To ask you? When I figured a way to tell you that didn't sound—"

"That wouldn't piss me off," she said.

I just followed her inside and watched her rooting around for breakfast fixings. It was still full dark.

"And you're sure this is the best idea?" she said. She just spit the words out.

"I feel like I got Sanchez into a risky deal. I can't wait to see if she lives or dies, then if she doesn't make it, just shrug and say, 'She knew the risks when she took the job.'"

"I know. I know. And if you don't go, there will be two motherless boys down in Rancho Cordova. I know all that."

She slammed the skillet so hard on the stove, I flinched.

"I'm thinking of dozens of units of high-end hardware in the hands of China or Russia or ISIS. The TV guy with the cufflinks was right about one thing. The task force is not any closer to the rifles than they were six days ago." I sipped my coffee and tried to look relaxed.

"And I'm thinking I can't leave two fatherless girls right here in this house—not to mention their mother. We can wait for the Feds if you want, but these monsters, these psychos with video of our ten-year-old? They ain't waitin'." I stopped for another second. "These monsters scare me, baby."

"Are you guys fightin'?" Audie was standing in the kitchen doorway in her pjs.

Sarah turned back to the stove. I could see her hands shake.

"No, Sis," she said. "We're not fighting."

Sarah got down a plate for Audie and a plate for me with pancakes and sausage and eggs on a platter. None of us said anything for a bit. Audie was giving me the once-over, chewing slow. Sarah came up behind my chair and put her arms around my neck.

"We're not fighting," she said again.

"Then get a *room*," Audie said. She laughed at herself.

Sarah gave the kid a semi-exhausted look and tousled her hair and sent her back to bed when she'd finished breakfast. Audie only made it halfway to the door.

"We gonna check them heifers when you get back?" she said. "Grandpa Dave said I could ride with you guys when you check 'em if I'm not in school." She laughed. "I'd rather work with you and Grandpa than go to school anyhow." She looked at the kitchen window. "Ain't it still kinda dark to go ridin' yet?"

"True enough," Sarah said.

"Dave said he won't leave here just 'cause them bastards from the prison are lurkin' around," Audie said. "He figures him and Burt and me can stand off a half dozen honyockers before the marshals and FBI guys get here."

"I'd be betting on you, Sis," Sarah said.

"Are you stayin' with us," Audie said, "or goin' with Tommy?"

"Neither. I've got to get to work."

"Well, shit-fire."

Sarah and I held hands across the kitchen table, not saying anything for a minute. The house was quiet. Then she let go of my hand and spoke firm and clear like she'd just put on her deputy hat.

"So how did they know? How did those pigs know she was driving north?"

"A rat?"

"But how did they know where exactly to find her? Those cons didn't just bump into her when they pulled over to get a bottle of Fireball and some Milk Duds. They knew she would be driving north today at three a.m. They had to know."

"She was definitely the target. Who else did she tell?"

"You think somebody at the task force leaked her flyover

plans?" she said. "Did she tell someone her specific schedule for tonight?"

"You can't have hundreds of Feds from a dozen agencies and not have somebody accidentally spill something."

"But this was no accident." She picked up my hand again and held it in both of hers. "I think they're after you. They knew if they took her, you'd come after her. You're the target, honey. Isela is just the bait."

She said out loud what I'd only been thinking.

After the early breakfast I hitched up the gooseneck to Sarah's Silverado and checked the lights and the brakes. Sarah had Mom come over in the snowy dark to watch the girls till she got back. I'd asked Sarah to drive me to the Hanging Valley turnoff and drop me off so I wouldn't tip my hand by leaving a recognizable rig like a billboard in sight of the Reno Highway.

Since the early snows, we'd been keeping the saddle horses in a pasture close to the barn and feeding them hay at dawn so they'd be easy to catch. We haltered my big red horse and a gray gelding from our pack string then stood under the single bulb in the barn alley brushing the snow and dirt from their backs and bellies as they ate.

"You're taking your best horse into a gunfight?" she said.

I almost said, "A guy doesn't want to risk dying riding an ugly horse," but I thought better of it and just said, "He's solid in a pinch."

"And when exactly are you planning on coming back?"

"Today. By sundown. That's what I hope, anyway. But I

don't want to be back in that canyon with no supplies and no options. You know. Just in case."

"Just in case," she said.

Sarah watched me throw one of the old saddles from the pack station on the gray. She asked me why I hadn't used a packsaddle.

"In case I find Isela alive. I don't want some non-rider hanging on to a sawbuck dodging bullets at a dead run through the snow."

I sensed that nothing I said was turning out to be very reassuring.

"When you first came back from Fort Benning and Dad was missing," Sarah said, "and it was just the two of us chasing Kip from the Buckskins to Sunrise Pass, I was never afraid for the two of us. Even with all Kip's crazy thugs and psycho killer stunts, I was still never really afraid." She smiled then. "I sort of felt the two of us were pretty invincible."

"Me too, babe. You and me against the world."

"If I were going with you now I wouldn't be afraid. But I can't. Not with Lorena and Audie . . . our preteen terror."

She choked on a laugh with tears in her eyes.

"One parent has got to stay back," she said, "when one has to go. We just can't risk . . ."

She walked up close and hit me in the chest with the bottom of her fist. "Why does it always have to be you?"

"I don't have a better answer now than the last time you asked me that."

We got to saddling. I packed jerky and cheese, a thermos of coffee, and Burt's bottle of Knob Creek in stuffsacks. Sarah checked I had a workable radio and put some of her extra batteries in my saddle pockets along with an old ski jacket of hers.

"When the goons snatched her, they left her snow stuff on the seat of the rental," she said. "You want me to get your down sleeping bag?"

"I don't want to get too comfortable."

She nodded at my answer, and all the ways it told her a different story than the one she'd been hoping for. I was surprised that as upset as she was, she didn't give me more grief.

I stowed the stuffsacks in a pair of old pack panniers along with hay and ziplocks of grain then gathered some hobbles and a couple of nose bags and stuffed them in the panniers, too. I buckled the panniers to the saddle on the gray then covered the load with a pack tarp and lashed them down. It was a pretty light load and a pretty Okie-looking outfit, packing a saddle horse like that, but I didn't expect I'd be running into any outfitters I knew that morning. Mostly, I didn't want to be packing the animals at the canyon mouth where anybody driving by at first light could see us. I wanted to unload the horses, tighten our cinches, and *move*.

I noticed the first hint of gray over the Monte Cristos to the east and a white-orange stripe laying across the deep blue Sierra crest across the valley to the west. The closer we came to my leaving, the quieter Sarah got. It had started to snow again, light but steady. She turned and walked back toward the truck, not saying a word, hugging herself against the cold, the yard lights picking up fat swirling snowflakes settling on her blond hair and making it shine.

She started her truck and let it idle. I fitted both horses with a couple of bosals and old mecates that would break if

I had a wreck, then led them over to the gooseneck to load. When they were tied up with their noses in a couple of feed bags, she swung the trailer door shut. The latch banged loud—echoing like the end of something.

Sarah turned the rig around, pointing it east toward the Monte Cristos. Mom stepped out into the porch light in her bathrobe and made a kind of helpless gesture. Audie ran out of the half-lit house into the porch light and skipped down the wood steps. She wore her cowboy boots and my old hat over her pjs and had wrapped herself in a blanket. The blanket dragged in the snow and dirt.

"The hell?"

"God," Sarah said. "She's just incorrigible."

Audie jerked open the passenger door and climbed up on my lap.

"Come on, Sarah," she said. "Let's rattle our hocks."

"Absolutely not," Sarah said. "This is just too dangerous for . . ."

"It's okay, babe. Let her ride along."

"You're *both* incorrigible," she said.

Sarah drove east along the edge of Dave's property, away from the Reno Highway and toward the Monte Cristos. In a mile she turned right on a little piece of paved road through the sagebrush that skirted the back side of the valley. We drove along the edge of strange pastures, ranch headquarters scattered along the highway the length of the valley, the houses and barns just far-off black shapes behind occasional yard lights looking murky in the snowy night. We came even with Three Flags then, red and blue police lights flashing in the predawn a mile west, marking the local and federal law that were still interviewing witnesses and processing the kid-napping scene of Isela Sanchez. A mile farther on the road dead-ended at the Reno Highway, and Sarah steered the rig left into the narrow West Frémont canyon. We sat quiet for the first few miles, watching the early light hit jaggedy granite hundreds of feet above us.

"If Isela's alive," Sarah said, "those killers will be . . ." She stopped herself. She'd said it all before.

"They won't be expecting me horseback. Four-wheeling or snowmobiling maybe, not horseback."

"Then you'll probably be able to hear better than half a dozen wet, cold, trigger-happy flatlanders in a couple of Kawasaki side-by-sides," she said. "Or whatever the heck they have. I doubt they're snowshoeing up that canyon."

"I was thinkin', better than half a dozen gunsels crammed in a stolen Marine Small Unit Support Vehicle."

She gave me a curious look. "How long have you had that idea?" she said.

"Since the day you and me saw the vandalized Susvee by the Sonora Pass turnoff. The one that ended up getting stolen. I figured that was too much of a coincidence for that to be parked there on the morning of the breakout."

"And you figured that was tied in to stolen Marine sniper rifles even then?"

"Well, yeah."

"That's why you've been bringing up the rifles every chance you get."

"Pretty much."

"And why you probably have been planning to scout the canyon horseback since that first morning."

"Probably."

"So worrying about you now . . ."

"Yeah."

I reached over and squeezed her hand without waking up Audie snoozing on my lap. "But I'm sure glad you do."

"I should have picked up on this before," she said. "The rifles were within a specific radius from the base, stashed where a tracked Marine Support Vehicle could access them."

"Yup. After being stored somewhere semi-flat and dry."

"Like the foundation of the old miners' cabin—" she said.

"—at the edge of that upper meadow. Then hauled where they could either be trucked out or choppered out."

"That's kind of brilliant," Sarah said. She squeezed back. "Let's hope we're not too late."

I looked at my phone. "I wanted to be off the highway and up the canyon a bit before first light."

"You almost made it," she said.

The West Frémont River flowed low over the boulders between the brush this time of year but would be roaring come the spring melt. First narrow and rocky, the canyon widened out with Jeffrey pine on either side the farther we drove. We were halfway up the canyon when we saw the lights of our first snowplow. It came fast around a rocky bend and passed us northbound, rattling and scraping on the asphalt in a white cloud of headlights and swirly snow, then was gone just as quick.

"Promise me," Sarah said, "if for whatever reason you can't get Isela, you get the hell out of there before they see you. You don't have to fight them all."

"I'll be careful. But if she's alive, I don't plan on coming back without her."

We broke out of the canyon and saw the shapes of open peaks beyond the Marine base poke above the clouds. The fog ahead up the road blocked the far reaches of Hanging Valley, but we could see the first mile or so through falling snow.

"Except for the county plow, there hasn't been a single car."

"It's like the whole mountain is already hibernating," Sarah said.

The canyon was getting light enough to see where this branch of the river flowed down from Sonora Pass in the early dawn.

"Can you pull off to the left just before the county yard?"

"Sure," she said. "Why?"

"Just want to check something."

She nodded. A mile or so farther along she crossed the oncoming northbound lane then pulled off onto the gravel. The Sonora turnoff was just ahead.

The electric highway sign said that the pass was closed. Sarah let the diesel idle, and I got out to study the ground like I'd done a few days before, this time with Sarah's good tactical flash. I kicked the snow with my boot toe now and then to see if I'd missed anything. Nothing had changed, not the leaking hydraulic hoses from the Small Unit Support Vehicle dripping into the rocky ground, not where the rubber tracks had dragged the tarred gravel as someone drove it off, heading south.

Right where the mark of the track had gouged the

ground, I did see something that was new. A bit of color in the slush under a couple of inches of wet powder. I picked it up with the tip of my knife. It was a bureau of Alcohol, Tobacco, Firearms and Explosives ID in a leather holder with a badge attached that probably looked better a few hours earlier. The picture was of ATF Special Agent Isela Sanchez with a smear of blood across the clear plastic cover. Whoever tossed it there might've guessed that somebody trying to track the Susvee might start looking right where I was standing. Or maybe Isela had dropped it herself, trying to leave me a bread crumb trail. If she wasn't dead already.

I got back in the cab and held the ID out to Sarah. She already had put on rubber gloves and took it in two fingers, careful not to smudge any possible prints, then put it in one of the evidence ziplocks she always carried in her glove box.

"I'll get this to Aaron," was all she said.

She waited for a northbound semi to pass then drove out on the road. At the junction I waved to a couple of Marines drinking coffee under the dome light in the cab of a pickup parked just off the pavement. I figured they were scouting for convicts, too. They didn't see me, and didn't wave back. As the road curved left, I looked over at the abandoned barn downhill from the highway. A quarter mile farther south, a wide gravel road joined the pavement. Sarah turned in and parked the rig against the slope.

Audie still slept while we got out and unloaded the horses. She started to stir when I pulled my chinks out from under her and she watched me when I draped my saddle pockets over my arm and got a grip on the rifle scabbard.

"Why don't you stay in the truck, Sis," Sarah said.

Audie stayed in the cab and fiddled with the radio while Sarah and I cinched up. The temperature was bearable until the smallest wind hit us and stirred up the snow. Sarah slipped and almost fell walking up close to me. She started untying my wild rag.

"You never tie these tight enough," she said. "I get cold just looking at you." She snugged the big silk square up tighter under my chin and pushed me away when I tried to kiss her. We both flinched when a bigger gust hit us, and we heard Audie cussing as she stumbled out of the truck.

"Come on, you two," she hollered. "Tommy's burning daylight."

"I don't see any daylight yet, Sis," Sarah said.

I buckled on my chinks and put on my coat then checked the magazines on my .270 and 9mm before I pulled on my gloves. Sarah had already snugged up the lash rope on the gray.

When everything was as squared away as it could be, I pulled her close and whispered a bunch of nonsense only she could hear. She gave me a long kiss, long enough that I didn't want to leave.

"Well, I guess I can't put this off any longer."

Sarah nodded and turned away. The real storm hadn't started yet, but it was coming.

I gave Audie a hug and told her to take care of Sarah and the baby and to not burn the ranch house down. She ran over to Sarah as I was swinging aboard my horse.

"Don't worry," she said to Sarah, "if Tommy gets shot, old Red'll haul ass down here to the highway and we'll know Tommy's in a bad fix."

Sarah gave the kid an exhausted look. I took the gray's lead and headed out. A hint of dawn light hit the far southern reaches of Hanging Valley Ridge far back in the canyon. Seeing that made me feel like I just might have a chance to pull this off.

Sarah turned her rig around and waited alongside the cutbank for a motor home to pass. I thought I saw her looking back over her shoulder, but the snow clouds easing down the sides of the peaks to the west shrunk my visibility. I was taking my time, the horses stepping slow down the slope until Sarah's rig disappeared around the curve above the old barn. Then I went exploring.

Sarah's text came about three minutes later.

"You're not back in good season," it said, "I'm coming to get you."

I texted back. "Wouldn't have it any other way."

Chapter Twelve

Instead of following the road up-canyon right away, I turned around and headed back north, dropping down the slope and crossing a creek to the old barn, stopping just outside what was left of the corrals. The place had been a homestead or stage stop on a tributary of the West Frémont a hundred-plus years before, so there must have been a house and out-buildings here once. One of the side doors of the barn was wide open and starting to rock back and forth in the fresh wind. I sat my horse and turned my flash down at the disturbed ground covered by yesterday's snow with tracks of vehicles and humans still easy to see. I stayed quiet a minute, the horses not moving except for eyes and nostrils taking in the sight and smell of the unfamiliar country.

I left the corrals and rode alongside the barn. The board-and-bat siding was still mostly intact but black from weather and age. I circled to the open door and stopped to unzip my coat. Then I rode inside, and the gray horse snorted at the gloom and at the shifting beams of occasional headlights spilling down through broken boards from the highway. I rode from one end of the center aisle to the other in the blackness, unsnapping the Beretta's holster as I rode. The place smelled like musty hay and the rot of old wood sitting in the seep of hillside springs. On top of that was a rank human smell and the smell of fried grease from takeout food. Then faint, but way too familiar, I picked up the smell of something dead.

I stopped the horses and waited, reins loose in my left hand, my right hand on my chap leg, close to the Beretta but not touching it. I didn't have to wait long.

"You're the guy," a voice said. I eased the flash out of my coat pocket and turned it on, pointing at the ground so's not to start a gunfight right away. I could see a shape move in the back of a draft horse stall about twenty-five feet away, close enough to hear him breathe. The parka he wore was too big for him and made his head look tiny. He carried a shovel in his left hand.

"The guy Kip's gonna kill."

"Who're you?"

That seemed to confuse him. "Gilbert Orosco. You heard 'a me, man?"

I shook my head. "Nope. But I know you."

"You say you know me, then you won't ask me nothin'," he said.

"All I know is, you're number seven."

"What you talkin' about?"

"Kip didn't tell you? After you, there's six."

He had to think about that a minute. Then he checked out my animals.

"You're ridin' a horse? Shit. Kip told us to scope out some dude on a snowmobile or somethin'. Not a freakin' horse."

I didn't say anything.

"Hey, man, Kip left me here to let him know you came by. So here you are, and here I am, man." He held up a big satellite phone in his right hand. "Be callin' Kip right now."

"Kip left you here to die."

He dropped the shovel and twisted his whole body to let me see an automatic on his belt.

I shifted the flash to my left hand. "You don't need to do this."

He raised his right hand. He was holding his gun now.

"Scared?" he said.

"'Fraid not."

He stopped to think. "What're you talkin' 'bout?" he said. "What's this 'seventh man' shit?"

"If your boy Kip was here, he could explain it to you." I slipped the flash into my coat pocket.

"Well . . . he ain't here, is he?"

"Then you're gonna die stupid."

He wasn't very good at this. It seemed to take him forever. The gray horse jumped at the pop of my Beretta in the dark. Two shots. The red horse under me never flinched.

When I looked back outside, it was gray dawn. The first real skiffs of new snow had already started falling. I tied the horses in the barn alley and looked around. Even in the uneven gloom it was easy to see the Susvee tracks and a damp spot of diesel fuel shiny on the dirt. The Susvee had been right here, almost in sight of the highway since a couple of mornings before when it only had to chug along in the predawn for a few hundred yards, snow covering its heavy tracks, then get hidden in the barn. Kip's crew could've reached here easy while his sister was leading the law on that low-speed chase in the other direction. At least until somebody tipped them off that Isela Sanchez was on the way.

Taking a closer look, I saw their human sign scattered from one end of the barn to the other. Even more of a mess than from the Placerville plane. From food wrappers and booze bottles to cigarette butts and toilet paper, this was the staging area as well as a hideout. And it was where they provisioned up for the trek into the canyon.

I checked Orosco's body. He was a small frail-looking guy. I found the satellite phone he'd been waving around when I first saw him, but it had taken one of my 9mm rounds full-on, and was dead useless. He'd fallen by the door to what was some sort of storeroom back in the stagecoach days. Maybe a grain room with hay hooks and wooden rakes hanging on what was left of a wall. I saw a pile of trash. Some of it old, like boards and rotting gunnysacks and dusty hay, and some new, like torn plastic tarps and paint buckets. My flash caught something shiny. I pushed some trash away with my boot and saw the headlight of a small car.

I pulled down a wooden rake and went to work scraping the trash away till the rake fell apart in my hands. By then I'd uncovered the front end of a late-nineties Camry. The body was dented, the paint oxidized. It looked like the Camry I'd seen Kip's mom and sister loading stuff into outside the Paiute Meadows NAPA the day after the Folsom escape.

The passenger-side window was gone. Moldy hay and trash and a torn tarp covered a mound in the dirt alongside the car. I was close enough to catch a faint whiff of rot. I flicked a gunnysack at the pile of trash so I wouldn't have to touch it. It was a stink not every person would catch over the old musty barn smell. I peeled back the tarp and the trash slid away.

The body of a middle-aged guy I'd never seen before sprawled next to the beginning of a hole in the black dirt. I didn't figure that Kip had ever planned on Orosco leaving this barn alive, much less finishing the damn hole. Once he'd told Kip on the satellite phone that I'd made it to the mouth of the canyon, Orosco's job was over. Besides, Kip loved leaving his dead where they fell. Hiding them was never his style.

The man had been shot between the shoulder blades and in the neck. Glass pebbles and shards from the side window still covered the body and reflected the beams of early light from the missing ceiling boards. The guy was dressed like a million other suburban dads. A red windbreaker lay in the dirt next to his body. His chinos were soiled, so I guessed his last seconds were pretty rough. I checked the pockets on the windbreaker. There was no ID, but I did see a service receipt from a Sacramento Chrysler dealership. He must've been one of Kip's carjacking hostages—until a better one like Agent Sanchez came along.

I rinsed my hands in the half-frozen spring out by the corrals then untied my horses and got out of there. A bit of eastern sky was clear, clear enough to spy the morning star, but clouds over Sonora Pass were getting darker by the minute. I took time to scan the country then worked my way back through the new snow on the sage up to the gravel road where Sarah had dropped me off. I wanted to put in some miles before full daylight. With Isela and Ridgely missing from Waingrow's radar, I wondered what his next move might be. Or maybe I was getting ahead of myself. Maybe Waingrow had connected the dots where I hadn't. Maybe Rod had checked in and Waingrow was cooking up some brilliant counterattack. That was better than thinking the boss marshal was planning to start a stampede of law and TV news that would turn this valley into a killing ground.

I hadn't ridden far when the wind picked up. Ahead was an unprotected rise just a few feet high where the wind blew harder and the snow wasn't sticking. I saw something moving on the bare ground in the growing light. Like deer, or maybe coyotes feasting on a carcass. I squinted until I could make it out—geese. Big Canada geese with banded necks. Just a few at first. Pretty soon I saw dozens, bunches of them covering the rise from side to side, then more as my eyes adjusted. There must've been a couple hundred of them, waddling along, pecking at the ground, grazing like goats. Some had formed vees on the dead meadow like they'd landed in formation. I rode closer. A few of them flapped their wings, then a few more, until the whole bunch took off yapping. My red horse eyed them, just wary as hell. It must've been a while since Kip's crew had passed this way. Enough time for the geese to resettle after a Susvee rattled through the middle of them.

The canyon mouth was more like a shallow valley with patches of dawn light cutting through the snow flurries so at first I could see a long way across that empty ground. Next to a plank shed half-hid in an aspen grove, I saw the orange shape of a Tucker Sno-Cat. It had steel pontoons and steel tracks, so I knew it was one of the old ones and worth some coin. Not something to leave unattended.

Ahead, cattle ate hay from feed cribs against a fence along the dirt road, and I saw fresh tire tracks following the fence. It looked like some cowboy had been out early with a flatbed truck to supplement the grass buried under the early snow. Sometimes when the nightmares came, I'd think I used to be that kind of cowboy, following hard and simple routines of a straightforward life with no blood on my hands except what came at the branding fire.

It was a half mile farther along that I caught my first clear trace of tracks that I hadn't noticed in the early dawn. Tracks like I'd seen by the Sonora Pass turnoff and again in the old barn. Small Unit Support Vehicle tracks—the Marines' stolen Susvee. From the wide rubber treads, it was climbing up to the road I was on, floating over the snow on the meadow then churning up the black dirt creekbank as it cut through fresh ice. It looked like they slid backward more than once. Judging by the depth of the tracks and the fresh snow on top of the tracks, I could calculate how far ahead they were and laugh that the Susvee was just ahead. The rifles must be right where Isela Sanchez and I knew they'd be.

Up-canyon was a last bit of blue sky over granite ridges. I'd forgot how deep this canyon could get and how far back in the canyon the ridges went. Purple-black clouds hung down above that patch of sky. I was watching the ground and the trees up ahead and noticing that the temperature was dropping as the wind gusts got more frequent. I listened to the muffled squeaking sound made by the horses' hooves as they picked their way through fresh snow. When I looked back up the canyon, the blue patch was gone and the ridge gone with it. I'd hoped that I could close the gap soon enough. Now I wasn't so sure.

I pulled up where the dirt road crossed a gully with a creek at the bottom. This was as far as I'd driven Isela Sanchez the morning before. The road made a hairpin turn to the right, and the Susvee tracks followed. If they kept following that turn they'd be heading back down the canyon before they knew they'd changed direction. I was guessing Billy Jack Kane was the only one of that bunch who'd ever been up here, and then only in early summer. Staring at the road and swirling snow through the Susvee windshield, he might've got turned around and missed the trail. I pulled up and made a quick check of the ground but didn't see a trace of man nor animal. I took the horseback and hunter trail away from the road, thinking maybe I could make up enough time to get ahead of them. If I could pull that off, things would get western fast.

A few hundred yards on, the trail joined the creek, winding through aspen and tamarack, climbing until the creek was thirty feet down a deep slope. Slabs of broken granite made a series of descending ponds and pools, half-frozen now, tangled with drowned trees. At the creek's edge the water ran fast under new ice. Away from the creek a scattering of tamarack had broken through the granite over the years.

Every couple of minutes I stopped to listen and to scan the trees and thickets and rocks for any rear guard the cons might have left behind and to take a fresh look at the fog slipping down the ridges and gullies ahead of me, bright white against the black of the storm. I wondered how a washed-out Marine like Ricky Lee Kane ever found this canyon. It was a rough spot even in the best of weather.

Sitting still on the red horse, I scanned the terrain in front of me, looking for any advantage, any cover. I pulled the Remington and tried to scope the tree line for movement, but now blowing snow stuck to the glass. That, and my horse shifting his weight made the riflescope useless as long as I was horseback. The early winter had come on so quick the aspen still had some of their yellow leaves to hide behind, and the red willow wasn't yet stripped to its stems.

The trail topped out on a ridge. I turned in the saddle to get a long view of where I'd been, scanning the land towards the old barn, but the galvanized roof had already disappeared behind the ridges and tamarack and fog. I pulled out my sheriff's radio and called Sarah, not sure if I'd reach her. When she answered, I could barely hear her voice, like she was afraid to ask me anything.

"How far have you gotten?"

I told her roughly where I was.

"Can you quit now? Come back?"

"I think I'm okay. I picked up their sign already. Clear as day."

"There's a hell of a storm rolling in, babe," she said.

There was no sound for a minute but my horses shifting their balance in the snow and the creak of saddle leather.

"The whole Sierra ridgeline will be socked-in pretty soon," she said, "from north of our ranch down to Mammoth Lakes." She sounded stiff and wary.

I told her about the two bodies her department would find in the barn and that one of them was Gilbert Orosco, an escapee.

"The other is lying next to a beat-up Camry that I saw Kip's sister drive."

"Another escapee?"

"No. A hostage." I described the guy who'd owned the minivan.

I heard Sarah suck in her breath. She told me that overnight, they'd found the faded blue truck Isela's kidnappers had used.

"Jack Harney told me a snowmobiler spotted it in some willows at the old hot springs just north of Hell Gate Summit," she said, "about a mile up the highway from the Hanging Valley turnoff. There was blood on the backseat and the headliner. You could see it from the highway—like Kip wanted us to find it."

She didn't say anything more. Her radio blasted static for a second then Sarah spoke loud and clear.

"Don't say another word, hon. This isn't a secure frequency."

"The hell—"

"You're flirting with obstruction of justice, Deputy," a woman's voice said.

"You told me I'd have a moment of privacy with my husband," Sarah said. "I just want to make sure that your word to a fellow law enforcement officer is truly not worth shit." Sarah rarely swore, so I was impressed.

It was US Attorney Kathy Avakian on the open line. She hissed and sputtered, and I heard Sarah telling me again to not say another word. When Avakian tried to come back with more threats to the both of us, Sarah killed the radio. Then my cell buzzed and Sarah came back on the line, talking to me like nothing had just happened.

"So you're on Kip's trail for sure?"

"Yup. They got the Susvee, just like we figured."

"Like *you* figured, babe."

"Sarah, what the hell was that all about? What's this 'obstruction of justice' crap?"

"Waingrow wants to look like he's cleaning house. Got things under control. He told the US attorney to lean on me so I'd lean on you." She sounded exhausted. "You know the drill. No stone left unturned."

"I just don't want my sweetie getting in trouble. Not over the US marshal. And not over Kip."

"Kip's simple," she said. "All he wants is revenge."

"I think he wants more than revenge now. I think he wants to die. He's not the crazy-eyed psycho we tracked down before. He looked like he's in pain all the time, and pain wears you out. I think he wants to commit suicide. You, me, him—all going out in a hail of bullets. A blaze of glory. He'll be a Folsom legend, but his crew just don't know it yet."

We said sweet goodbyes. Sarah being on my side made the trail ahead somehow a lot easier. A couple of hours on, after steady snow, the sun tried to burn through patches of fog then disappeared just as fast. The tips of the willows were almost pink when the dawn light hit them just right. I stepped off my horse and scraped the balled-up snow from the gray's feet, gave the red gelding's feet a quick glance, then got moving again.

The trail opened out on another, smaller meadow, but I was seeing less and less with every step. Every time I took my bearings, the fog got thicker and moved closer down the canyon. Fresh powder smoothed out the terrain, and hard winds came and went. I caught glimpses through the fog of the granite ledge of Hanging Valley Ridge. Then I thought I heard voices. I kept the horses as quiet as I could, listening for Kip's team, hoping to locate them even before I saw them. I was pretty sure I was hearing bits of cussing and complaining and raging against the freezing fog. With the weather, it was hard to tell if I was listening to a pair of them or the whole bunch or just the wind. Then I felt the fog turn to ice on my face, and I couldn't even see my horses' ears ahead of me. I'd felt that ice before.

The first time I remembered old-timers calling the killer fog pogonip, I was a kid in maybe the seventh grade. Bigger kids said it was an Indian name for the ice fog that lay so thick across western mountain valleys and canyons you couldn't see your hand in front of you. Kind of like now. Sarah Cathcart was a senior in high school, so I figured she knew everything. She told me that story was all crap and to not pay the other kids any mind. She said "pogonip" was a made-up name because the miners and hayshakers and bartenders who were the grandparents of these grade-school smartasses were too thickheaded to remember the Shoshone word was *payinappih*. And in Shoshone it didn't mean fog, it meant cloud. Being a smartass myself, I liked knowing stuff other kids didn't know. I pulled my wild rag tight so it covered most of my face and thought of Sarah at seventeen as I rode. I looked at the darkening sky and got worried that she would head out to find my trail too early. Before it was safe. I still pretty much figured she knew everything, but sometimes I worried about her just the same.

I let the horses rest every few minutes now. They were glad to quit fighting the snow and fog and stood quiet, vapor puffing from their nostrils then turning to ice with every breath. They'd left deep furrows in the low spots as they heaved their weight against the growing drifts, furrows that looked deep enough to be seen for miles. Now I looked back at my tracks but couldn't see a trace.

I pulled my Beretta from the holster under my coat and slipped it into an outside pocket so it would be handy. I eased the horses forward one slow step at a time, trying to remember the terrain. Moving forward made me feel better. I was never much good at standing still.

The wind and cold and fog were getting worse, and the horses were getting tired. They didn't have wild rags like I did to keep the airborne ice out of their lungs. My only way of telling where I was heading was crossing the occasional ditch or creek and seeing which way the water was flowing when my horses' feet busted through. Beside the hard freeze, I had to fight the drowsiness. I was thinking of that, and trying to concentrate, shaking my head to keep alert. If I didn't jump-start this whole deal pretty soon, the cons would be lighting cigars in Vegas, toasting the honyocker who couldn't find his way out of a box canyon. Then I heard voices echoing in the fog again, and I knew the voices were real.

I stopped. The fog had covered the ground, and when

the wind pushed down the canyon I was at a dead stop till the wind eased. When it did let up, I was surprised that the wall of fog just kept on coming, slow but steady. I tried to focus on my numb fingers as I slid the .270 from the scabbard.

The first gunfire was a surprise, so close it seemed like it was coming right from under my horse. I heard the red horse squeal as he jumped to the left with the gray right behind. I'd rode right over a little propane heater at the edge of a snow cave dug into a bank, and it must've singed my gelding. I got off a single shot at the direction of the gunfire then saw white shapes dive for cover. Somebody got off a couple more wild shots. One of the shooters I recognized even in the fog, the spiky-haired con, Chester Livermore, the guy who raped little kids. A second guy stumbled into the willows along a frozen creek and vanished in the whiteness with a big revolver in his fist. I located him when he started to return fire, his pistol shots making circles in the airborne ice. Then there was silence except for the wind until I heard a third convict crashing in the willow and fog.

I didn't see that guy till he'd covered half the distance from the timber behind me, slogging along in the tracks I'd made, then dragging himself up a ridge above the creek. It was the wild-haired Mexican guy, his beard crusted with so much frost he looked like a grizzly.

I made a quick one-handed shot over my left shoulder just to dust him back then balanced the rifle in the crook of my rein hand. I was pulling the bolt for another shot when the gray stumbled. Since he was still dallied tight, he almost jerked my red horse down. I loosened the gray's lead, tossing it a few feet to leave him at liberty, but not before the .270

slipped off my arm and dropped in the snow. I cussed myself and gigged my horse in a wide circle heading up toward the guy on the ridge, the packhorse trotting and stumbling behind, not wanting to be separated. The second gunsel fired twice then headed toward the trees, too, falling on all fours in a willow thicket. The gray spooked good that time, sucking back and running off. When I looked up, the Mexican on the ridge had vanished.

I rode back to where I'd dropped my rifle and jumped down to pick it up, wiping the snow off the scope and slipping it back in the scabbard. Then I got mounted to chase the damn gray. If Kip's guys didn't kill me then and there, I'd have died from shame for dropping the Remington. Still, I'd found three of the cons, or they found me, and the weather was equally crappy for us all. And now I knew it wasn't going to be hard to cut these chowderheads from the herd.

I watched for a sign of more shooters as I circled the red horse wide, wanting to face the ice cave from a distance. That let both the horse and me gather our wits while I dropped a fresh magazine into the .270. Hard wind followed me as I crept up the second shooter's trail. I saw a touch of blood on the snow but that could've been the guy just snagging his face or hand on a tree limb. Either way, he'd gone to ground, and I couldn't waste any more time on him. I had to keep moving.

If I circled away from the cave, I might beat these three to Kip and the rifles, but odds were they had satellite phones or something like, and now they'd know I was close. I patted my pocket just to feel my 9mm, but I left it where it was. Even horseback I shot more true with the .270, and I figured I needed to disable at least one more of them. I yanked a round into the chamber and pushed that red horse into something that looked like a gallop, heading right for the ice cave where I'd last seen Livermore, shooting as I came. I felt like Custer riding into a Cheyenne winter camp but was a tad less sanguine about the outcome.

Chapter Thirteen

I'd closed the distance to about fifty yards when the gunsel rose up wrapped in a ratty sleeping bag, popping away with an AR-15 as he yelled like he remembered me as the guy that broke his nose. The red horse's stride and my shot fell into perfect sync for half a second as I fired a third time. The guy fell, tangled in his sleeping bag as he stumbled across the propane heater. He screamed as the polyester bag caught fire and started to melt. I pointed the rifle at the cave and listened to the guy take his last breaths as I scanned the fog for a way forward. The noise the dying convict made was something I could've done without, but considering what he was locked up for, I wouldn't lose any sleep on his account.

Then I heard another sound behind me and twisted in the saddle. It was only my gray horse. He was used to traveling head-to-tail in a pack string, so he hadn't gone far. I scooped up his lead then dallied, looser this time, and headed back to where I'd last seen the second shooter.

The next sound I heard wasn't gunfire. It was the tinny,

soft *pop-pop-buzz* of a two-stroke engine firing up. I held my breath. It was some sort of Ski-Doo, and I wanted to hear which way it was headed, though the whiteout played tricks with noise.

The sound faded, and I rode slow up to the cave. It was more of a shallow spot in the bank than a cave, but it had given the cons shelter from the wind, and the propane heater gave them some warmth. It looked like the one thing that kept them from sitting in ice puddles was a couple of blue tarps. It told me how well planned some of this slaughter was, and how half-assed the other half was. These boys had been low on the totem pole to be stuck down-canyon alone and in a blizzard, guarding the main event. At least Orosco had the shelter of the old barn.

I stepped off and checked my horse's legs and belly for burns or wounds, but he seemed okay, more surprised than hurt. I hobbled both horses and pulled hay from the panniers on the gray and set out two piles on the snow. Then I poked around the camp till I found the tramped-down snow and frozen mud and the Ski-Doo tracks heading up-canyon. After the horses ate I tied the gray behind the sorrel again and started walking, face down, leading my horse and following the Ski-Doo tracks as fast as I could move on foot. With my cold lungs pounding, I covered ground without really noticing. I straightened up to see a little break in the weather, a hint of visibility far to the east.

I looked around to get my bearings. Behind me was a rocky treeless slope that I remembered had a passible hiking trail in summer. It was nothing but wind-whipped snow now with a bit of mahogany poking through every ten feet or so.

A hiker fit enough to make that climb would pass a small lake then top the ridge below Rickey Peak and be able to look east down into Paiute Meadows. In this weather, I didn't figure I could make it even halfway to the crest. Then the wind picked up and cut visibility back almost to nothing again.

I climbed back on my horse and waited till the next lull to scan the country. The canyon had split behind me in the whiteout. I was following the left fork of the canyon along the semi-frozen watercourse of Molybdenite Creek. Since this was where the two shooters had their camp, I knew I was heading the right direction. To the right side of the creek was the big wall of granite called Hanging Valley Ridge. To the left side was the second rock wall, Flatiron Ridge. I had to be getting close to where Ricky Lee Kane had stashed those rifles. Once those two ridges merged somewhere ahead of me, there was nowhere left to go.

I'd lost the Ski-Doo tracks in the new snow but the second shooter still left me traces of his blood. Looking ahead through the fog, I saw an unfrozen beaver pond, small and rippley from the fresh snow landing on its surface. It was just a wide spot in the creek with no way to tell how deep it was or if the bottom was sandy or rocky. I circled the pond, keeping my distance as I headed for some tamarack, all the time scanning the ridgetops for any sign of the third convict, the bearded guy. I kept my eyes on the fresh snow, trying to not lose the wounded con's trail altogether when the ground under my horse started to give way. The gelding spun and thrashed. He was already in belly-deep water before he got turned around, fighting to keep his feet under him. Behind him, the gray stumbled and almost dragged him down.

It took some spur rattling and mecate popping to get the gray upright and keep him moving, his brisket and forelegs breaking the ice till he reached the shallows. The near-wreck seemed to take forever.

When the horses were back on solid ground, they shook the water off their bellies and backs. I checked their feet again before I mounted. Then I went back to searching for the second shooter.

With a shift in the wind, I spied the Ski-Doo poking half out of the water, wedged against the beaver dam. I saw the gunman's body just beyond. The icy edge of the pond came up to his waist like he died trying to climb out but didn't have the strength.

I stepped down from my horse and stomped to shake the water off before it seeped into my boots. I wanted to keep the horses saddled and ready to ride if Sanchez was alive, so I tied them in the tamarack and spread the last fistfuls of hay to keep them occupied. The snow was up to my knees now in the low spots, and when the wind slammed into me, the snow around my legs was all that kept me upright.

The part of the man poking out of the water was already covered with ice crystals, his dead eyes frozen white. One hand gripped a rotted length of tamarack a beaver had left behind. The other held a .44 Magnum revolver so big he'd rested it on an ice-slick log, the revolver just barely visible under fresh snow.

Shooting blind, I had still hit the guy twice, once in the arm, once in the ribs. The shots might not have been fatal in better weather. By just the shape of him, I was convinced it was Dennis Wang, the flyer and meth smuggler who'd murdered the charter pilot. Him being one of the rear guard told me he was out of the action and not part of any future play, except to grunt and carry. I was guessing the rifles were close, but I didn't know how close. If Wang was expendable, it meant the stash was too heavy to move by air, and there must be more rifles missing than the Marines let on, with more profit to be had for whoever could traffic them. Or the two campers were just rear-guard troops waiting to see if I'd passed their checkpoint. Either way it didn't matter. I wouldn't make a move on the rifles until I'd located Sanchez.

I left the horses tied and rounded the edge of the pond. I saw the Susvee tracks ahead of me. Tracks I hadn't noticed in the killer fog. They went straight into the waters of the pond and were still visible under the snow even though they had to be at least twenty-four hours old. I circled the pond until I saw the tread marks coming out of the water and up on to the bank. Kip had always acted like he walked on water. Now he had a contraption that let him do it for real.

I climbed the slope above the pond. Close to the rim I tried my sheriff's radio, then my phone, but got no service. I texted both Sarah and Aaron my approximate position and the rough number of Kip's crew still standing. Minus Orosco, Livermore, and Wang, that would leave four—Billy Jack, Esparza, Vasiliev, and Kip himself. Always Kip, the guy in charge.

I circled the Susvee tracks until I reached the creek. I looked for an easy place to ford on foot then followed the creek bed back to the horses. I filled a canvas bucket and watered them from the beaver pond till they'd had their fill. My hay'd run short, so I broke off some dead cottonwood bark like I'd heard the Shoshone did in the old days when winter feed was scarce. I'd wait till dark to make a move.

I tried to call Sarah one last time but still no luck. I figured she might already be on my trail, maybe with Jack Harney, a guy who knew the canyon and wasn't fazed by a blizzard.

I loosened the saddle pad on my red horse then spread the blankets flat and doubled the pack tarp on the snow. I lay back and pulled my saddle against my chest and drew what warmth I could from it. I'd brought the tarp in case I needed to pack out Isela's body, but there was no call to freeze to death myself while I waited. I sat under my blankets bundled in my coat eating jerky and an apple and washing it down with cold water and a gulp of Knob Creek. Then I let myself doze a few minutes.

I sat up in the half dark. For the first time in days I'd had the dream of the cave as I drifted in and out of sleep. This time, though, I was getting buzzed by a helicopter gunship, and I'd taken some of God's Warriors down with me before they overran my position. I got another drink of water, panting like some old bear as I gathered my wits.

I rolled up the pack tarp and brushed the snow off my gelding with it then resaddled him and left both animals in sheltering tamarack while I headed up-canyon on foot, trying to keep the circulation in my feet going. It was almost full dark.

Squinting ahead, I picked up a bit of color, a little flicker of blue, then more ice and fog until I caught a glimpse of something large and dark hanging back in the timber. I wiped the riflescope with a corner of my wildrag and scanned the bank until I got a good look. I could see the convicts drifting through the trees, kind of floating in the soft electric light like I was a lone Washoe watching the Donner party through the pines and knowing that no good would ever come of it.

I saw the Mexican watcher from the ridge up close. The same guy who'd drugged the folks at East Fork. He was taking a leak in the snow. Next to him was the Russian, Vanya Vasiliev, in a yellow slicker, pouring something into a Styrofoam cup. Behind them I saw the one who must be Billy Jack Kane, reaching into a big wood box sitting on a forklift pallet with a battery lantern on the pallet next to him. The box still had scraps of tree branches and brush they'd used for camouflage the year before. Billy Jack was wrapped in a blanket, typing into a phone with a tan-colored rifle across his lap. Probably taking inventory. He seemed to be examining the rifles—the new Mk 13s—one at a time. This was his score, after all. His and his dead brother's. He'd take his time unless someone had the sand to tell him he couldn't.

That's when I figured Billy Jack had precious little idea just how big or small his baby brother's original haul was. Billy Jack had never seen the rifles up close. Probably had no idea how many of them there were. But then, for that matter, neither had I.

Behind Kane I saw heavy brownish tarps covering rectangles of what I guessed were more of his stolen goods. I swept the reticle across the hideout but didn't see a fourth con. I didn't see Kip. If these four were all that was left, they'd picked a heavy load to haul in hard country.

Then I took my first good look at the stolen Susvee. Its front windshield stared out in the storm, battery lights putting a low glow on falling snow. The thing was two boxy, camo-painted units powered by wide rubber tracks. The rear unit wasn't a trailer, but almost like a pusher. It could be used for troop transport, medevac, you name it. A handy piece of hardware, but small as it was, the thing still made too big a target for my taste. I wondered if Billy Jack felt the same way.

They'd parked it inside the stone foundation of an old miners' cabin, now just broken bits of rock and concrete ringed by tamarack tucked against a steep slope. If the light hadn't been on inside the front unit, the camo plate would've been hard to spot against the dirt bank in deep shadow and thick trees. It was a pretty smart place for the rifles to be hidden. Not easy to find but easy to defend—in the short term, anyhow. The personnel carrier was turned around so it faced the trail down-canyon for a semi-quick getaway. The side door to the rear unit was open, and faint lights outlined the interior, but I could only guess how far along Billy Jack was with his counting. I was too close to use the riflescope but not too close to use the rifle if I had to. I knew I couldn't jeopardize Isela Sanchez, but the hunter in me was tempted to try to end it all then and there.

The wind had come and gone in bursts. Billy Jack stood up and yelled something to Vasiliev, grabbing him by the front of his yellow slicker. Billy Jack was still wrapped in his blanket. He pointed to the exposed crates he'd been sitting on, then pushed the Russian hard in that direction, complaining about missing a chance to head down-canyon when they still had some daylight. It was the first time I'd heard Billy Jack Kane's voice.

I circled the Susvee on foot, using trees for cover, then came at it from the rear. For a few minutes, I hadn't seen a soul. I held back forty or fifty feet so the vehicle was almost invisible in the snow and fog, the running lights just a dim glow. Then the interior lights popped and brightened and I faded back farther into the trees.

I pivoted slow to check my surroundings and the brighter light gave me a surprise. Not more than fifty feet behind the Susvee was an old orange Sno-Cat, just like the one I'd seen down-canyon only a few hours before. I brushed the snow off my rifle and eased up on it from the side. The windshield had been wiper-ed clean not long before, the housing around the engine was cool but not cold, and there were greasy finger-prints on the sheet metal where the wet snow didn't stick, like someone had been working on the motor. I threw the cab's door open and leveled my .270 inside but the interior was tiny like a prewar pickup, so no one could be hiding there. I heard voices and hustled back toward the Susvee, looking for Sanchez but turning back to check out the Sno-Cat more than once. The odds that there was two of those orange relics in the same canyon the same day were pretty slim.

I eased open the rear door of the Susvee's second unit. In the faint light I could see a body lying twisted against a stack of rifles wrapped in tarps like the ones Billy Jack had been sort-ing. The man's ankles were bound together with duct tape and his hands were pinned behind him. Another strip of tape covered his mouth, but not real well. He looked unconscious, either beaten or drugged. It was deputy US Marshal Rod Ridgely, and he was a long way from Plumas County.

I stepped outside into the snow. I could see Kip now in the dim light, sitting at the controls of the forward unit. He wore a brand-new black parka and looked a lot less seedy than the last time I saw him. He was talking loud to someone on a satellite phone like the one Orosco had been using. He had all the earmarks of a man in charge, like the old Kip when I first met him, except skinnier. The dangerous Kip. Maybe I'd been wrong about him being played out. Maybe all he needed was just some fresh cocaine. I couldn't hear what he was saying over the hum of a generator, and couldn't tell if Kip was just jabbering to himself. I stepped to the side for a better look and saw the back of agent Sanchez's head on the steel deck. I took another step, then Kip swiveled in his seat. When he was partly turned away from me, I stepped closer to the window. My movement must've caught Sanchez's attention. She twisted her neck and shifted her eyes, but that was enough. I could see her tense up. She was tied and taped just like Ridgely, and they'd roughed her up pretty bad.

Kip stood up, still talking on his phone. He looked alert, eyes popping. After a minute he opened the Susvee's side hatch and stepped down into the snow, hobbling a bit as he went. I could hear him shouting orders to someone in the wind, hurrying them up.

I stepped inside the opposite hatch as soon as Kip limped away into wind-ripped aspen. I dropped to my knees and pulled my knife to cut the tape and set Sanchez free.

"We were right," she said soft, coughing up blood. Her

voice was a hoarse whisper like she'd been punched in the throat. "They were right where we thought they'd be."

I yanked more tape. She'd busted a tooth since I'd last seen her.

"We *did it*."

I shushed her. "We gotta get you outta here."

Sanchez looked out the door Kip had just disappeared through.

"Where's the cavalry?"

"Ridgely is drugged and unconscious in the back of this thing, so you're lookin' at all the horse soldiers you're going to get tonight."

"You're shittin' me," she said.

"I got two horses tied down-canyon. We make a little noise to divert these rat-heads, then make a run for it."

"That's all you got?"

"Yeah, unless I can roust Ridgely, that's how it is." I stood up. "You hear anybody coming, play dead."

She started to say don't go, but fell into a coughing fit.

I stepped out of the front unit into the wind the way I'd come. I held the .270 in my left hand as I steadied myself against the Susvee with my right. I worked my way along to the rear door then grabbed a-holt and pulled myself up.

"Hey, cowboy. *Wassup?*"

It was Deputy US Marshal Rod Ridgely. He was sitting on a stack of tarped-up boxes, peeling a piece of half-cut duct tape from the ankle of his boot with one hand like he hadn't a care in the world. He stood up, brushing dirt and sawdust and scraps of tape off his skinny jeans. He had a Sig 9mm in his other hand, and it was pointed right at me.

Chapter Fourteen

"You still packin' that Beretta?"

I nodded.

"Hand it over."

"Want me to drop the magazine first?"

"Nah," he said. "I trust ya."

"When did you know I was here?"

"We heard gunshots a long-ass time ago. Sound carries, bud. Then Tito Esparza saw you pokin' around in the trees. Looking for Kip?"

"Nope. Moved on, old son."

He cocked his head.

"Trackin' guns, now."

"Well," he said. "Fuchs *said* you were a tracking fool, fool."

"Somebody had to know I was coming. Just didn't figure it'd be you."

"No way Sanchez got carjacked by accident," he said, cheerful as could be.

"No, I guess not. Looks like you got some new partners."

Ridgely looked past me out the rear door towards flashlight beams in the dark.

"Yeah," he said. "They might take some breakin' in."

"So let's go see 'em anyway."

"Might be good if you left that rifle right here, though," he said.

I set the Remington on a pile of tarped boxes that were most likely neatly stacked and wrapped sniper rifles, already counted and cataloged by Billy Jack Kane. Looking at wet spots drying on the canvas, I was guessing I was seeing one of his early batches. I stepped up close to Ridgely. Even though he was armed and now I wasn't, he took a step back. That told me something.

"Let's go get Sanchez. See what Kip wants to do with her."

"Why would I give a shit?"

"Then you should worry about what Kip wants to do to you."

"Like what?"

"That revenge motive for stealin' his woman? Puttin' him in lockdown? Shootin' his ass? You forget about all that?" Ridgely sort of shivered. "I figure he's gonna drag those bad times out till you squeal."

I waved him off. "Kip ain't gonna live that long. He's used up."

Ridgely gave me a strange look. A real jolt, actually. "He's lived *this* long," he said.

"Every dead convict in this canyon makes the pot richer for the few guys left alive. But I bet you already figured that out for yourself."

"You're the boy takin' out Kip's guys," he said.

"And that puts an even bigger target on his back."

Ridgely scrunched up his face. "Dude, you are *such* a pessimist."

"All I'm sayin' is, you'd best watch your own back. *Dude.*"

I walked around the tail end of the Susvee through the snow to the front unit with my own Beretta jammed in my back. Agent Sanchez lay on her side on the steel deck like every breath hurt. I figured she might have some broken ribs when I helped her sit upright. She froze when she saw Ridgely.

"*Cabrón!*"

Ridgely pushed his Raiders' cap back on his head, trying to look super casual.

"We all thought you were up around Beckwourth in Plumas County," she said. "But when Tommy made the case that the rifles were stashed down near Paiute Meadows and the Marine base, I thought you were walking into a convict trap." She wiped her nose with her fingers. "Boy was I wrong. I had my peeps ping all the area cell towers to track you down. I called to *warn* you, you damn *sellout.*"

Isela glanced up at me. She looked whipped.

"With all this country crawling with law, nobody copped to this jerk, including me. I can't believe I was still trying to warn him when the two creeps grabbed me."

Isela stopped talking when Kip dragged himself stumbling into the Susvee.

"Hey Ridgely," he said, all chipper and cheerful. "How's my go-to guy?"

Now it was Ridgely's turn to tense up.

"Wherever this lady Fed showed, I knew Tommy Smith'd be right behind." Kip laughed and flipped the interior lights to bright but kept his eye on me. "Read you like a damn book, chump."

I looked at Ridgely. "So what's your story? You figure to get out of this mess alive?"

"No big thing, Tommy," he said. "Just a half dozen rifles to look the other way. Maybe give the occasional heads-up to Kip and his crew."

"Seems like a big risk for such a small reward."

Ridgely shrugged. "Another couple hours, anybody left in this canyon will have zero credibility—like you—or they be dead." He laughed. "*Also* like you. Meanwhile, I'll be back in the warm bosom of the US Marshal's office nodding at every word that comes out of Waingrow's stupid mouth."

"So that's your plan?"

Kip shuffled over to the windshield and stared out at the snow swirling in the faint lights in the trees. "You about done here with this loser, Rod?" he said.

I grabbed Kip by his parka collar with one hand and jerked him around then jammed his face into the windshield. No real plan, actually. I just wanted to see who would do what. The tempered glass didn't crack, but Kip's face did. It came back kinda messed up. The fresh blood around his mouth made him look like a wolf caught feeding on a calf.

That got Billy Jack's attention. The shaved-headed thug climbed into the Susvee and parked himself at the controls with a can of Red Bull in one fist and a bottle of Cuervo in the other. He watched Kip hyperventilate and seemed pretty amused at the whole deal.

"*Jee*-sus," Kip said. "Will somebody *do* something?"

He was pointing at me like he expected the con to take a swing at me for him. Instead, Billy Jack motioned for Vasiliev to come inside. The Russian climbed up and handed Billy Jack one of the Mk 13s, setting it across his lap, then Billy Jack waved him back outside. I'd bet my good red horse that this was the Mk 13 that blew Mitch's brains out. He pulled an open box of Winchester .300s fresh from the armory and set them on the deck by his feet, tossing a cleaning rag at Kip so the evil mastermind could wipe the snot and blood off his face. The stink of unwashed convict in the inside of that cramped little Susvee was getting way worse all the time, but at least I had most of the players in the same room.

I was surprised when it was Sanchez who exploded, but I shouldn't have been. She'd been crumpled on the floor, acting like every bone in her body hurt. Before Kip got his balance on his good leg so he could wipe himself off, Sanchez sprang up and grabbed him, then spun him around. She got him in a headlock with her left arm and jerked a combat knife with her right. She must've had the knife Velcro-ed to her shin under her pants and was counting on the cons being too sloppy to find it. Comes from lack of protocols. Sanchez must've known that with Billy Jack in such close quarters, she could be dying a nasty death within a minute or two, so she had nothing to lose. She laid that blade across Kip's Adam's apple, daring Billy Jack to make the next move. I was glad that woman was on my side.

"Shoot 'er!" Kip yelled at Ridgely. It came out kind of

gurgley and muffled. He looked from Rod to Billy Jack and back, all wild-eyed. "*Shoot* the damn bitch."

I watched Ridgely raise my 9mm. Billy Jack grinned and took a big gulp of Cuervo. Kip's eyes bugged out and more bloody snot bubbles blew out his nose. Ridgely paused half a second, then he smiled and dropped two 9mm rounds into Kip's chest at close range. Kip's expression was pretty surprised when the blood pumped out of his rib cage. Sanchez let go of him and put her hand on her own chest to make sure none of the blood was hers. Then she took a step back, letting Kip fall in a neat little pile. All the time he was staring up at Ridgely like he couldn't believe what had just happened. Kip had been shot before—by me—but I didn't know if he figured exactly how many seconds he had left before he lost consciousness. I thought how much he had changed, and about his comedown from the over-amped iron-pumping hard-guy days when I first came back west from Fort Benning and he was terrorizing Sarah with his steroid rages.

I looked at Ridgely. "So that's how it is?"

"That's how it is, *pahd*-nuh," he said.

Billy Jack stood up and pointed the Mk 13 at my heart. I had no clue what was coming next. From what Sarah'd told me about his psych profile, Billy Jack had wasted guys for a lot less reason—or for no reason at all.

Just as quick, Billy Jack lowered the rifle. He had to step over Kip's body when he slogged back outside to sort and stack more stolen weapons in the steady snowfall. He gave Isela a hard-guy look as he left, but that was it.

Ridgely reached over and killed the bright light. "Amateurs."

"You used this piece of crap as a decoy."

"Yup," Ridgely said. "You were right that I wouldn't take a big risk for a small payday. Kip thinkin' *he* was in charge was the ultimate head-fake."

He ejected the magazine from my Beretta and thumbed out the remaining rounds, then stood in the open hatchway and threw the bullets out into the growing snow one by one. When he was done, he contemplated the Beretta, then chucked it backhand out into the dark as well. I must've given him a curious look.

"You know after this, there's no going back."

"I know," he said. "Hey, by the time FBI forensic dudes start diggin' around this dump, we'll all be long gone." He paused. "At least *I'll* be long gone."

Sanchez spit blood. She looked ready to go another round with whoever was handy.

"Now," he said, "with Sarah's ex on the slab, the narrative is back to betrayed sweeties, not Marine rifles. And betrayed sweeties is *right* where you come in, you romantic horndog, you."

He reached for his phone, scrolling till he found a picture Kip had snapped a couple years before. A photo of Sarah in a hot bikini at Summers Lake when she and Kip were courting.

"There she be. The do-able deputy who married both you chumps. She'll be the poster girl for the horny and weak-minded in every lockup in the country. Cons'll be dreaming she's one of those sick hotties that marry dudes in prison. Shheesh. And Kip thinking that *his* sick mind was driving shit, not Billy Jack. Damn."

Ridgely watched Billy Jack standing out in the snow
with his ammo boxes and rifle cases, carefully cranking the
ratchet on another cargo strap, his new rifle no more than
arm's reach away. He looked up when he heard us talk then
hollered for Vasiliev to come help him.

Isela pulled herself up, moving as far away as she could
when Billy Jack stepped inside the front unit.

"Don't be long," he said to Ridgely. "Take your victory
lap so we can bail on this shit-box. And figure what you're
gonna do with this guy." Billy Jack looked at me. "I know
what I'd do."

I watched Billy Jack and Vasiliev each grab one of Kip's
armpits and hoist him almost upright. Then they shoved
the corpse and Kip fell outside without a sound, facedown
in new snow. Billy Jack sneered and pushed the Russian out
after him. When they were both gone, Isela shuffled to the
side window, watching them.

"I got to pee," she said.

"Knock yourself out, buttercup," Ridgely said.

She disappeared out the hatchway into the snow and
was back just as quick. Then she curled up on the steel deck
for what little warmth it could give. I could've swore I saw
her smile.

With Billy Jack out of earshot, it was just the three of us.

"How'd you get mixed up with this bunch?"

"Back in the day," Ridgely said, "I was Billy Jack Kane's
transport officer. That boy and I had a long trip together in
the prison van. Talked some shit. Told some lies. You know

how that goes. When he was in the lockdown, his brother paid me a visit on the Q-T. Said he'd heard I was a guy a guy could do business with. Ricky Lee and me talked some *more* shit. High-dollar rifles and stuff. Then when Ricky Lee gets popped by the ATF in Idaho, we ain't talkin' money anymore, we're talking blood. Family blood." He turned to Sanchez. "So if Billy Jack walks back in here again, don't be surprised if it's to cut your pretty little self all to pieces."

Ridgely looked at the time on his phone. "Oops. I got to be gettin'. Come on. There's a shovel just outside. Grab it, wouldja?"

"You gonna make me dig my own grave?"

He laughed. "Hell, boy, I ain't *that* cold-blooded."

I stepped outside and found the shovel leaning against the unit's exterior bulkhead. Isela hobbled a few steps behind me. She grabbed my coat as Ridgely stuck his head in the rear compartment like he was looking for something. Isela spoke soft, like every word hurt.

"What's our play?" she said.

I shushed her but nodded down-canyon. "I got the two horses tied in the trees. That's about it. So just follow my lead. If they take me out, grab the gray horse and git, hear me?" I bent down and whispered in her ear. "And don't waste time on revenge."

"I'm *waaii*-ting," Ridgely said. His voice rattled in the wind.

"Right behind you."

When I slogged past the rear unit I saw Ridgely out ahead, already halfway to the Sno-Cat. He was carrying my .270.

"You could dig your own grave if you want," he said when I caught up, "but it might be better if it looks like all you folks killed each other in one big-ass shoot-out. *Yeah.* Like Kip getting plugged with your nine-millimeter, it's kinda perfect."

"Folks'll get wise soon enough."

"Don't bet on it. Falling-out among thieves? Oldest story in the book. Falling-out over a hot honey like your wife, second-oldest story. I even had a smart guy like you going for a while."

He crossed his arms over his chest and hugged himself.

"I'm from South Texas, son, and I surely do hate the cold."

The cargo deck on the back of the Sno-Cat was piled with tarped bundles stacked neat and strapped tight, way more firepower than just a half dozen. I wondered if Ridgely might be a tad overloaded but kept that to myself. When I looked up, he still had me covered, this time with my .270.

"Come on," he said. "Help me dig myself out."

"Too late for that."

It took him a second, then he laughed.

"Right."

"What I mean is, you don't need a shovel. This's what the Sno-Cat *does*."

"Riiight. Right."

"Who drove this thing up here?"

"Me."

"Funny. I didn't see any trace of you on the trail."

He climbed up into the cab.

"Maybe I wasn't on the trail."

The motor didn't start right away.

"How come you didn't follow the same trail your boys and me followed?"

He didn't answer right off.

"Maybe them and me wasn't going the same direction."

He gave the motor another minute, then it started right up.

"Got a buyer?"

He looked surprised. "Well, *yeah.* Kind've a big risk if I didn't."

"How's that work?"

"Uh-uh-uh. 'Fraid I can't tell you that." He laughed. "The woods have ears, if you know what I mean."

"Who'm I gonna tell?"

Ridgely laughed again. "You are the *only* guy in this whole little shitkicker hoedown who was worth talking to." He looked up then, just as wary as could be.

I glanced back to the Susvee. "Looks like you got company, bud."

Two bulky lumps slogged towards us, lit from behind by the Susvee's running lights. It was Billy Jack and Vasiliev. Tito Esparza followed a few yards behind, dragging Isela by the hair. Ridgely climbed out of the Sno-Cat, watching what was left of his crew from just a half dozen yards away.

"Can't believe they're down to three," he said.

I squinted into the dark, talking soft. "What's Esparza's story?"

"Tito was a special pal of both Kane boys," Ridgely said.

"You know—from the joint. Folsom, in BJ's case. Esparza's one guy you don't wanna turn your back on."

Isela broke free of Esparza and stumbled back towards the Susvee. Vasiliev and Esparza scrambled after her. Billy Jack watched, pleased, while his cons caught her and roughed her up more along the way.

In the tussle, Ridgely had eased out of the Sno-Cat carrying my .270. He circled around by the cargo deck, keeping the Cat between him and the three cons like he was checking his load. He reached over to an old tamarack and leaned the Remington against it, almost out of sight. Just as quick, he was back by the Sno-Cat's door. For a change, Ridgely looked at me dead serious.

"What you said? I know. There's no going back."

"Afraid of your crew?"

"Not exactly afraid," he said, "but it does get me ponderin'."

Billy Jack slogged over to the Sno-Cat. Ridgely shot me a glance then met him halfway. "You better get movin', Rod," Billy Jack said, "before these two clowns get me to change my mind."

They kinda grunted and did a little fist bump like they were back in the prison van planning their next big score. Then Billy Jack turned and walked back to his crew.

"Clever shooter like you might take a run at these last three." Ridgely turned toward me and squared his cap. "Just a thought."

"You want me to even the odds for you?"

"Works both ways," he said. "From where you're standing to that pine tree just might be the longest walk or the shortest run you ever take, cowboy."

Ridgely climbed into the Sno-Cat. He spun it in as much of a circle as the trees allowed, and I watched it lug in the drifts from the weight of the cargo. Then he waved, and he was the old Deputy Rod Ridgely again. The guy who had the world by the short and curlies.

"Just-A-Thought," he hollered as he passed me a last time.

"Watch out for the other guy."

"Hey, man," he said. "I *am* the other guy."

Chapter Fifteen

Crunching back through the snow to the Susvee with a new sniper rifle digging in my back got me doing some contemplating of my own. Pondering how and when these clowns planned to get rid of Isela and me once we'd helped them sort and bundle the hardware that had been buried in a damp hillside for way too long. I'd set aside a few of the guns damaged by corrosion from seepage. Rifles that could be salvaged and one that was beyond repair. Billy Jack grunted like he was glad to have the extra eyes on his prize. I'd figured we'd be semi-safe while we were some sort of use. But now they looked to be about done.

I'd got some grease on my hands from the cowling of the Sno-Cat where somebody had been checking the oil or something. I figured it wasn't Rod. He wasn't a greasy-knuckled kind of guy. I wiped my hands on the cuff of my jeans, never more than a few steps from one of the three goons. Billy Jack nodded from Esparza to Vasiliev. They traded custody of Sanchez, then with me assisting at gunpoint, Billy Jack and Esparza started cinching down the last of the loads.

The Susvee had filled up with tarped boxes pretty quick. Vasiliev sat ignoring Isela on a stack of empty packing pallets just outside the front unit, smoking his crap cigarettes, swigging his crap vodka, and blocking any chance I had of grabbing the Remington without being seen. As much of a grunt as he seemed to be, Vasiliev was sort of his own boss. Maybe what news reports said about him working for some other Russians was true.

The other two disappeared inside the Susvee, cinching poorly balanced boxes with canvas cargo straps stiff from the cold. Billy Jack had set his personal Mk 13 on a tarp in the front Susvee to keep it handy, but the whole manifest was a tight fit. I guessed Isela and I didn't make the passenger list. That Mk 13 would be Billy Jack's souvenir. His other souvenir would be Isela's scalp.

I saw that Billy Jack had gone to the same school as me, military-wise. I'd caught him watching me scope out their camp as his boys wrapped things up. He motioned me over, covering me with his new rifle, each step in that snow taking me farther from my weapon.

"So you're the sniper," he said. "I could tell."

"Was."

"Once you are you always are."

"Some things are better left behind."

"I hear you were pretty good."

"I came back."

He looked around at his load of guns. "Some didn't . . . Come back, I mean. My brother . . ."

"A guy's got to know when to leave it behind."

"Some of us don't seem to be much good at the leavin' it behind part. Always pickin' new fights."

"Sometimes I think the fights pick me."

He looked at the blizzard covering us both as we stood there.

"Amen," he said. "Kip said you're a throwback. Didn't use the M-one-ten."

"Kip always remembered the wrong stuff."

"But the old M-twenty-four? Crap, mister. Talk about hard-core."

Now it was my turn to squint through the blizzard. "You ask a lot of questions for a guy in a hurry."

Their campsite was still a scattered mess. Billy Jack motioned for Vasiliev to sit tight with Isela and me while he and Esparza started cleaning up the most obvious human sign. The big guy saw Isela limp back to the Susvee, but he didn't make a move to stop her or follow. Just puffed on another cigarette with his eyes fixed on her. I guess to him she was about done for and not worth his trouble. Then she stumbled on Kip's body in the snow. Vasiliev laughed and started walking over. I got a whiff of him as he went by. He smelled like a corpse.

Sanchez was smart. To some muscle-for-hire like the Russian, she looked tired and pathetic, someone to kill or not kill depending on what he'd been told to do. But Ricky Lee Kane probably wasn't the first lowlife who underestimated her.

Billy Jack and Esparza were still stashing smashed ammo

boxes and rifle cases behind boulders and tamarack so they couldn't be seen as easy from the air. If Isela and I were going to run for it, now'd be the time. I asked Vasiliev if I could step into the Susvee to get out of the wind and light a smoke. He stuck his head inside the cramped quarters then looked back at me with a shrug that I took as an okay. Isela kept her eyes on me as she pulled something out of her coat. It was my Beretta. She must have seen where it landed when Ridgely tossed it from the Susvee. She slipped it onto my palm when I helped her to her feet.

"Time to go."

She nodded affirmative.

I stuck my head out. Vasiliev looked up.

I patted the pockets of my coat. "Got a smoke for a condemned man?"

He got a confused look.

I held two fingers to my mouth.

Vasiliev pulled a ratty pack out of the pocket of his slicker and looked down at it like he was sorry to part with even one of those soggy, gray beauties. His face was clammy from his cleanup work and his head as red as a big country ham from the booze. He held out the pack, grinning like we were old smoking buddies. He took the full force of the Beretta's trigger guard under his nose and dropped like a rock. I grabbed Sanchez's arm and whispered, "Come on."

We could hear Billy Jack and Esparza like they were standing right next to us as we headed down-canyon away from that place. Billy Jack complained he was whipped from carrying all that heavy cargo and antsy that he was so close to pulling the whole job off. I heard Tito Esparza bitch that

cleaning up their campsite was a waste of time. Billy Jack
said if they cleaned up the big stuff, the small stuff would
be covered in snow in no time and hard to spy from the air.
Otherwise, the law would have an easy starting point if they
had to make a run for it. They bickered like an old married
couple.

Billy Jack yelled for me to help the Mexican hoist something. By then we were too far down-canyon for me to answer
without giving up the game. I peered behind us into the blizzard, but all I saw was the dim Susvee beams reflecting swirly
white cones of light. By now Rod Ridgely was a good ten
minutes gone. Then I heard Billy Jack yelling for the Russian.
He was silent a long moment when he didn't get an answer.

"Well *shit*," he said, figuring it out.

It took a few minutes till we heard the sound of the Susvee's
diesel humming to life, ready to travel as the high-beams
popped on all at once. The convicts had their weapons
stacked and most of their enemies killed and some sort of
arms-smuggling contact waiting down close by the highway.
Billy Jack had beat the odds to get those rifles that his baby
brother had died for. Now he had the odds-on promise of a
pretty fine payday, and he was free of Folsom Prison like he
was living out some old Johnny Cash song, but he didn't have
Sanchez and he didn't have me.

At first we could see faint bits of the rising half moon
through the treetops, but once we were beyond the headlights and close in against the granite wall of the canyon, it
was dark as hell. Sanchez stumbled and fell then stumbled

again, panting deep. I was puffing and sweating myself, slogging through the drifts, relying on memory to keep us on what I hoped was the right track. I heard Billy Jack yell my name, faint in the distance but clear, even over the diesel hum. It almost sounded like a question. I laughed then and thought, if Billy Jack took Isela and me out before we got to the horses, cable news would have a hell of a time sorting us all out.

I could see the Susvee lights swing left, then right, like Billy Jack was trying to catch us in the beams, but his visibility was crap with the headlights reflecting off the snow swirl. I half expected him to straighten out and hightail down-canyon, but I guess he needed to kill Sanchez pretty bad. He wanted that as much as he wanted to close the deal for his brother. And he probably knew if he didn't take us out right now, we could bring the whole task force down on his head by noon tomorrow.

Then I heard the first two rounds of the Winchester .300s. They sounded close, echoing on that mountain granite, but they only clipped trees and chipped rocks far from our position. Billy Jack must not've had a visual on us yet. He was just shooting to be shooting and having sport with me to keep me pinned down and on the defensive.

We ran for the horses as soon as we caught sight of them. It was like slow motion running, but we were finally on the move. They stood tied with their butts to the wind, the remnants of their hay and tree bark stomped on and covered with ice, their piss puddles frozen under their bellies. They almost seemed glad to see us. I grabbed the gray first and cleaned the balled-up snow from his hooves and cinched him up.

"I'm not much of a rider," Sanchez said.

"Don't worry. He ain't much of a horse."

I rooted in a pannier and pulled out Sarah's ski parka. Isela gave me a worried look. I stuffed her arms in the sleeves.

"You're not freezing on Sarah's watch."

Sanchez nodded.

"This old guy will go where you tell him, and since he's a deer hunting horse he won't run off at gunfire." I finished wiping the snow off the gray's saddle and zipped up the parka.

That didn't seem to encourage her.

"He's a gullumper, but he's sure-footed and will want to get back to the trailer and out of the wind. We get split up, don't try to steer him, just let him lead the way. Pretend you're back in Oakdale."

I hoisted her into the saddle and handed her the hacka-more rein then swung up on my red horse, and we beat it out of there at a slow walk-trot. Our visibility was less than zero, but the rifle fire behind us was real enough. We had about a three-minute head start.

We hadn't gone far when I pulled up. Sanchez already looked frazzled.

"What are we doing?" she said.

"I'm sending you on while I divert Billy Jack. Let the horse follow the canyon and keep thumping on him. Just try not to let him turn around."

I held out the Beretta to her.

"Won't you need this more?"

"Just take it. You let this horse backtrack, Billy Jack'll find you and kill you."

I pulled the extra magazines from my pocket and loaded

one in the pistol to replace the one Ridgely had tossed, racked the slide, and lowered the hammer and held the Beretta out to her.

She didn't take it right away. "You sure?"

"As sure as Ricky Lee Kane is dead and buried in Idaho."

She looked scared then gave me a broken-tooth smile. Just as quick she got serious again.

"Why are you doing this?" she said.

"Doing what?"

"These mountains will be crawling with federal personnel by tomorrow. But you're the only guy I see ass-deep in snow with these losers in his gunsights."

I had to stop and catch my breath, ice in my lungs burning with every inhale.

"I figure I got you into this mess. I should get you out."

"That's it?"

"Ain't it enough?"

She took the pistol, then the spare magazines, and shoved them in her pockets.

"What happens if we make it?" she said.

"If my wife gets the Feds in place, maybe we can keep these gunsels from ever leaving this canyon with the rifles."

"And if you can't?"

I didn't answer.

"Your wife's a smart woman."

"Tell me about it."

She looked down-canyon at the way she'd be heading.

"I guess there are worse places to die," she said.

I nodded and wheeled around and headed back the way we'd come.

For about fifteen minutes I heard the diesel rumble fading in and out, muffled by the snow. Then the rattling sound got closer, bouncing off the high rock ridges. Still, I couldn't see the Susvee or even a hint of its running lights. Just as fast, the diesel faded altogether then stopped. I couldn't hear a thing except the breathing of my horse in the motionless air. I let him stand in that deep quiet as long as I dared, trying to focus on where I was heading, the black mass of Flatiron Ridge ahead of me in the darkness. Billy Jack was fiddling with me, so I didn't linger.

I rode slower as I neared the cabin site, pausing to listen but still not hearing in the wind. I got closer. There was just darkness in the hillside trees while the snowy meadow faded in and out in the shifting moonrise. I found the square clearing where the miners' cabin had stood. With the Susvee gone, the bare rectangles the two units left in the dirt were already disappearing under growing skiffs of snow, and Kip's remains right along with them. I slipped off my horse and examined the ground. A last wooden box on the pallet was empty and even fresh snow wasn't covering all the trash the cons had scattered. I didn't linger. I still had to flank Billy Jack in the dark so he could chase me a while. It seemed the snow was falling harder now.

Dad's .270 was still leaning against the tamarack right where Ridgely had left it. Half-covered with frost, but otherwise okay. Strange guy, Ridgely. I told myself to be more careful of that Remington. Since the morning of the breakout that rifle had been to hell and gone while in careless hands, including mine.

I tightened my wild rag, zipped my coat up snug, screwed

down my hat, and swung aboard my horse, the Remington in my free hand. I kept at a fast walk when I could, nothing more. The horse and I had a long ways to go, yet. I took off my gloves, popped the magazine and checked the load as I rode. Just out of habit. The horse's warm hide felt good against my cold damp hands.

Even in that dark canyon, getting a decent visual of the Susvee wasn't hard. Terrain permitting, Billy Jack was making big, wide S curves and stopping every couple of minutes, probably to check the ground for fresh hoofprints and hold his head to the wind in case we were stupid enough to be speaking loud. The guy was thorough. He'd been on the hunt before.

I goosed my horse across the valley on the diagonal then pulled up behind a screen of willows, hobbled the horse and waited. The next time the Susvee stopped and Billy Jack got out to study the ground, he was only about a hundred fifty yards downrange. I waited for him to bend low then blew out one of the Susvee's searchlights just over his bent-down head. I bet that got his attention. In that windy dark he wouldn't be able to pinpoint where I'd fired from, at least not right away.

Billy Jack was more cautious after that. He examined the shattered light socket and the dimple in the armored sheet metal. Pretty quick he had a rough idea of where my shot came from and started rattling on toward the willows. I unhobbled my horse and jogged off down the canyon and into the trees. I made a big circle across the canyon, which was getting wider and flatter all the time. When I thought

I could chance it, I rode out into the open and popped a fresh round at the Susvee from horseback, listening to another faint ping against the steel as I skedaddled off into the dark.

I caught up with Isela in another fifteen minutes. If I didn't have her to worry about, I would've kept pestering Billy Jack all the way to the Reno Highway. As it was, she was traveling way too slow.

I asked her how she was, and all she did was nod. We rode on, quiet and watchful, stopping when the Susvee lights swung over us from a quarter mile back, not making a move, then pushing on when the light probed in a wrong direction.

"Won't they pick up our tracks?" she said.

"These chowderheads couldn't tell the difference between the tracks of two horses or four in these drifts, or if the tracks were passing east to west or west to east."

"Could you tell?" she said. "If it was you chasing them?"

"Most likely."

She nodded like that sort of made sense.

"Just for the record, we *are* chasing them." I had to say it again louder. "They just don't know it yet." That made her laugh, busted tooth, bruises and all.

Now and again, I caught her rubbing her feet against the gray's flanks and told her she didn't need to do that. When she stopped I could see the convicts had taken her boots. I should've noticed that first thing. We were in open country only protected by darkness, and I didn't want to stop but didn't see any way around it. We pulled up to rest in some rocks sheltered by aspen. I cut long strips from the pack tarp with my skinning knife and bound her feet till she looked like some freezing G.I. at Bastogne from one of Dad's Time-Life books on World War II.

I tried to be cheerful and jokey, but I knew we'd have to pick up our pace when all we were doing was slowing down. I stomped my feet and told her to do the same, but she didn't have the energy.

I got her back on the horse and rubbed her feet hard. It made me remember an Army captain from the Afghan high country. He was a beet farmer from South Dakota who called the Hindu Kush a barren windy bitch. The serious way he said it always made us laugh, right up until an IED cut him in half. By then he'd already lost four toes to frostbite in just two weeks.

I was winded and light-headed, and it was messing with my perception. I looked back behind from time to time. There was the glow of the waxing moon that had cleared the ridges and treetops and lit up the fresh snow on the meadow. Then the clouds rolled back in, and the snow gusted and again blackness covered us.

We kept to the trees till we got to where I'd left the body of Chester Livermore. He was in the open already covered with half a foot of snow. I left Isela mounted while I rooted around the convicts' campsite for their weapons and their boots. The AR was right where Livermore had dropped it in the snow, but if any of the guys who'd been camped there had spare AR magazines or rounds for a revolver, they weren't where I could spot 'em. I slogged across the drifts and kicked the snow away. I yanked his frozen-stiff legs up one at a time, ice breaking away from burned flesh. His boots were burned too bad to be of any use.

I tried their propane heater, hoping to warm up Isela's feet, but the tank was empty—burned down to nothing. Then I made a last quick reconnoiter.

"What are we looking for?" she said.

I had to laugh at myself. "Clues, I guess."

I shook drifting snow off a plastic tarp and rooted around among burger wrappers and beer cans and a mostly empty tequila bottle. I found a couple of prescription bottles mixed with the trash. I pulled out my phone and read her the names. "Any of these ring a bell?"

"No," she said. "Should they?"

"One of the cons is a prescription drug thief called Tito Esparza. These must be his."

"I know exactly the guy you mean," she said. She pushed her lip back to show me her broken tooth. "Hand me the tequila, wouldja?"

"You don't want to touch the mouth of this bottle with your mouth, lady."

I pulled the Knob Creek bottle from my saddle pockets and she took a couple of pulls of that instead.

I turned around when I heard the diesel rattle. The Susvee popped up less than a quarter mile behind us, making more big curves across the canyon floor to flush us out, coming slow and steady.

"Where are we?"

"About halfway."

She watched me check the magazine of the .270 and pat my coat pockets for the half-full box of soft points. I watched her imitating me, patting her parka pocket for the box of 9mm rounds I'd given her, almost like she'd forgot she had 'em.

I'd lost some of the feeling in my right toes so I stood up and stomped the ground. By the light of my phone I looked down at blood seeping through Isela's socks into the canvas around her feet, freezing fast as it hit the air. I dropped to my knees and untied the wrapped canvas and rubbed her feet again hard. She winced but didn't say anything.

"Did they hurt you?"

She nodded.

I told her to rest as I checked the horses. The gray didn't have any injuries, but the old guy was just whipped from fighting the balled-up snow pushing against his soles. I could see Isela's eyes on me every time I looked up.

"Is he injured?" she said.

"No, just tired. I wanted a gentle horse for you to ride, but he's got some age on him. Next time we do this, remind me to fit both horses with pads, not just one."

"Next time," she said, "I'll try not to get myself kidnapped. Give you more time to plan."

I rewrapped her feet and got mounted.

"You ever ride since the horse camp at Oakdale?"

"At Girl Scout camp on Carson Pass a couple years later, and Baja on the beach two years ago during my divorce," she said. "But that time I was kinda drunk."

"Happens to the best of us."

We pushed the horses as hard as we dared, but the gray was losing steam. The trace of moon was close to overhead now—when we could see it—which in the storm wasn't very often. I could make out where the creek meandered from one side of the canyon to the other then back again following its course. Even with snow on the ground, staying on the trail gave the gray easier footing. The contours of the flattening canyon got more and more visible in the random moonlight, but the snow kept coming steady with no letup.

I had to stop again to let the gray catch up. Isela was just hanging on, not doing much to keep the horse moving.

"Will I be seeing Agent Fuchs?"

"I expect so. We'll see him together."

"What do I tell him?"

"Tell him what you saw and heard. Tell him I won't let those guys out of my sight."

"Fuchs told me that he was afraid you planned to kill Kip Isringhausen no matter how this plays out."

"Aaron knows me pretty well."

"What about you? Will you be okay?"

"Don't worry about me."

"Will you kill Isringhausen?"

I got worried quick. She'd stopped making sense.

"He's already dead, remember? Ridgely shot him, and he died in your arms."

Chapter Sixteen

I'd hung hackamores on both horses when I started out a lifetime ago, so if I had to tie them and leave them and then got myself killed, they could rub the bosals off on a tree or pull back and bust the mecates that tied them when they got hungry enough, then trot for home. I was pretty fried now, but that was my thinking at the time.

I unbuckled my chinks and walked up behind Isela and started buckling them around her waist.

"What are you doing?" she said.

"Giving you my chinks. An extra layer of leather to keep out the cold and damp." I showed her how to buckle the leg straps around her thighs then went back to shortening the stirrups on my dad's old saddle.

"What next?" she said.

I walked her over to the red horse.

"We're swapping horses."

I helped her aboard, then unbuckled a set of hobbles

and slid them through the saddle gullet, then rebuckled them into a single loop.

"What's this?" she said.

"Old-time buckaroos call it a night latch. Watching the herd at night, they could doze on horseback and still have something to grab a-holt of so's not to fall off."

"You must drive your wife crazy sometimes."

"Sometimes."

I showed her how to hang on tight to that loop like a kid bucking out their first pony.

"Easier to hang on to than a saddle horn."

"I don't know if I can do this," she said.

"Look. The gray needs a rest. He'll follow you, but he'll have more easy traveling without you on his back."

"How do I steer?"

"You don't. Just hang tight and keep moving down-canyon. Leave the steering to this guy." I walked around my horse, checking things for the umpteenth time and hoping it wouldn't be the last time I saw him.

"You set?"

She nodded.

I fished the Knob Creek out of my saddle pockets and took a couple of pulls then offered her some. She shook her head no. I grabbed a couple of strips of jerky for myself then left the rest for her. I was worried she was too out of it to remember to eat or drink. I hollered and waved my hat and watched that red horse head off down the trail as fast as the deep snow and darkness would let him. I knew I'd get my chance at Billy Jack before this was over, but it wasn't worth getting such a good horse killed to push the odds. I sat on a rock and took a bite of jerky and right away wished I'd kept the whiskey. I could see the Susvee coming out of the trees in the distance.

I walked along creekside willows, not making great time but giving myself quick cover if I needed it. The Susvee was about even with my position as it hummed down the far side of the canyon scouting for any trace of Sanchez or me. I got tired of that contraption setting the pace, so I stopped to catch my breath and let it get ahead, watching its route. It slipped into the trees till all I could see was flashes of running lights then blackness as the night just swallowed it up.

I walked slow, circling west across open country, stumbling and panting and falling more and more on gentle ridges that would have been green grass just a couple weeks before. I tried to pace myself, stopping when my lungs got raw and when the wind picked up and cut my visibility down to nothing. I could bear the cold and the snow until the wind blew hard and cut through every layer of clothes I had on. Then I'd shiver and couldn't feel my feet. For the first time I faced the fact that I might not get out of this alive.

I'd never been on this side of the valley before. The wind slackened for a second, and I caught a glimpse of the contours of the country and the glacier-cut granite of Hanging Valley Ridge. That's when I saw the orange Sno-Cat. It was tucked against the slope, its two small headlights still giving off a weak yellow glow from either side of the grille. This was the Sno-Cat that had been driven just hours before by US Marshal Rod Ridgely when he left Sanchez and me to the mercy of the convicts.

I checked my .270 and walked slower now. I stopped to listen, but there was no noise, either from voices or the motor. I circled around it from the rear. The cargo deck was packed and strapped just as neat and snug as it had been back in the escapees' camp. The cargo was covered with a fresh layer of snow. I thought maybe Billy Jack's crew had missed seeing it on their way down-canyon. It was like Ridgely had made a big circle to the west so he and the cons wouldn't cross paths. Now it looked like he'd succeeded a bit too well.

Deep snow covered the pontoons and steel tracks and was piled up past the bottom of the cab. The door on the driver's side was half-open with blowing snow wedging it so it couldn't close. A small decal on the corner of the windshield said the Cat was the property of a rinky-dink snow park in Tahoe City. The cab itself wasn't much more than a yard across and there were lots of small animal tracks around the half-open door.

Ridgely sat behind the wheel, his chin on his chest, his hands crossed against his belly. His Vegas Raiders cap was gone, probably blown away in the wind. His face and hair were covered thick with ice crystals from the *payinappih*, and his eyes were frozen shut. I thought how Sarah would be proud I thought of the Shoshone word instead of pogo-nip, and would be even happier if I didn't freeze to death like Ridgely had.

What really gave me the fantods were the fresh rips in the soft parts of his face, the rips to the cheek and lip and bites down to the bone in more than one place and the fact that half of his nose was missing. Then I heard hints of whining and turned to look. Not more than twenty feet away, three good-sized coyotes stood in the snow watching me. It's like they were waiting to see if I'd poach the rest of their dinner.

I shooed them away, but they only took a few steps back and crouched as they started their whining again. The biggest of the three began to creep closer, his eyes glowing in bits of moonlight. That made it easier to see the blood frozen on his muzzle. Then his whine turned into more of a snarl. I wanted to get out of there, but I needed to know just what happened to Rod.

I circled the Cat again, running my gloved hand over the cowling as I kept one eye out for the hungry coyotes. My hand found the slick spot where oil had been smeared on the sheet metal. It all may have been harmless sloppiness, but since Rod died probably not knowing that his machine had been tampered with, I figured I better not make the same mistake.

I popped the latches on either side of the grille and, after some pounding to break loose icy hinges, I opened the hood. The engine block was already cooling, and in the dark I couldn't see anything that looked like tampering. I dropped down and crawled between the pontoons, rooting around. By the light of my phone I could look at the motor from the underside. As I lay sprawled in fresh powder I could see coyote paws moving through the drifts just a few feet away. They were curious little bastards.

I took off my right glove and ran my fingers along the sides of the block and the oil pan. A guy didn't need to be a mechanic to feel that the fuel line was filed partway through.

Ridgely had enough fuel to go so far and no farther. I should've felt bad for the marshal, but I didn't. He'd been dead for a while before the coyotes started eating his face. The men who died because of him didn't have the same luxury.

Rod double-crosses Kip. Billy Jack double-crosses Rod. Whoever cut the fuel line might've tried to outsmart Billy Jack. Half the rifles added up to a fair amount of coin, but I didn't guess I'd ever know. Vasiliev didn't seem savvy enough to double-cross a border collie, but if he was the guy who tampered with Rod's motor, and who maybe tipped Rod off about a route less traveled, then maybe Vanya Vasiliev got the last laugh. Maybe the talk of some hard-assed Russian friends in Vegas or back east had some truth to it. Then all of a sudden one of the 'yotees let loose a howl that'd raise the dead. I didn't want to hang around to see what was next.

The effort of the slog through the snow and digging under the Sno-Cat wore me out. I put my glove back on and stumbled into the dark timber, looking for somewhere dry to sit and catch my breath.

I cut a diagonal into a grove of tamarack where the drifts wouldn't be as deep and I could put some distance between me and the Sno-Cat. Whether it was Vasiliev's guys or Billy Jack who'd cut the fuel line, somebody'd be hunting that machine on their way out of that canyon once they got tired of hunting for me. No way would anybody just walk away from the rest of that swag. And if there was a third party like the Russians who might be eying that loot, I didn't want to get caught in that crossfire.

I stopped to reconnoiter. With the thick tree cover, black clouds, and windblown snow, I was back to zero visibility. I could hear my own heartbeat, but I couldn't hear the Susvee anymore. I held my breath, steadying myself in the gusts. What I finally did hear was the slow tick of a hot engine cooling down.

It sounded too close to be real. The single bead of sweat running down the small of my back was real enough. I turned slow, careful where I put my feet, almost not wanting to look. Then I turned enough to see the Susvee, just two black shapes on a small rise in the tamarack not more than a few dozen feet away. Its lights and engines were off, but it seemed close enough to touch. I shifted my weight. A dead limb buried in snow cracked when I took a wrong step. I wondered if they'd been watching all along.

The diesel roared and the headlights popped on so close to me that the beams showed in the snow of the tree canopy just above me, the grove of trees now bright as noon. I dove for cover. I couldn't quite tell if they had me spotted or if I'd just rousted the beast. It turned in my direction, and I made it to my feet, running and stumbling in knee-deep snow toward the darkest part of the forest.

The rubber tracks of the Susvee didn't make the metallic clank or the deep ruts that a US personnel carrier or tank would, which was probably why the Marines commissioned these for mountain combat. Still, the soft rumble of the new top-end diesel with its damn Scandinavian efficiency somehow made the whole deal even creepier.

I moved out fast. When the Susvee turned away from the trees to cut across open country I did my best to circle behind it, keeping it in sight without getting caught by surprise a second time. I kept my eyes on the trail the rubber tracks made as best I could, but the steady snow was burying the faint trace almost as quick as they were made. The sky stayed clouded up.

A canyon below a shallow rise finally lit up for a second, snow swirling and blinding and white. The diesel hummed and whined as the Susvee turned sharp, heading back toward me, light beams probing. The headlights caught me dead-on, and I couldn't see a thing except that the Susvee was coming at me faster than I'd seen it go before. But maybe it wasn't me they were looking for. Maybe it was Sanchez. They could've taken me out a half dozen times in the couple of minutes they'd been circling. Billy Jack didn't want to leave that canyon without Isela's head on a stick. It was cold comfort either way.

I dropped and rolled, sighting my .270 and getting off two quick shots. I heard a crack of glass and a ping of metal plate as I fired into the light. Someone in the forward unit returned fire. I squeezed off a third round then got moving out of the headlights. From the cartridge boxes in my coat pockets I reloaded the magazines for the .270 for one last dance. I could tell by the lack of heft of the boxes that I was getting low. The Susvee crept along the creekbank with spotlights bobbing and probing, trying to catch me as I crawled. It paused at the creek like it knew exactly where I was. Fire from what sounded like three different weapons popped and tore in my direction.

One was an AR, no different than the sound Burt's AR makes when he's target shooting behind the barn. Second was the sharp snap of a 9mm. The third was that faraway sound, dim and metallic like the whip of a steel spring. I'd heard that round close before, from less than a couple hundred yards away. It was the day Mitch Mendenhall took the shot to the head. Billy Jack was drawing the curtain on this chapter with his very own Mk 13, sending those Winchester loads my way, fast, steady and methodical. I figured he was lurking behind the Susvee, hiding in the contrasting dark, maybe off to the side a bit. The peckerwood sonofabitch had learned something from his instructors at Fort Benning after all.

I found a sandy stock-crossing and waded back to the other bank in the knee-deep slush. From there, I tried to conceal myself as best I could as I worked my way downstream. And I tried not to dwell on the fact I was losing sensation in my right foot. Billy Jack kept slamming rounds in my direction out there in the dark as he got the feel of the gun. I'd seen the boxes of Nightforce scopes in the big crate by the miners' cabin, so I knew he was pretty well fixed. I was facing an awesome weapon with way more range and wallop and precision than Dad's old deer rifle. My Leupold scope, good as it was for hunting, was no match for the Marines' new night vision optics.

Then the shooting stopped and I heard a rumble and swoosh and crack of tree limbs off in the dark. Billy Jack had unleashed a mini-avalanche that I could hear but not see. Neither of us fired for a minute. The next look I got at the Susvee, it was cocked off-center and a snowbank was piled up against the far doors. I used the diversion to find a safer nest.

It took a few minutes for the Susvee to work its way out from under the avalanche, rocking back and forth and sending clouds of snow and diesel smoke across the canyon's mouth as the engines revved. It finally loosened the ground under it and moved away from my position across the creek then doubled back across the course of the snowfall, taking full command of the canyon like it was daring me to make a move.

The wind was picking up more now and the temperature still dropping. I huddled behind rocks for cover then retied my wildrag and snugged it up over my mouth and ears. The front-facing spotlights on the Susvee went dark and I lost a visual of my target until Billy Jack fired a single round. Maybe a faint reflection on his nearside door gave him away. Maybe it was just my dry eye or that sound of the Win-mag. Maybe just wishful thinking. Now the idling diesel was no louder than the wind.

I hadn't seen Vasiliev since Isela and I had made our break. With the canyon dark, the Russian might have been sent out to flank me—if he was still with them. That would be a tough guy's errand, and Tito Esparza struck me as more cunning than tough. It was still before midnight.

Then the Susvee's lights popped back on. I saw it rocking in my direction and saw a single figure—probably Billy Jack—stumble out a side hatch for cover in the snow. I hadn't been seeing things after all. It looked like he'd positioned himself outside the Susvee, keeping low to draw me out. I listened for any hint of the Russian, but no trace. Wind was howling now, and visibility went from thirty yards in the headlights back to zero when the wind blasted. Then in an instant a hole in the sky let in the light of the flickering moon before a blast of wind pulled the curtain back down.

I was pretty sure I saw the Russian trying to flank me on the opposite side, using the wind to cover his creep away from Billy Jack. A sixty-plus-mile-an-hour gust knocked him on his ass as the headlights lit him up. He came up shooting, and I returned a single round. He grabbed his right leg above the knee and dropped. I could see movement as he crawled back toward the Susvee.

The only sound for the next few minutes was the wind whipping over me in the trees. The diesel revved, but nothing moved and the lights were still out. My best chance was to stay put and hold out, making them keep their distance as best I could. I tried not to think about the siege of the cave but without much success.

I concentrated on the escapees, taking a mental tally to focus my brain and keep from falling asleep and freezing to death. I counted backward and forward from the twelve guys who broke out of Folsom. I kept losing my place and having to start over.

I gotta admit I didn't see the Kip fake-out coming. I'd had him on the brain since I'd heard he'd married Sarah a couple of years before. With nothing to do in Folsom, he had plenty of time to ponder how to mess with my head. And I had plenty of sweaty sleepless nights to let him do just that. Even if he was dead, Kip was still the last man. That fried my brain, and I had to start counting all over. It was way harder than I thought.

The Susvee idled. The headlights blazed. The soft humming diesel whine still rattled in my skull. The running lights must've come on when I dozed off or I must've been dreaming or counting dead men. I saw the front doors both open, then close. Fire commenced from both sides, but this time from the rear, using the whole vehicle as cover. The next volley came bunched, like maybe the shooters were all taking cover behind the Susvee. Just as quick, the shooting stopped. I was still facing three escapees, so I was guessing the Russian's wound must have been minor. Still, only three guys? Piece of cake. Then the lights dimmed a last time. The little steel box just sat there, waiting me out, engine idling, guns pointing my way.

I shook myself to keep awake and keep the dreams at a distance. I cleared my eyes with a glove full of snow. I needed to slip out of that place. If I dozed off again, I'd either freeze to death or take a shot to the head. I was keeping my eyes on the trees, watching for any movement, any sign that one of the cons was slipping out to flank me. A crashing in the trees made me think for a second that one already had.

But it was a horse, running hard in the dark, splashing through the creek behind me. It whinnied once at the human scent, coming close enough I could make out that it was the gray. His saddle was still on his back and his frayed and busted mecate dragged between his forelegs. The lights of the Susvee blasted on for real, now, turning the night sky white. I figured that if the gray was still this far up the canyon, maybe my red horse and Isela might still be here, too. Maybe she couldn't get one horse to move without the other, or maybe she just fell off. I hollered her name but heard only my voice echo against the rocks. There was the chance that she'd made it all the way down to the old barn, but more likely she had a wreck with my horse. That would leave her on foot and bootless in the middle of the night, and miles from help.

The gray was one of my saddle horses from the pack station, solid, big-footed and unremarkable. Still, he was mine to care for. My responsibility. The glaring lights spooked him, but the Susvee wasn't the first diesel he'd heard clattering in the middle of the night. The horse made a big circle off to the side of the Susvee, checking things out. A side door opened a foot, and more gunfire popped from inside. I hunkered down, sighting the Remington, looking for a target. Then I realized whoever was shooting, they weren't shooting at me. They were shooting at the gray.

I crawled up the slope, keeping my eye on the Susvee but calling the horse just so he could hear a familiar voice. When he got close enough I took the chance to rise up, more crouching than standing. The horse was backed against an aspen thicket about thirty feet away. If I kept low and moved fast I might get to him before Billy Jack picked up the movement. I slogged ahead, deciding as I went that it was time to just grab that horse and get on down the road. I'd done about all I could. The Feds could kill the rest if they ever caught up.

I was only ten feet away from the horse when I heard a shot. He grunted and took a single step, one foreleg to the side like he was bracing himself, his head lowered. Then I saw a bubble of blood appear in a nostril like maybe he'd been hit in the lung. I'd been ready to reach out to grab the dragging rein, get mounted and make a run for it. Now all I wanted was one last shot. I was guessing Billy Jack hadn't stayed in the Susvee. That would draw and concentrate my fire, making his sniper nest a hard target despite its armored sides. Instead, he'd be out in the open, where dark country would hide him. I locked on to the Susvee's forward unit then inch by inch sighted more and more to my left. I found Kane prone in the snow with his Mk 13 just barely poking between the forks of two tamaracks. It was a good nest, but he'd stayed just a touch too close to the headlights. Then he rose up just a hair more, like he was saying something to one of his crew in the support vehicle. What a cocky bastard. I laid the cross-hairs right on Billy Jack's left cheekbone. I took my shot, but thought I heard an overlapping echo, more like two simulta-neous shots, then a sort of slap as I flattened into the snow. I felt a stinging in my left hand and saw the gray drop hard. He was dead before he hit the ground. Billy Jack was more marksman than I'd expected, even if his recklessness cost him his life. And he was the kind who'd kill an animal just to rattle my cage.

My hand burned more now, sharp like a hot spike in the middle of the palm. I was inching over to the gray to see if I could use the dead horse for cover when the Susvee began to hum and rumble my way. I felt dizzy and dropped to my knees, the headlights sweeping over me. I was kneeling in what must've been a spring or a pocket of snowmelt but instead of feeling icy it felt warm, instead of white, the snow was red. I was kneeling in my own blood.

I could feel it wet and warm, running down my arm to my elbow. Kane had hit an artery. Maybe even severed one.

I pulled off my left glove, held it with my right and scooped up a handful of snow, putting pressure on the wound like a compress. The warm blood melted the snow faster than it could slow the bleeding. I heard voices over the diesel and looked up to see silhouettes coming my way in the white halogen beams, floating in the swirling snow. I'd been wounded three times before. Once in Iraq from a sniper round when I was pretty green, once in Afghanistan from an IED, and once from a bullet out on Dave Cathcart's winter grazing permit when Kip had kidnapped Dave after Sarah had walked out on him. All three had been somewhere in the legs. None had bled like this.

A shadow fell over me from the first convict. It was Vasiliev. The tough bastard was limping on his right leg but mostly ignoring it. The second black shape held back, almost impossible to see. I guessed that to be Tito Esparza. Neither one of them seemed in any particular hurry. Vasiliev looked down at the blood all over my coat and hands. Then he grinned.

"Well, *you're* done," he said.

He poked my arm with his toe. I liked to pass out when he did that. I shifted my arm just a little. Another bunch of blood poured down and disappeared into my sleeve.

"Billy Jack dead?" I could hardly hear the sound of my own voice.

"You better hope so, soldier boy," Vasiliev said. He hacked and spit on the snow next to me.

Esparza was still just a black shape rimmed by the blinding glow of Susvee headlights about ten yards away. I thought maybe I was dreaming until I heard Vasiliev yell at him to get in the Susvee. Until he moved, Esparza did kinda look like an angel of death.

Vasiliev turned to me and grunted. "Not so tough now, eh?"

I tried to say something, but I was saving my breath.

"Why you stick your nose in this, chump?" he said. "Shitkickers. Brooklyn guys. Moscow boys. Why you care?"

Since Kip wasn't the evil mastermind after all, I didn't have a good answer for that. I shifted my arm, but it didn't do anything to slow the bleeding.

"This guy says you're going into shock." The Russian nodded back over his shoulder toward Esparza. "You bleed out pretty soon."

I was getting more and more heavy-headed.

Vasiliev made a belch that passed for a laugh. "Or you freeze to death first."

I heard a voice over the hum of the Susvee. "Hey, man, we gotta meet your Russian amigos pretty damn quick or they won't be your amigos no more."

With the Russian and Esparza the last escapees left standing, one of them could play evil mastermind for a while. Then Vasiliev disappeared into the dark. The lights of the Susvee turned. I was lying on my back, so I didn't see it chug away down the canyon.

The Russian was right about one thing. I was going into shock. Then I would pass out. Then I would bleed out. That was the order of things. I knew the feeling. I tried to change my position. When I took the pressure off the palm of my hand, I felt more warm blood washing down my forearm, filling up the elbow of my coat like a water balloon.

I thought of Sarah when she first called me back to these mountains a year and a half before, and thought of failing to stop Kip and protect her, even if that would've meant killing him so he never went to Folsom in the first place. I always figured it could end like this. If I wasn't careful. I fought to stay conscious but would black out for a few seconds at a time. Maybe more. I always tried to be the careful one. I knew I wouldn't last long once I passed out. Then I drifted away, and it all went black.

III
BACKTRACK

III
BACKTRACK

Chapter Seventeen

I was in the cave again seeing lights in the distance. Maybe I just imagined I did, but they were so bright they blinded me. I saw somebody running toward me and I reached for my rifle, not finding it or knowing where it went. Everything was bright and flashing, with snow spinning in the dark and a roaring sound all around like I was back under fire, back in the thick of it. The sky was lighter than I remembered, and I saw a piece of moon with a planet crowding next to it like the flag of some far-off country. My left arm couldn't move. I tried to pull it toward me, but it wouldn't budge and that worried me. Lights dimmed, and I saw Audie lying next to me, bracing my left hand to her body, with her right hand hugging a towel against my palm, pulling it to her to slow the bleeding, holding on like death. She wasn't looking at me, but I could see her clenched face, the towel and the front of her hoody soaked in blood. Sarah knelt and handed Audie a folded dry towel, all the time watching the people stumbling toward us through the snow, hands full of what, I couldn't tell, and Sarah's whole body shaking. Blood ran down my arm when Audie swapped out the drenched towel for the dry one that Sarah handed her. Audie's tears left frozen places on her cheeks.

Sarah looked up as a Marine EMT brought bandages from a medevac chopper. I must have said something.

"They're here to help, honey," she said.

I nodded.

"Don't try to move," the woman said.

"Okay."

Sarah spread a blanket over me. She tucked it under my chin without really making eye contact. She felt me shiver.

The first EMT waved to someone in a helicopter that had landed in a clearing beyond the trees. A second EMT carried a long board from the chopper, stumbling in the snow. I saw Burt step out of the dark and grab a side of the board to help.

"You've lost a lot of blood," the first EMT said. "Better not exert yourself anymore."

The woman wrapped my hand hard with pressure right on the wound then laid it across my stomach. It was basically what Sarah and Audie did with the towel, but with less mess.

"Artery?" It was about all I could say.

"You were shot right through the hand," the woman said. "About an inch below where your index and middle finger come together. The artery looks severed. If you're lucky, just torn. Might have tendon and nerve damage, too." The Marine looked at Sarah and Audie. "If these folks hadn't found you . . ." She let it hang, and gave me a shot of something in my right arm.

They got the board under me and the two EMTs, a third Marine, Sarah, Burt, and the medevac pilot all carried me across the snow. Audie walked alongside holding my good hand. Balancing that board over such uneven ground in three-foot drifts, they couldn't help but jostle me and almost dropped me once. It must have been coming on dawn, and I thought I saw black smoke down-canyon, but with the chopper blades swirling the snow near us it was hard to tell. They carried me from under the tree canopy out toward the chopper. Clear of the trees, I turned my head and watched the piece of moon slide behind the ridge and disappear. I saw a single star or maybe a planet alone in the predawn, like those pack station mornings when we'd been up since full dark then noticed the morning star alone in the east just before first light when we were busy brushing and saddling the mules.

They slid me off the board and onto a stretcher then strapped me down as they secured my left hand. They hoisted me aboard through a side door. Someone put a dry blanket over me. Sarah stood outside talking to the second EMT. I couldn't hear the words over the prop noise, but I could tell by her tone she was telling, not asking, saying that she and Audie would be riding along. She was out of uniform but showing her badge. Sarah and Audie climbed in after me. I had no clue where Burt disappeared. The big Marine chopper had space for him with room to spare.

We lifted off. I could see the lights of another vehicle, maybe a smaller search-and-rescue Sno-Cat or something like it. In the gray dawn, all I could see was that it was red, like a newer version of the Cat that Rod Ridgely froze to death in. Sarah stroked my hair.

"Isela Sanchez?" I had to stop to catch my breath.

"FBI SWAT personnel found her half-conscious about a

mile from here," Sarah said. "Her feet were wrapped in canvas and she was about half-frozen. She was riding your horse and saddle."

"I told you old Red would get 'er done," Audie said. She was still pretty sniffly and wiped her nose with the back of her wrist.

I tried to ask something about my horse being okay, but the words didn't make sense.

She nodded at the window a few minutes later. I moved my head and saw flames down below, receding as we gained altitude to clear the trees, fading as the day began. We flew through black smoke, and I thought about Afghanistan and Hendershott again and wondered how he was getting along.

"Holy shit," Audie said.

"It's a Marine vehicle, Sis," Sarah said. "Something set it on fire during the shoot-out."

"Oh, that is *so* creepy," Audie said.

"They get away?"

Sarah stroked my hair some more. She nodded. "Some, I guess. Maybe only one. But Billy Jack Kane is right where you left him." She took a breath. "With a hole under his left eye. From the tracks, he was ten feet from where the Marine vehicle had been parked, but his body hasn't been recovered."

"Hendershott?"

"He's gone, baby." Sarah clenched her whole face like she was trying not to cry. "Remember?"

Audie started some tough talk about dead guys. When Sarah asked if I remembered telling her about Hendershott, Audie broke down crying again. "Is Tommy gonna live?"

Sarah held her close. "Yeah, Sis. He's going to live. Didn't you just help save his life?"

All hospitals are pretty much the same. When I broke my collarbone playing high school football. In a medic's tent in Fallujah. In Walter Reed a couple years after that. No huge difference. You see the world pass you by when you're flat on your back, looking up, with maybe one part of you hurting more than another or only hurting when you moved and then hurting more than anything you ever remembered. I was in a two-bed room. My bed was the one closest to the door. Each bed was surrounded by a curtain that ran on a track in the ceiling. It was all super exciting, but it beat the alternative.

I tried to sleep until the time Sarah and Audie were let in. I had a wad of gauze taped to the crook of my good arm, so I figured they gave me some blood or fluids to replace what I'd lost, maybe starting in the medevac chopper, though I didn't remember. I did remember an ER nurse telling someone that he thought they could save the toes that he'd been afraid I'd lose. I'd had my hand cleaned up and stitched up in the ER and was told I'd get it operated on the next morning. An ER doctor told us it would be a long operation but that the hand surgeon coming up from Mammoth Lakes was really a pro. He'd be rebuilding a blood vessel as best he could, repairing nerves and patching up and debriding ragged tendons. I don't remember much of what the ER doc said except the specialist was going skiing when he was done with me. I don't know why that made me feel more optimistic, but it did. The doc was hoping the storm was the beginning of a long snow season. I had no other real memory of anything beyond Audie in the snow slowing the bleeding. The .300 Win-Mag had made its own incision.

I was dozing when Audie's laugh woke me up. She was holding up a pair of my sweatpants and doing a sort of dance. Sarah shushed her and pointed to the curtain blocking our view of the second bed and of the man in it. Sarah went back to checking out my half of the room, pulling out drawers and opening closets, then being quiet as she peeked into the other half of the place. Finally, Sarah grabbed the sweatpants away from Audie and draped them over the bed rail.

"Can I turn on the TV now?" Audie said.

Sarah must have nodded yes, and in a second I could hear Audie clicking from Tahoe weather to University of Nevada football to *Bewitched* reruns. She stopped on a news channel that I couldn't see and could barely hear.

"Lookit," Audie said, "Tommy's on TV."

I caught a glimpse of the Marine chopper in footage taken from above, before the chopper lifted off with all of us inside.

Sarah must've grabbed the remote because the sound clicked off.

"What did I tell you about that?" she said.

Audie said something about how I oughta put the sweats on so folks couldn't see my butt, but beyond that she didn't argue.

I turned my head enough to see the TV had gone dark and that Sarah was pulling my bloody clothes and boots out of the closet.

Audie laughed as Sarah emptied my pockets and unthreaded my belt and the skinning knife hanging from it.

"Don't take his knife," Audie said, loud enough for somebody in the hallway to hear.

"I really don't think Tommy will be needing it," Sarah said, "at least not for the next few days."

"You don't never know," Audie said.

"You keep it safe for me, Scamp."

"Yessir," Audie said. As tough as she acted, I could tell she was still kinda shook, but she was pretty proud of herself for staying so calm and tough when she was up to her elbows in blood the night before. I was pretty proud of her myself. She took the sheathed knife and slipped it on her belt. God help the orderlies.

Sarah just shook her head at the pair of us. She spoke in a ragged whisper. "We'll be burning the rest of these clothes."

"Except the belt, boots and hat," Audie said.

"Except the belt, boots and hat."

I woke up around dark. Across the room three nurses stood over the second bed, changing an old man's sheets and sponging him down. An IV bag hung from a chrome hook up by his head. He had no teeth and his mouth hung open and his skin went from purple to yellow. He wore what looked like a Korean War Vet ball cap that made him look about a thousand years old. He was too far away for me to read what was written on the cap. He had a couple of visitors a half hour later. A pair of ladies, one older, one not so much, who were arguing about money, ignoring the old man like he wasn't even there, and for that matter, damn heedless about bothering me, either.

I stared at the ceiling half-awake. I don't know how much later it was when a heavy nurse with a tattooed ankle wheeled a portable stand up to my bed and took my blood pressure and temperature and respiration and such. I thought the woman was as big a grump as me till I realized she might be hard of hearing or maybe just exhausted. When she was done with me, she opened my curtain to wheel the contraption to the next bed to check the old guy's numbers. The women were still standing around his bed bickering away until the nurse asked them if they could please step back a minute. They moved aside, but the young one kept talking, like the nurse was the intruder. With the curtains pushed open, the old guy looked between his visitors across the room and straight at me. I couldn't tell if he was conscious or if he just had some sort of muscle spasm. Just in case there was some consciousness there, I gave him a quick thumbs-up. The women never even noticed. The nurse must've seen, because she laughed.

Next morning I was awake well before sunup, which was usual. No food or water because of the surgery. Also SOP. Then I had nothing to do but just wait for Sarah, who'd be walking me into pre-op in an hour or so. I stared at the ceiling. I heard a rustle and clank on the other side of the curtain. I called to the old guy, asking if he was okay. He didn't look like a guy who should take a fall. I pushed the red call button clipped to my blanket and waited a few minutes, but no one came. I leaned halfway out of my bunk. His ceiling curtain was partly open, but I only could see the foot of his bed. I asked him if he was okay. Nothing moved under the sheet.

My nightstand was on my right side. The side the old guy was on. I pushed it away from the bed and swung my legs out so I could see better.

"Hey, mister. You okay in there? Want me to get a nurse?"

I listened but didn't hear a thing. I grabbed the portable IV stand for balance and pushed off. There was five or six steps from the side of my bed to the foot of his, but with the load of drugs I had in me, I was pretty short-strided.

I shuffled over, but nothing moved under the guy's sheet. I thought maybe he'd died during the night. Dead bodies didn't faze me anymore, though there were times I wish they did. The old guy's eyes were rolled back and his mouth hung open, but his breathing was still regular. Then one purple hand gripped the top of the sheet, bony fingers curled tight. His eyes still stared straight ahead as his other hand rose up, shaking like crazy. I could've swore he was giving me a thumbs-up, but maybe that's just what I wanted to see.

Sarah showed up fifteen minutes later in time for sunrise. She walked next to my gurney as they wheeled me down a hallway to the pre-op room. Nurses stuck an IV needle in the back of my right hand and gave me some pills in a paper cup. They asked me a bunch of questions then wrote something on my left forearm with a Sharpie. Then they wheeled me across the hall. I don't remember much after that till I woke up in recovery. I remember a wall clock saying it was past noon. The wound dressing on my left hand was as big as a catcher's mitt. It was another hour before they wheeled me back to my room.

As cranky and loopy as I was, Sarah was a rock. She told me that Audie would be by after school and that Mom and Burt would be bringing her while Sarah watched the baby. I asked her about Vanya Vasiliev and Tito Esparza. She told me Vasiliev had been killed along with some other Russians by FBI SWAT in a shoot-out near the Reno Highway during the weapons swap. Verified kills. The burning Susvee was the smoke we saw when I was choppered out. That, and part of the old barn. Sarah wasn't sure if the Feds or the cons set that afire. Aaron had texted her that his team recovered a sizable amount of missing ordnance from the shoot-out site, verifying what Sanchez and I had been pushing about since the escape. The fact that the rifles were in the news tickled me as much as it was going to frost Waingrow. Still, that wouldn't stop him from taking credit for wrapping up a year-old cold case, or from making the announcement on TV news.

The tattooed nurse came in to take my vitals while we were talking. I asked her about the cap the old guy in the other bed wore, and if he was a veteran.

"Yeah," she said. "He was an army guy that fought at some place in Korea. Pork Chop Hill, I think."

"Why did they call it that?" Sarah said.

"I guess it looked like a pork chop," the nurse said.

The woman and Sarah talked for a few minutes more.

She told us her name was Annie Goff, and that her uncle had been a gunner on a Swift Boat on the Mekong in 1966.

"And I used to think *he* was old," Goff said.

She laughed and pushed her testing unit past the curtain to the old soldier's bed.

The missing and the dead were harder for my memory to track. Hanging Valley was wide deep country covered with drifting snow and shifting winds. There was a body recovered in the fire in the barn that matched the minivan dad, and another that might have been Esparza's, but based on the location was probably Gilbert Orosco's. I asked Sarah for more details. She told me to quit thinking and get some rest. Instead, I kept her talking another half hour, telling her what I knew and what she might not know. About Kip, about how he was killed, how Billy Jack Kane had double-crossed Kip since the beginning, letting him think he was the boss. When she asked about Ridgely, I told her how he died, and how close he came to getting away with half the rifles for himself.

When she asked, I told Sarah where Kip was killed. That his body was under a foot of snow inside the stone foundation of the old miners' cabin on Molybdenite Creek, and that she was finally free of him. She kissed me goodbye and headed home, alone with her thoughts.

I was in a deep post-op sleep when a couple of nurses, one male and one female, closed the circular curtain around my bed. One was Annie. She gave me a quick nod, then I heard the curtain around the old soldier pulled open. I could hear the nurses talking, but not loud enough to catch what they said. There was the sound of hospital hardware getting moved around, drawers getting opened and closed and a few quiet words like the two of them were trying not to roust me. After a few minutes I heard the squeak of the rubber wheels of the bed rolling by. The nurses bumped a cabinet door with the metal corner of the bed on their way out.

The IV needle was still stuck in the back of my right hand. It itched and burned but I'd had way worse and knew the nurses probably needed to keep it in place. None of this was new to me, so I didn't yank it out like I might've done a few years before. I eased out of the bed, steadying myself with my own IV drip-stand and careful not to get tangled or bang my new bandage as I walked barefoot through the curtains.

An open window put a chill on the room. The old man's bed was gone, and he was gone with it. The drawers were empty and soiled bedding was piled in the middle of the floor. His Korean War Veteran ball cap lay on the heater under the window like the nurses had set it off to the side then forgot about it. I'd seen younger versions of that old guy. I was a younger version of him myself, just like Billy Jack was. All members of the same tribe, taught by the same code, but this is where we all end up. Some guys check in to a place they know they're never checking out of. Some fight and some just stop fighting.

I bent over slow and picked up the cap, mindful to keep my balance. It was new, with no sweat marks or greasy spots on the bill. Like somebody had just given it to him. I looked back out to the hallway door to make sure I was alone. I straightened up and stood at attention for a second then gave the empty half of the room a quick nod. Not exactly a Viking funeral, but what the hell. The old soldier had gone to his last post.

The sky out the window was moonless and black. When I got up to piss, it felt like another storm had blown in. With the gauze catcher's mitt, pissing was a process. I could've called a nurse for help, but I wanted to do as much for myself as I could. Even that short walk tired me out. I was halfway back to my bed when I heard footsteps shuffling in the hallway, then my door opening. It was Annie Goff.

"I'm going off duty," she said. "Just wanted to make sure you're doing okay."

"Never better."

"You need help getting back in bed?"

"Nah, I'm good. But thanks."

"G'night, then." She started to pull the curtain.

"There is something."

"Yeah?"

"The old GI. Was it just his time?"

"I think his family parked him here to die."

"He deserved better."

"All you guys do," she said. "You have a peaceful night, now, hear?"

"I will, thanks."

A kitchen staffer pulled open my end of the curtain and brought a covered dish with a piece of microwaved chicken plus a side of olive-drab broccoli and red Jell-O. Basic hospital stuff but nothing to complain about either. I'd be eating again in eight or ten hours. She said she was sorry she was late. She'd brought my dinner a couple of times already, but I'd been sleeping like a dead man. She gave me a pen and a breakfast menu. I checked off coffee and orange juice and toast. She put the menu in her pocket and left the pen on the nightstand. On her way out she left the curtain open behind her. I looked at the clock on the wall and remembered to charge my phone. I was hoping that the old soldier wasn't some spirit messenger sent to fetch me along behind him. You think a lot of crazy bullshit when you're full of drugs and semi-helpless after a brush with eternity.

This wasn't like a military hospital. Here time just dragged. I wondered if that must be how it is for guys in prison. I started thinking about Kip and his crew and if the slow time passing had been the same for them or if they just went from one freaky intense minute to the next with no letup for years. Then the whole mess of violent dreams and bad memories came full circle.

The food service lady came back and picked up my tray a half hour later. When she saw I hadn't touched my dinner, she offered to make me a grilled cheese. I thanked her but said I was fine. I had a sweet goodnight text from Sarah with an xoxo from Audie. The window was still open, and it felt like I was back in the canyon. I pushed the call button, but no one came this time either. I was so cold I got up to shut it then got back in the narrow bed. I was thinking I should tell Annie Goff they needed to fix the call button. Then I must've dozed off again and had loud angry dreams, worse than most.

Something moved in the gloom, but it was only one of the night nurses coming to take my readings. This time it was a shaved-headed Latin-looking guy pushing one of the portable testing stands. Maybe he wasn't Latin. He could've been Native American, I guess, or maybe Hawaiian. With a cap and a mask, I couldn't really tell. Not that I cared.

"Time to check your vitals," he said. He sounded cheerful enough.

I just nodded, the drugs still fogging me up.

"So, how are we doing?"

"Not bad, I guess."

The nightstand blocked his access to my bed from the right. I held my right hand across my body so he could get to the index finger from the other side. He attached a little clamp to the last joint, and I wriggled to sit up straighter. Then he took off the clamp and reached for a thermometer attached to a spiral cord and I opened my mouth.

"Any pain tonight?"

I shook my head no.

"Just hit the call button if you need anything. From hydrocodone to Tylenol." He smiled under the mask. "We're full service here, *amigo*."

He took the thermometer out of my mouth and ejected the disposable sleeve into the disposable bag. Then he turned and reached for something on the tray behind him I couldn't see. I grabbed the food lady's pen from the nightstand and stabbed him in the throat.

Chapter Eighteen

Agent Fuchs's evidence recovery team had started in my old room hours before sunup, examining every bit of tissue, bone, broken medical equipment, and blood, poring over the mess I'd made when I stabbed my visitor the night before. After the FBI briefed the US marshals and local sheriffs, the folks with the mops started cleaning up the gore. Hospital administrators, more out of curiosity than duty, kept poking their heads in. I was already long gone—across the hall to a new room. That place smelled like disinfectant, too, but the view was different and even the weather looked like it was taking a turn. Like maybe I'd only dreamed the killing of the last convict.

Fuchs was sitting in a chair at the foot of my new bed, which was identical to my old bed, debriefing me himself while Sarah sat next to me. She'd beat Aaron to the hospital by half an hour. I didn't know if she was on duty that morning or not, but after I told her over the phone what had happened, she showed up in full uniform, hair pinned up, packing her 9mm on her hip.

"They made a quick preliminary ID of Tito Esparza from dental work and tattoos," Aaron said. "There'll be further confirmation once the DNA is a match, but it's him all right."

"Was there ever any doubt?" Sarah said. The bloody scene in my room had her shook.

"Some folks always doubt."

She scooted her chair closer to my bed and reached out to take my good hand.

"Don't worry," Aaron said. "You're solid. Photos of the body from just an hour ago have been ID'd as Esparza by the Folsom medical staff." He laughed. "We had to wake them up." He held out a plastic evidence bag full of something wet and black. "Then there's this."

"The hell?"

"Our crew found it in the sink of a vacant room at the end of the corridor," Aaron said. He held it out to Sarah. "Along with three or four disposable razors."

"Human hair?" she said.

He nodded.

"Gross."

After more talk about Tito Esparza and the other dead convicts, I asked Aaron where Arvin Waingrow was going from here.

"Congress," he said. "If he gets his way."

"He wishes."

"Well, he's definitely putting this in his 'win' column," Aaron said.

"It could have been a big loss for him if you'd guessed wrong," Sarah said

"I wasn't wrong."

"And you probably weren't guessing, either," she said.

"I 'guess' maybe I noticed he had diesel under his fingernails."

"You knew all that in an instant?"

"You can't scrub oil or diesel fuel off real easy in a blizzard."

"Only you would think of that," she said. She smiled when she said it, so I was hoping I was out of the woods.

"One thing I can't quite figure," Aaron said. "Is why? Why try to take you out now? Esparza wasn't exactly home free, but he was in the wind with a fair chance of disappearing if he set his mind to it. Why would he risk sneaking into a busy hospital in a pair of stolen scrubs?"

"Revenge?" Sarah said. "What other motive could there be other than trying to kill . . . ?" Her voice tapered off.

"Esparza needed the manhunt to be over, at least for a few days. He needed to buy himself some time. Time to regroup. And that would take more than just shaving his head. If I'm still alive, he'll figure I'll be giving your task force a tour of the canyon so you can retrieve the bodies. Then you'd come up one short—one killer still on the loose—and the sights will all be on Esparza. But if it was me who's dead, there'd be nobody left to rat Esparza out, at least not till things got sorted. The task force would be matching up names with corpses, assuming that they found 'em all and assuming the coyotes hadn't beat you to it. Esparza could move free for a couple days, maybe longer. It would be at least a little while till a bunch of busy FBI medical examiners in a killer blizzard with a half dozen corpses on their hands figured out who was who and that the dead Latin guy in the barn was Gilbert Orosco, not Esparza. How I died would be a puzzle for a few days at least. That is if anybody even bothered to order a tox screen for some dead civilian."

I could feel Sarah flinch when I said that.

"If he pocketed the syringe after he stuck you with it," she said, "we might never have known why . . . you know. We might never have had a cause of . . . death."

The room got real quiet.

"Which is why you did what you . . ."

It was hard for her to say the words. I looked out my open door at a maintenance guy with a tool bag who was asking nurses about faulty call lights and punching numbers into his phone.

"My guys should have results on what was in that syringe PDQ," Aaron said.

"Another thing if Esparza took me out. He could use the time that bought him to hunt for whatever guns he could still locate. Whatever ones you folks haven't found. Salvage a busted crime. He rounds up some muscle from his ex-prison pals or skinhead friends of Billy Jack's little brother Ricky Lee and cuts a deal for the remaining hardware. Then he can get the hell out of Dodge with a pocket full of traveling money. Being on the run is lot less lonesome with a wad of cash in your jeans."

"You think there are still more guns up in Hanging Valley?" Sarah said.

"Did either Frémont County or any of your Feds find

an old orange Sno-Cat on the west side of the canyon with a half-eaten body inside and bundles of rifles stacked on the flatbed just neat as you please?"

"Ridgely?" Sarah said. She and Aaron swapped glances. He just shook his head.

"I guess that would be a no," Sarah said. "That's a lot of country back in that canyon we haven't searched."

"Then you only found half the rifles."

"If Waingrow thinks all the weapons are accounted for," Aaron said, "he'll declare victory ASAP and tell the world. Case closed."

"Except it's not."

Sarah tried to hide a smile. "If more rifles show up after the fact, he'll look like a prize chump." She laughed out loud.

"Be like Mitch all over again."

"Tommy," she said. "Don't."

Aaron stood up and walked to the window where Sarah couldn't see his face.

"Not you, too, Aaron," Sarah said.

"I was just wondering it Tommy's offer still stands."

"The, 'if I'm still alive, I'd be giving you a tour of the canyon' offer?"

"Right."

We kicked that notion around. I could smell the food cart in the hall, and the smell made me queasy. The idea of riding back into the canyon where, by my count, four or five dead were still waiting where they fell made Sarah even queasier. But covering the ground horseback kinda made sense.

"Want to borrow one of my horses, Aaron?"

"The task force has been deciding the best way to locate the rest of the bodies," he said. "Then move them out."

"I know where they all are except for Billy Jack Kane. He's kind of vague at the moment."

"The FBI advance team going horseback would totally frost Waingrow's keister," Aaron said.

Sarah laughed out loud. Again.

I was sitting in a hospital chair in my new room watching Sarah bag up what little personal stuff she'd brought for me two days before. I was surprised she sounded so game. I told Aaron I could lead him and Sarah to the rest of the bodies easy enough.

"With Orosco, Vasiliev, and Ezparza dead, there's only four left to locate. Five if nobody's moved Rod Ridgely."

"That is a *big* canyon," Aaron said.

"Billy Jack will be the hardest for me. I got him in open country at night when I was about played out, but you want, I'll find him, too."

"I'll get a Marine chopper to follow us," Aaron said, "and GPS each death site as we go."

"Waingrow is going to want the task force to do the recovery." Sarah said.

"He's got a weak argument with all the escapees being dead," Aaron said. "And since not all the ordnance has been accounted for and Tommy can lead them right to it, the Marines are going to want to run the show from here on out."

"How did they know just when and where half their new rifles had been found?" she said.

"ATF Special Agent Sanchez," Aaron said. "She's been pretty much right about all of this from the beginning."

"Don'tcha just hate that."

Aaron laughed.

"It makes sense for the Marines to want the first look. Stolen top-of-the-line weapons makes this a national security deal for them now and takes priority. Sanchez is right about that, too." I stretched to look out the window. "Snow's melting. We best do this quick before those guys rot."

They released me that afternoon. Nurse Goff pushed my wheelchair out the front door of the hospital then set the brakes so I could stand. I walked out semi-stiff into the sunlight, waiting for Sarah to bring her truck around. I was surprised at how warm the air felt. On the grass I stepped over lumps of melting snow where hard winds had pushed dead maple leaves around still-green juniper shrubs. From what I could see across Carson Valley to the Sierra, the snow on those ridges was receding fast. Sarah held the passenger door for me so I wouldn't snag my stitches. Then Nurse Goff gave her a hug and asked her to keep in touch. I got the feeling that woman didn't have a lot of friends.

Audie sulked when Sarah told her she couldn't go with us on the body hunt. Sarah had skipped the "Sis" and "Kiddo" and went straight to "young lady," so Audie knew she was sunk. Sarah promised her she could go with us the next time we rode out to move cows on Dave's winter permit. She could pack her own bedroll and sleep in the old cow camp cabin with the grown-ups. That took the edge off her—at least until Dave let slip that I'd killed Esparza with a ballpoint pen.

"I *told* you guys Tommy might need his skinnin' knife in that damn hospital. You guys *never* listen."

Aaron briefed his own bosses first in person at South Shore, then by teleconference for bureau honchos in Washington. If the Marines weren't up to speed before, they sure were now. They were relieved that their new rifles were about to be returned, but could've done without the publicity.

Two days later, TV news vans and government trucks parked at the edge of the tamarack a quarter mile up the canyon. A couple dozen men and women climbed out, some in uniform, some carrying cameras and video gear, some dressed like fly fishermen who'd lost their bearings. Waingrow was about to start his wrap-up of the escape, an outdoor press conference at the canyon mouth for *his* higher-ups and some Congress folks who'd flown in to Reno for what everyone hoped was a killer visual with the guy who was calling himself "America's Marshal." As Waingrow's row of microphones was getting set up, we could hear the marshal rehearsing his talk, saying basically that all the Folsom Prison escapees had been killed and that the threat to public safety was over. He was getting wound up as he went. All he needed was a horse to ride and a new hat to wave. But when he started in for real, he got drowned out by a big Marine Sikorsky that rattled the canyon walls and set down on a patch of muddy, snowmelt sagebrush a hundred yards up-trail. Our horses plunged and reporters' hats blew off and mud spit in every direction. A side door opened and a Marine Medical Officer jumped out to touch base with Aaron. Inside the bird I could see a few more Marines and maybe some of Aaron's FBI evidence team and what looked like half a dozen body bags stacked neat and ready to go.

Once the chopper blades slowed down, Waingrow started talking again. He pointed to Aaron and Sarah and me holding our horses off to the side, calling this an example of federal law and local law and community volunteers operating seamlessly under the command of the US Marshals—or some such nonsense. He was still talking when two riders crested an east-facing slope up-canyon of us. One of them was Jack Harney.

"Who's that with him?" Sarah said.

"Agent Sanchez."

Sarah laughed.

We waited till they caught up with us. Instead of a riding boot on her right foot, Isela wore some sort of plastic and Velcro surgical boot where her three frostbit toes had been removed.

"Hey, Tommy," she said as loud as she could. "We *got* 'em! Right where you said they'd be." She described the rifles neatly bundled on the cargo deck of the Sno-Cat, and Jack confirmed the terrain. What they described sounded like the Cat hadn't moved a whisker since I crawled underneath it in the storm. Isela said Burt Kelly and two of his Marine packing instructors had made winter camp at the Sno-Cat site to secure the place until Aaron's forensic team did their work.

The side door of the Sikorsky slammed shut and the big blades tore the air. That was about when Waingrow completely lost his audience.

Aaron and Sarah and I picked up the trail through the tamarack above the creek until it broke into open country. The snow had mostly melted off the granite peaks that rose up on all sides, shining in clear air. The rush and roar of the Sikorsky rumbling across the mountain sky behind us was like morning in Afghanistan.

We pulled up two hours later when we got to the ruins of the old miners' cabin.

"You doin' okay?"

"I'm good," Sarah said.

I wasn't sure how she'd take seeing Kip's body lying face-down in the slush. She said she needed to see it, and that was all. Then she'd be done. To see it by daylight so she could put it behind her, at least for now. You could never know what would be waiting for you down the road. That was the measure of what to take and what to leave behind.

A few days later Sarah and I climbed into my old truck and drove down from Dave's ranch to Paiute Meadows for dinner with Aaron and Jack Harney at the Sierra Peaks. We hardly said a word the whole way.

"You've been sleeping better," she said, pretty much out of nowhere when the lights of town were only two miles ahead. "No more night sweats anyway." She waited for me to say something. "That's got to be a relief."

"Yeah." I was quiet a minute. "Pretty much."

I reached for an envelope stuck behind the visor and handed it to her. Inside the envelope was a brochure from a Reno VA-sponsored PTSD clinic with a handwritten note about an appointment I'd made. Sarah kept her eyes on the road, but a smile came over her. She reached across the cab of the truck and gave my neck a squeeze, like she used to do when we were first figuring that we could never live without each other.

We walked into the side door of the Sierra Peaks past the lunch counter to the dining room where Jack and Aaron were waiting. Aaron watched a busboy standing on a milk crate taking down the red-white-and-blue election banners that said DON'T FORGET TO VOTE! with the date two days earlier. The owner of the Sierra Peaks didn't want to take sides, so there were no photos of Mitch or the undersheriff from Mammoth Lakes running against him. The owner knew these small county elections could go south quick with bad feelings that could last for years and eat into his bar revenue.

"So who won the election?" Aaron said.

"Mitch," Sarah said. "It was too late to change the ballots."

"Yeah," Jack said. "We elected a dead guy sheriff."

"Sounds about right."

The waitress took our orders, so for a minute I didn't get

asked any questions. She came back with a round of drinks and I noticed Cedric the bartender standing under the neon Budweiser sign watching us. He was a moody, buffed-out guy always getting in fights who Sarah had arrested more than once. I was curious seeing him carrying a mostly full whiskey decanter to our table.

"Hey, Tommy," Cedric said. "Mitch wanted you to have this." He held out the decanter. "You know, when he was alive. I was gonna give it to you a few days ago but you looked busy."

"The hell?" I was going to laugh it off, but the guy was dead serious.

"He told me if anything ever happened to him, I should give you this."

It was the decanter Mitch had won at the political fund-raiser he'd gone to the night before the Folsom escape, about as expensive a bourbon as a guy could buy. That all seemed like forever ago. I took the decanter, then passed it around the table for the other three to see. Then I set it down, not sure what the hell to do with it.

"It's pretty much full," Cedric said. "He only ordered a pour from it one time I can remember. He was showing off, acting like he's a big shot for some of the county supervisors from Mammoth. Ordering from his own private stock and all that bullcrap."

"Pappy Van Winkle," Aaron said. "That is a *fine* bottle of bourbon." He laughed. "So I hear."

"When was this?"

"About the time of the prison deal," Cedric said. "He told me it should go to some friend of his who cared about good whiskey. He said that would be you."

"That's quite a nice compliment," Sarah said.

"Yeah," Jack said. "Be a shame to waste it on somebody who wouldn't appreciate it."

Sarah laughed. "You are *so* transparent."

"I'd feel better you took it off my hands," Cedric said. "I'd hate something happens to it and you blame me, you know?"

"I wouldn't blame you, okay. Hey, leave the bottle and bring us four glasses."

"Three will be fine," Sarah said. She touched the top of her wineglass with her fingertips.

Cedric left the bottle and disappeared into the bar. When he came back, I asked him to pour us three shots. Sarah watched the three of us sip and smile and sip again. It really *was* good whiskey. Cedric stopped in the doorway of the bar again, watching us. Sarah picked up my glass and took a sip herself, then nodded.

"How much do you think this cost, hon?" she said.

"I don't know. Hundred. Hundred fifty?"

"Try five or ten times that," Jack said.

"Boy," she said. "Don't get too used to it."

When we were finished, I motioned Cedric over.

"Thanks, Cedric. That was mighty fine. You can take it away now, I guess. Maybe put it in a safe place?"

"The idea was you just keep it." Cedric said.

I picked the decanter up by the neck and looked at the label. "Tell you what. How 'bout you keep it behind the bar."

"Then what?"

"Then every time I come in with these folks, you pour us a shot from that bottle, and we'll drink a toast to old Mitch."

"What'll I do when it's all gone?" Cedric said.

Sarah set the empty glass back on the table while I tried to come up with an answer. Since Afghanistan, I'd always figured that you lived as long as the last person alive who remembers you.

I tossed down a final swallow and handed the bottle back.

"Nobody lives forever."